Dear Reader,

My job with the
me to Nuev
small town,
working alo
comfortable,

Until I met Kri... ...ien.

Beautiful, golden-haired and blue-eyed,
wealthy and sophisticated, she was everything
I'd ever wanted, everything I knew I couldn't
have. Worse, her father was the subject of an
ongoing smuggling investigation, and I was the
agent on the case. How could I get involved
with her when I was trying to arrest her father?
All I could do was keep my distance and try to
protect myself from her.

But Krista had other ideas. Maybe it was
her privileged upbringing, or just pure
stubbornness, but she wasn't about to be
denied something she wanted — and what she
wanted was me.

I thought I knew what love was before I met
Krista, but she taught me new meanings for the
word. She brought light into my life.

She brought peace into my heart.

Rafael Contreras

New Mexico

MEN
MADE IN AMERICA

MARILYN PAPPANO
Within Reach

New Mexico

Silhouette® Books

Published by Silhouette Books New York

America's Publisher of Contemporary Romance

If you purchased this book without a cover you should be aware
that this book is stolen property. It was reported as "unsold and
destroyed" to the publisher, and neither the author nor the
publisher has received any payment for this "stripped book."

 SILHOUETTE BOOKS
300 East 42nd St., New York, N.Y. 10017

WITHIN REACH

Copyright © 1987 by Marilyn Pappano

All rights reserved. Except for use in any review, the reproduction
or utilization of this work in whole or in part in any form by any
electronic, mechanical or other means, now known or hereafter
invented, including xerography, photocopying and recording, or in
any information storage or retrieval system, is forbidden without
the permission of the publisher, Silhouette Books, 300 E. 42nd St.,
New York, N.Y. 10017

ISBN: 0-373-45181-4

Published Silhouette Books 1987, 1993

All the characters in this book have no existence outside the
imagination of the author and have no relation whatsoever to
anyone bearing the same name or names. They are not even
distantly inspired by any individual known or unknown to the
author, and all incidents are pure invention.

® and ™ are trademarks used under license. Trademarks recorded
with ® are registered in the United States Patent and Trademark
Office, the Canadian Trade Marks Office and in other countries.

Printed in the U.S.A.

Chapter 1

It was quiet in the desert under the midafternoon sun. Its rays beat down unmercifully, sending out shimmering waves of heat to be absorbed by the sandy ground. There wasn't even a hint of a breeze to offer relief, and movement among the desert's natural inhabitants—snakes, lizards, kangaroo rats—had ceased completely. Only its unnatural inhabitants—men—were out.

Rafael Contreras was as quiet and still as his surroundings. The baseball cap he wore in place of the usual uniform cowboy hat offered little protection from the heat, but he hardly noticed. His attention was on the six men coming toward him.

They were young, ranging in age from sixteen to twenty. Unaware that they were being watched by the border-patrol agent, they were talking good-naturedly, calling out to each other in rapid Spanish. One of them was relating the details of his latest encounter with his girlfriend's disapproving father, bringing bursts of laughter from his friends, when Rafael stepped into view.

The gaiety disappeared, but none of them made a move to run. They knew the procedure. Their trip to the north had ended within three miles of the border, but they would at least be given a free ride back. There was no reason to run.

Rafael's hands hung loosely at his sides. He didn't consider drawing his revolver from its holster. He knew these six from their previous attempts. They wouldn't threaten him. They would return to their homes in San Ignacio, and another day, when they were bored or restless, they would make another try. Unlike many of the undocumented aliens, or illegals, apprehended by the border patrol, these six weren't desperate for the better life offered in the United States.

Rafael understood all the reasons the illegals had for crossing the border. He knew firsthand what it was like to be poor and hungry, to dream of a better life. Twenty years ago he had made the illegal journey many times himself, but with better luck than the six young men before him now. He had gotten caught only once.

Some of the people he caught berated him, cursed him for his job, but Rafael didn't mind. He understood their reasons, but he also understood why the United States couldn't open its border to all the aliens who wanted to enter. It was his job to stop as many as he could.

He'd been with the border patrol ten years, the first five in San Diego. The illegals crossing into San Diego County had to deal with their smugglers, corrupt police officials in the Mexican border towns, bandits who prowled the network of canyons on the border, and the patrol. The agents in turn also had to deal with these groups. Assaults, rapes and robberies weren't uncommon; neither were shootings. It was a tough place to work.

Now he worked the desert in southern New Mexico. He liked the desert—liked the heat, the barrenness, the quiet. There was a lot of room in which to be alone, and Rafael liked being alone.

Jim Stone pulled up near the small group in a border-patrol van. "Is this it, Rafe?"

The casual nickname grated, but he made no comment. Most of the men he worked with spoke only enough Spanish to get by and didn't care much about their accents. They seemed to have trouble pronouncing all three syllables of his name; it usually came out "Ra-fell." Rafe was the obvious nickname, one they could handle. The fact that he didn't like it didn't matter.

They loaded the six men into the van. The last one was a cocky sixteen-year-old named Eduardo. He flashed a grin at Rafael. "Haven't seen you lately."

"Often enough." He picked up Eduardo an average of once every couple of weeks—sometimes as often as twice in one day. It was that way with a lot of them.

"My English is getting better, isn't it?"

"Yes." He gestured to the boy to get into the van.

"Someday I'm going to live in the United States, where I can use it, like you, Contreras," Eduardo vowed as he took a seat beside his friends. "Only I will enjoy it better than you."

Rafael heaved a silent sigh. It was near the end of their shift, and he was looking forward to going home. It was Friday and a long, empty weekend stretched ahead. He liked that kind best. He would see Constancia, do a little work around the house, do some reading. All very boring—except, of course, Constancia. She was . . . comfortable.

The van bounced over the rutted trail that passed for a road, but Rafael didn't notice. He ignored things that irritated him, such as being bounced to death or being called Rafe. He continued his thoughts undisturbed.

He liked his relationship with Constancia. He felt genuine fondness for her, but he knew it would never become anything stronger. Fortunately, she didn't seem to want anything more than he could give. They were satisfied with what they had.

It was another hour before he was able to leave work. He changed from his uniform into jeans and a red shirt, the sleeves rolled up to reveal muscular forearms, then climbed into his black Bronco parked outside the Nueva Vida Bor-

der Patrol Station. The parking lot was filled with the cars
of agents coming and going with the shift change, and official vehicles—cars, vans, four-wheel drives—all painted in
the distinctive white-and-pale green colors of the patrol, and
all Dodges. Nueva Vida was a small station; it didn't rate
any of the department's new Chevy Blazers.

When he was able to back out of his parking space he did
so, intending to go straight home, but the idea of a cold beer
to wash away the day's heat tempted him. By the time he'd
driven north through the small town to the Blue Parrot, he
was too thirsty to pass it by. He parked in the gravel lot next
to a brand-new Mustang and went inside. The bar's name-
sake squawked as he walked in the door. Rafael ignored it.

Jim Stone was already there, two women seated at his table. There were only two other customers at that time of
day, one seated at each end of the bar. Rafael walked past
Stone's table, neither man looking at the other, and went to
sit at a small table in the back, facing the door.

"I swear, the temperature drops twenty degrees when that
man's around," Royce Ann Stone said in a thick Southern
drawl. She had moved to Nueva Vida from Georgia twelve
years ago, but she had never lost her charming accent.
"Does he ever talk, Jim? Why, he walked right by, as if he
didn't even know you."

"Unlike some of us, Rafe talks only when he has something to say," Jim replied dryly. His wife was as well-known
for how much she talked as the way she talked.

"That's rude." She pouted. "You are so lucky to still be
single, Krista. The men I know just aren't worth putting up
with."

The woman across from her smiled fondly. "Neither are
the men I know, which is *why* I'm still single. Who is he,
Jim? He couldn't have lived here before, when I did."

"Rafe—Rafael Contreras. He's one of ours."

"One of—oh, you mean he's with the border patrol."
Krista leaned forward to pick up her Coke, all the while
studying Rafael. "I don't suppose *he's* single."

"Of course he's single!" Royce Ann replied, shocked by the question. "Look at him, Krista. What woman in her right mind would have him?"

Krista was certainly enjoying looking, but she could find no obvious answer to the question. "What woman in her right mind *wouldn't* have him? He's gorgeous. Does he drink? Beat his girlfriends? Mistreat animals? There must be *some* flaw."

Royce Ann leaned cross the table to reply in a low voice. "He doesn't talk. He never smiles. I don't think he knows how to laugh. He's the most unfriendly, coldest, most inhuman person I've ever met. You just wipe that smile off your face right now, Krista. Rafe Contreras is no one you want to know."

Krista sat back in her seat, slowly tilting the Coke bottle to her lips. She knew better than to argue with Royce Ann, but she also knew her friend was wrong. Rafael Contreras was most definitely someone she wanted to know. Inhuman or not, he was the most attractive man she'd seen in years. In her lifetime, she amended. He was the man she had dreamed about since she was a girl—dark, handsome and sexy, though he missed out on "tall" by several inches; he was only about five foot ten. And that mustache! He was definitely someone she would like to meet.

"Does he live in town?"

"Krista! Don't tell her, Jim. She's liable to do something crazy like go to his house."

"As a matter of fact, he owns a piece of land out there near your dad. Remember the old Moreno place?"

She nodded slowly. She remembered it, but only vaguely. She had lived in Nueva Vida only eight years, and six of those had been from birth. She had returned when she was sixteen and left again when she was eighteen. This was her first visit in ten years.

"That's where he lives. Runs along the south border of your dad's place."

"Does he have a girlfriend?"

Royce Ann gave a very unladylike snort. "There's not a woman in town who would let him touch her. He's spooky."

Again Jim offered information. "He sees a woman in San Ignacio, across the border. Really pretty little thing."

Rafael had long since finished his beer, but he was still in his chair. He was aware of the blonde's frequent glances, and he was curious. One look had committed her image to memory, from the blond hair to sky-blue eyes to a gorgeous, sensuous mouth. Though she looked vaguely familiar, he was certain she was new in town; if she'd been around long, he would have seen or heard about her.

He didn't care much who she was or why she was there. His curiosity extended to one question: why did she keep looking at him like that? Stone's wife was probably telling her all the stories about him. Rafael had a tendency not to make friends, and in a small town like this, what the people didn't know, they suspected and distrusted. This woman was different, though. She openly watched him, when most people were afraid to stare at him for fear of meeting his eyes. This woman didn't seem to mind when he stared back.

Krista finished her Coke and set the empty bottle on the table. "Well, guys, I'm going to head home. It's been nice seeing you, Jim. We'll get together soon, okay?" She stood up and reached for her purse. Out of the corner of her eye she saw that Rafael Contreras was also rising.

When he left the bar he found her leaning against the Mustang next to his truck. She straightened, moved to stand in front of the door of the Bronco and extended her hand. "Hello."

Rafael looked at it as if he had never seen one before and didn't know what to do with it.

Her brilliant smile faded. "I'm Krista."

He reached into his shirt pocket, pulled out a pair of mirrored sunglasses and put them on. Next he drew a set of keys from his jeans pocket and slid his finger through the ring, letting them dangle.

Though she had purposely omitted her last name, he knew immediately who she was and why she looked familiar. Krista wasn't exactly a common name. He had come across it, along with an old photo and a note that she would be coming to town for a visit, in one of his files at work just last week: Krista McLaren, age twenty-eight, only child of Art McLaren. Now he knew more about her than he wanted to. Still, he took the hand she offered.

His hand was warm, the palm callused and rough against the cool smoothness of hers. The small gesture brought her smile back full power. "I understand we're neighbors."

"Are we?"

She wished he would take the glasses off so she could see his eyes. It was disconcerting to talk facing dual images of herself. "My father owns the property next to yours, according to Jim Stone. You work with Jim, don't you?" At his brief nod she continued, "He's a friend of mine from school."

"You used to live here?" he asked, his voice low and rough. He knew the answer, of course, but it seemed like the right question to ask.

"For a while. I'm visiting my dad—Art McLaren. Do you know him?"

Rafael shook his head. "We've never met." A border-patrol agent wasn't powerful or influential enough to be included in Art McLaren's circle of friends.

He looked down at the hand he still held, and his fingers moved fractionally over it. Her fingers were slender, the nails neatly clipped and painted a pale rose. Her grip held just the right degree of firmness, and her skin was pleasingly soft. He wondered how that softness would feel against him, touching him. . . .

Abruptly he dropped her hand and took a step back. "Enjoy your visit," he said brusquely as he reached for the door of the truck.

Krista moved away and watched him climb inside. "Hey, you didn't tell me your name."

He hesitated. Obviously Stone had already done the honors, but if she wanted to pretend he hadn't, Rafael could go along. "Rafael."

She smiled. "You'll probably be seeing me around, Rafael."

That was what he was afraid of, he thought grimly as he drove away. Art McLaren's pretty daughter could be a problem. He couldn't afford any kind of involvement with her, for both personal and professional reasons. Fortunately for him, beautiful, rich women like Krista McLaren lost interest *real* fast. They weren't interested in maintaining an honest relationship; their entire lives were a whim, nothing planned, nothing worked for, nothing serious. And Rafael Contreras was nothing if not serious. Nothing on earth could force him to do something he didn't want to do, and seeing more of Krista definitely fell into that category.

He could handle her—he hoped.

Krista's smile was gone by the time the Bronco disappeared from sight. She walked around the midnight-blue Mustang convertible, slid into the driver's seat and headed for home.

Unfriendly, cold and inhuman—the words Royce Ann had used to describe Rafael Contreras. But Krista knew her friend was wrong. There was a difference between not being friendly and being unfriendly. She suspected that Rafael was a very private person, a loner who simply didn't conform to Royce Ann's idea of what he should be, and so he got the labels.

Krista didn't need labels. She trusted her instincts, and they told her that Rafael was a complex, interesting man— one she was going to enjoy getting to know.

She pulled into the driveway of her father's house, circled the fountain out front and stopped directly in front of the double doors. She left the keys in the ignition—one of the servants would put the car away, freshly washed and waxed, until she wanted it again.

The main part of the house was over eighty years old, authentic adobe with two-foot-thick walls. The additions on either side were only about thirty years old, built by Art McLaren for his new bride Selena. The house was big and beautiful, but Selena hadn't been happy there. She had never cared for the desert, New Mexico, her husband or her daughter, and she had left them all behind when Krista was barely six.

Servants were waiting. They opened the heavy, carved door as Krista approached, and one hurried out to move her car. The housekeeper, Juana Morales, took Krista's purse and asked, "Would you like something cold to drink?"

Krista gave her a warm smile. "Yes, some tea, please." She started to go into the living room, then changed direction and followed Juana into the kitchen.

"Is there something you need, *señorita*?"

"Please, Juana, I know it's been a long time since I've been here, but I'm still Krista." She leaned against the counter and watched the woman who had practically raised her in the few years she had lived there. "Do you know Rafael Contreras?" She pronounced the first name in the same two syllables that made most of his fellow workers fall back on the nickname Rafo.

"He's a border-patrol *agente*."

"Do you *know* him?"

Juana shook her head. "No one knows Señor Contreras."

Krista accepted the tea the woman offered and thanked her. "Did I say it right?" She repeated the name, and Juana shook her head.

"It's Rah-fah-el." She trilled the *r* and after several tries Krista was able to mimic her perfectly.

"Hasn't he been here long? Is that why no one knows him?"

"Four years, maybe five. He doesn't want to know anyone. He keeps to himself." Juana's eyes narrowed suspiciously. "Why are you so interested in Rafael Contreras? He isn't a man your father would welcome into this house."

"You mean because he's with the border patrol?"

The black eyes seemed fathomless when they studied her. At last Juana decided the younger woman was sincere, and she sighed, shaking her head. "Because he's Mexican."

Krista still didn't understand. "But so are you—and Marta and Ruben and Luis and just about everyone else who works around here."

"Everyone who *works* here," Juana repeated with an indulgent smile. "Your father has no objections to hiring us as employees, but do you think he would let his daughter take a Mexican lover? He'd send you back to New York so quickly you wouldn't know what happened."

"Oh, no, Juana. He wouldn't care. He never cares."

"He would care about *this*," the housekeeper stubbornly insisted. "You stay away from Rafael Contreras, Krista."

She thanked the older woman for her advice without agreeing to follow it. For reasons she couldn't quite explain, Rafael interested her, and she had no intention of staying away from him. Too many people, she thought, had already stayed away from him, and she wasn't going to join the crowd.

The small house sat at the end of the street, several empty, overgrown lots separating it from the nearest neighbor. Rafael sat on the top step, his back against the porch railing. A can of beer was nearby, next to a hammer and a handful of nails.

Constancia Aranas was surveying the repairs Rafael had finished only moments earlier. She turned and smiled at him. "It looks good." She sat down near him and took a sip from his beer before handing it to him. "*¿Quieres pasar la noche?*"

Rafael shook his head. He didn't want to stay the night. He'd driven to San Ignacio to spend the evening with Constancia, but he'd been there only an hour—and that time had been spent fixing the loose porch railing—and now he was ready to return home. He didn't know what was wrong with him. He finished his beer and pushed himself to his feet. "*¿Necesitas alguna cosa?*"

No, she replied, she didn't need anything. She didn't question why he was leaving so soon. *"Ten cuidado,"* she called softly as he walked away.

Be careful. He was always careful. That was how he survived.

The customs agent at the border crossing recognized him and waved him through. A mile into Nueva Vida, then seventeen home. He was tired, anxious to get there.

Alone in his bed he slept, and he dreamed of a blond-haired, blue-eyed woman. He awoke disoriented, breathing rapidly, his entire body aching. He expected to see the IVs, the smiling nurses, the somber doctors, but he was alone.

He hadn't dreamed about Rebecca in years, but the dream tonight had been just as vivid, just as real as the first dream twelve years ago. He lay in the center of his bed and listened to the sounds of the night until his breathing slowed. He knew what had brought about the dream, after years of being free from it: another blue-eyed blonde, one who'd said that he'd be seeing her again.

Well, this dream, this nightmare, was one more very good reason why he should avoid Krista McLaren. He didn't want to be reminded of a past best left forgotten.

The talk at work on Monday morning was all about Art McLaren's daughter's return to Nueva Vida. Rafael sat at his desk, pretending to look at a file, and listened. It wasn't because he was interested in Krista, of course. It was just that anything that affected McLaren interested him. Any bit of information he could gather on the man to add to the file would help.

"So you went to school with her, Jim?" Mike Hughes asked.

"Yeah. She and Royce Ann are good friends."

"She's beautiful," Nick Morris put in. "Ah, the things I could do with her!"

"And what if Carla found out?" Jim asked, referring to Nick's wife.

"She wouldn't, and what she doesn't know can't hurt her." Nick propped his feet on the desk and leaned back. "Too bad she didn't come back two years ago, before I got myself tied down. But I could still show her a very good time."

"Krista takes care of her own amusement, Morris, so back off," Jim said, only half-teasing. "You married guys leave her alone."

"Say, that leaves just you and me, Darren," Mike called.

"And Rafe," Darren Carter added.

They all looked at Rafael, diligently working on his file, and Mike shook his head. "Just you and me, buddy."

Rafael's jaw tightened. If he decided he wanted Krista McLaren, nothing would stop him from getting her—not Hughes, or Carter, or Krista herself. She could hate him, but before he was finished, she would welcome him into her bed.

But he didn't want her. Rafael recognized one important fact about Krista: she was a very dangerous woman for him. He didn't need to know her, to talk to her or to touch her to know that she represented danger and risk to him. She was a woman who could take control of his life, his thoughts, even his heart. Instinct told him that.

But he had decided long ago that he would never, as long as he lived, give his love freely to any woman. Especially to a blond-haired, blue-eyed woman.

Whatever she wanted from him—proper respect for her position as Art McLaren's daughter, adoration for her beauty, her superiority—he would give her nothing willingly. She would have to satisfy her need for worship with the other men in Nueva Vida, men like Hughes and Carter and Morris.

The file in front of him wasn't thick, and he'd been over it several times already, but Rafael read it again. He knew Art McLaren's life history as well as his own, but as he read it now he included a mental image of Krista. Now she was part of it.

McLaren had been born to a poor farmer and his wife in Oklahoma. He quit school at the age of sixteen and went to work. By the time he was twenty-two, he'd saved enough money to gamble in oil. Some extremely risky deals paid off, and he became an overnight millionaire. A year later he married Selena Whiteford, the daughter of a wealthy New York businessman, and settled on the property outside Nueva Vida, devoting a portion of the property to farming, which required extensive irrigation, and the rest to raising cattle.

Two years after their marriage Selena gave birth to their only child, Krista Larie Alise. Rafael gave a shake of his head. Selena had saddled her baby girl with one hell of a name, apparently not considering the child who would have to answer to it.

During the next few years Art worked at making more money, and Selena worked at spending it. The marriage was stormy, and the divorce six years after Krista's birth surprised no one. It was a particularly nasty case, involving fights over money, property and custody of their daughter. Selena took a large sum of money, Art took the girl and they split the property.

The girl. The "girl" was now twenty-eight and absolutely gorgeous. She had inherited her mother's beauty and, he suspected, her father's persistence—a lethal combination.

Rafael wondered how her presence in Nueva Vida would affect McLaren's activities. There was no reason to suspect that she was involved with—or even aware—of her father's major source of income. Rafael thought that maybe Mc-Laren would call a temporary halt to his side business until Krista was safely back in New York. No father would want to risk exposing his daughter to that kind of danger.

Richard Houseman, the DEA agent who had put the file together for Rafael, disagreed. The daughter's visit would be for an indefinite period of time; each shipment her father canceled or postponed would cost a fortune and lose him customers. He wasn't likely to stop in deference to her visit.

DEA. Drug Enforcement Agency. Rafael had occasionally worked with the DEA before. Sometimes people who smuggled illegals found it was an easy step to smuggle other things, too, from animals sold without quarantine to babies sold to the highest bidder—to drugs. He wished McLaren were involved with the animals. Even the babies—they were well taken care of and sold to people who desperately wanted them. But no, McLaren had chosen the most profitable—the drugs. The most profitable—and the most dangerous.

He didn't feel good about this investigation, and Rafael was a man who trusted his feelings. He wanted out of it, but he knew what Martin Thompson would say; his boss's answer would be a flat no, without even asking his reasons. And what reasons could he give? *My instincts say back off; it doesn't feel right. And I'm worried about what his daughter might do to me.* Thompson would laugh and tell him to ignore his instincts and do his job.

Forget the drugs, forget Krista, he counseled himself. His part of the case didn't involve either; he was working on it because McLaren's people smuggled in a hundred to two hundred illegals a week. His job was to work with Houseman so that when McLaren was arrested there would be enough evidence to convict him for both types of smuggling—the people and the drugs. The joint investigation was to ensure that neither agency blew the other's case.

In the back of the file was the photograph of Krista McLaren. It was six years old and revealed a very pretty, laughing, happy girl. It didn't do her justice, though Rafael doubted any photograph could.

She would leave soon. She belonged to the city, where her friends and admirers were. She wouldn't stay long in a town like Nueva Vida. It couldn't satisfy her. Whenever she left, he thought grimly, it couldn't be too soon for him.

Krista was working Monday, too. With the help of Juana and one of the men, she set about turning an unoccupied room next to her bedroom into a workroom. The furniture was removed, replaced with several long tables, a sewing machine, a drafting table, shelves to hold supplies, and chairs.

"Your father won't approve."

Krista's retort was flippant. "He won't event notice. If I don't work, Juana, I don't get paid, and I've grown rather fond of eating."

Black eyes moved critically over Krista's slender frame. "It doesn't show," Juana grumbled. "You're too thin."

"Thank you. Here, let's move this table over here." Krista lifted one end of the table, but the housekeeper shooed her away and she and Ruben moved it.

Deciding she liked the arrangement, Krista thanked Ruben and wandered to the doors that opened onto the balcony. For miles around she saw nothing but desert, though she knew Rafael Contreras's house was only about five miles southeast, and Nueva Vida was about eight miles southwest, though it was twelve miles by the road.

"How long will you be staying?"

She didn't turn at the sound of Juana's voice. "I don't know," she replied. "Until I get his attention." Her eyes drifted back to the southeast, and Juana, coming to stand beside her, noticed.

"Until you get whose attention, Krista? Your father's? Or Rafael's?"

Krista's cheeks turned pink. All weekend the dark, silent man had been in her thoughts. She wasn't quite sure why he attracted her so. There was the obvious—that he was simply one of the most handsome men she'd ever seen—but there was more to it than that. She just didn't have the answers yet.

The ringing phone prevented further questions from Juana, who answered, spoke for a few minutes, then hung up. "A package has arrived in town for you. They can't deliver it until tomorrow, so I told them one of the men will pick it up."

"Oh, that's all right. I'll get it. I wanted to go into town anyway. Thanks for the help, Juana." She went to her room next door to change clothes, then pulled her hair into a ponytail before leaving the house.

The town of Nueva Vida didn't require a large shipping office. The facilities consisted of one large room and one harried clerk, who was trying to deal with an irate customer when Krista entered. While she waited several other customers came in, running errands on their lunch hours, and finally a second employee, the deliveryman, appeared.

"We could've brought this out tomorrow," he said, searching through the invoices for Krista's.

"That's okay. I wanted it today."

"Truck's broken down. In the garage down the street. They promised to have it ready in the morning." He pulled out a crumpled invoice and squinted at it while reaching for a smoldering cigar in a nearby ashtray. "So you're Art McLaren's daughter."

She made no reply. By now she assumed that everyone in town knew she was a McLaren—including one border-patrol agent who probably couldn't care less.

"I'll get this for you. Just a minute."

As he disappeared into the maze of shelves that served as storage, Krista left the counter. It was growing too crowded, so she chose an out-of-the-way spot to stand, near a high stack of cartons, and waited restlessly.

Behind her the bell over the door jangled as it opened to admit another customer. Idly curious, Krista started to turn her head to look, but just then the delivery man rounded the boxes at the end of the aisle and started toward her with a rapid gait.

"Here it is, ma'am. You need help with this?"

Krista watched as the box slipped in his grip, bumped against his knee, then began to fall. The man grabbed for it with too much force, lost his footing and pitched toward her, shouting both a warning and a curse. She quickly backed away, past the stack of boxes and into the main aisle—and into a body that was hard and unyielding.

The deliveryman hit the floor and rolled against Krista's legs, sending her off balance against the man she'd bumped.

She tried to grab something for support, but the man lost his balance, and they crashed to the floor together.

She heard a sound from the man she was lying on top of, a very distinct grunt as the impact of her body knocked the breath from him. She opened her eyes and found her face pressed against a dark green uniform shirt, and on that shirt was a name tag. She could only see the last six letters of the name, but that was enough.

She had just gotten Rafael Contreras's attention.

Chapter 2

Rafael looked at the head of blond hair that had struck him in the chest and silently groaned. He didn't need any more encounters with Krista McLaren, accidental or otherwise, and he knew this had to be her. No other woman in Nueva Vida had hair so soft, so sweet-smelling or so blond—at least, not naturally.

They had landed in a tangle, Krista's leg thrust between Rafael's. As each realized who the other was, the position became far too intimate. She pushed against his chest, raising herself a few inches before she slipped and fell on him again. Embarrassment burning her cheeks, she mumbled, "Sorry."

There were effusive apologies and anxious questions about injuries. Rafael ignored them. Lifting Krista over him, he rolled to his feet, took her hands and pulled her up. "Are you all right?"

She was wearing that ever-ready smile despite her embarrassment. "I think so. What about you?"

He nodded. He released her hands and immediately wished he could take them back. He liked the physical contact.

"Nice seeing you again," she said in a husky voice. Blue eyes held black eyes for a long moment before she slowly moved away. She accepted more apologies on her way out, her box safe in her grip. After stowing it in the trunk of the Mustang she went to the nearest service station to get gas.

The pale green-and-white border-patrol truck caught her eye when it passed. There were plenty of similar vehicles around the country, but this one was being driven by Rafael. When he pulled into a restaurant parking lot a block and half away, Krista impulsively decided to follow.

He had already been served by the time Krista paid for the gas, drove to the restaurant, found a parking space and found him. "We seem to be destined to run into each other today."

Rafael felt a sinking feeling as he recognized her voice. His gaze traveled up long, golden legs, over skimpy white shorts and a tight white tank top to a golden face and golden hair. He wasn't ready to see her again, not so soon. That brief contact in the shipping office had affected him more than he liked, and he needed time to forget it.

"Mind if I sit down?"

He shrugged, and she slid into the seat across from him. She leaned forward slightly, her elbows on the table. "Sorry about that accident. I hope I didn't hurt you."

"It wasn't your fault." He looked back down at his food, dragging his eyes from her.

The silence lengthened as Krista waited for him to speak again. He continued eating his lunch as if she weren't there, but at first she didn't mind. She was stubborn, and she was also patient, but after almost ten minutes of being ignored she ran out of patience.

"Listen, *Rafe*." She knew instinctively that the nickname Jim Stone had used would irritate him, and she was rewarded with the slight tightening of his jaw. "I can be as stubborn as you can, so why don't you relax and tell me a little about yourself, and then I'll tell you about myself."

He looked up, fixing a steady, cool stare on her, and said in a dry, gravelly voice, "I don't want to know about you, Krista." He already knew more than he wanted—that she was beautiful, that she affected him like no other woman and that she was one woman he absolutely could not get involved with. He rose from his chair, picked up the check and walked away.

Krista sat back, undisturbed by his utter lack of interest in her. She was confident that somehow she would change that—she just didn't know how.

She wasn't used to pursuing a man, but she could always learn. She wanted to get to know Rafael Contreras, and it looked as though the only way to accomplish that was to convince him that she was worth his time. There had to be some way to melt through that ice-hard exterior of his, and she was determined to find it.

She remembered the sound of his voice, and it intrigued her. It was low pitched, a little gravelly and completely sexy. The last words he'd said had been rude, but she forgot the insult and concentrated on the voice. It was a voice made for whispering sweet love words to a woman while his body showed her what they meant, a voice to make her feel secure in the aftermath of their passionate lovemaking.

A honeyed drawl interrupted her thoughts. "That smile is almost obscene. I'd like to take a peek inside your head and see what it's about."

Krista's smile became dreamy. "I was thinking about a man who must be the world's best lover."

Royce Ann Stone sat down in the seat vacated by Rafael only moments earlier. "Oh, tell me more."

"Nope, that's all. I didn't see you come in."

"That's because you were lost in your own little world with your fantasy lover." Royce Ann indicated the dirty dishes in front of her. "You already eaten?"

"No, those are Rafael's."

"You were having lunch with Rafe Contreras?" Even the idea upset Royce Ann. She couldn't possibly imagine sitting down to a meal with that man.

"I just told you I haven't eaten. I sat down with him while he ate. When I tried to get him to talk he insulted me and left." She toyed with the menu, turning it in her hands. "Unfortunately, he doesn't say much—just stares with those gorgeous black eyes."

"Stay away from him, Krista. Rafe Contreras is trouble—more trouble than you can handle."

"When have I ever listened to warnings? Besides, if you ask Rafael, I think he'd probably say *I'm* trouble, not the other way around."

Royce Ann was worried. She had known Krista for twelve years. She had moved to Nueva Vida at the same time that Krista returned to the small town from her Swiss boarding school. They had been naturally drawn to each other and had been close friends ever since, despite Krista's ten-year absence. Royce Ann knew how stubborn her friend could be, how single-minded she could become once she'd made up her mind about something. She was worried about Krista's interest in Rafael.

"Look, there's this guy who works with Jim named Mike Hughes. He's really nice, Krista, and he thinks you're pretty. How about a date, you and Mike, and Jim and me? We could go out to dinner—" She let the sentence end abruptly. It was obvious that Krista had no interest in the unseen Mike Hughes. "Let's see…there's also Darren Carter. He's kind of shy but good-looking and nice. Or maybe…"

"Or maybe no one. Don't set me up with anyone, Royce Ann, okay?" Krista pushed her chair back. "I've got to get home—work to do. Why don't you come over to the house tomorrow for lunch? Around one?"

Royce Ann heaved a sigh even as she accepted the invitation. She didn't like Krista's interest in the Mexican, especially now that it had reached the point that she didn't even want to meet other men. Royce Ann knew that, despite her money and sophisticated air, Krista McLaren was still rather naive and innocent. Rafael Contreras could hurt her—hurt her badly. Royce Ann had to persuade her to leave the man alone.

Richard Houseman was waiting for Rafael outside the border-patrol station. He looked hot and out of place in his three-piece suit, and as Rafael parked the truck, Houseman pulled off the jacket and tossed it through the open window of his car. "Contreras."

Rafael returned the curt greeting with a nod.

"I hear McLaren's daughter has arrived." Houseman wiped at the sweat that trickled down his forehead. Damn. Contreras looks like it's fifty degrees out here instead of a hundred, he thought crossly. "You seen her?"

"Yes."

He waited for the other man's opinion of the woman, but none was forthcoming. "Well? Is she going to be a problem?"

For the case, probably not. For Rafael himself, undoubtedly. Already he'd spent too much of his time thinking about her, both hoping to see her and praying he wouldn't. Wanting her and knowing he couldn't have her.

Rafael shook his head, and the midday sun glinted off his mirrored sunglasses. Ordinarily Houseman preferred to see the eyes of the person he was talking to, but with Contreras it didn't matter. Those black eyes revealed no more of his thoughts, his feelings, than the mirrored lenses did.

"I don't think she'll stay long," Rafael finally volunteered.

"Do you think she's involved?"

Rafael trusted his instincts, and though he sought to dislike the woman, his instincts said she had nothing to do with the smuggling. "No."

"I've got to get back to New York. The next shipment from McLaren is due there tomorrow. Did you check the shipping office here?"

"I was there today. So was Krista McLaren."

That caught Houseman's interest. "Was she sending or receiving?"

"Receiving."

"Any idea what?"

Rafael shrugged.

"Can you find out who and where it was from?"

"New York. She sent it herself. A week before she left." Rafael had seen the invoice on the floor after the fall he, Krista and the deliveryman had taken. It had been very easy to pocket it without being seen.

That killed Houseman's interest. "Probably personal things she couldn't bring with her. Keep an eye on her anyway, will you?" He glanced at the expensive gold watch on his wrist. "I've got to go. I'll be in touch."

Rafael watched him get in the rental car, loosen his tie and start the engine. The next thing he did was reach for the air-conditioner controls. Some people never got used to the desert heat. *He* liked the desert, and he liked the heat. He leaned back against his truck for a moment and just let himself feel the sun's rays. For that moment he was relaxed, at ease, and into his unguarded thoughts came Krista. Did *she* like the heat? Or was she like her fellow New Yorker, Houseman, who thought eighty degrees was a heat wave, or her Southern-belle friend, Royce Ann, who simply refused, according to her husband, to go anyplace that wasn't air-conditioned?

He summoned up a mental picture of Krista as she had looked the last time he'd seen her, less than thirty minutes ago, in those white shorts that were almost indecent and that flimsy white garment that passed as a shirt. She was a beauty, with those sky-blue eyes and that smile that seemed to appear from nowhere, and the body—the body was nice, too. All that perfectly tanned skin that looked baby soft.

Rafael wanted her. He wanted to make love to her. He desired her in a way he hadn't desired any woman—not even Rebecca. Was he doomed to unwise affairs with beautiful, rich, blue-eyed blondes who didn't understand words like honesty, trust and commitment?

He imagined himself touching her, raising that skimpy shirt and pulling it over her head. Her breasts would be bare underneath; he'd seen that she wasn't wearing a bra. Her breasts were rather small but very nicely shaped, and he pictured his hands on them. Her nipples would harden beneath his fingers, and when she was moaning for more, he would take one in his mouth and suckle it till it grew even harder....

Rafael felt a corresponding swelling in his own body, and he muttered a vile curse. He squeezed his eyes tightly shut, and the enticing, arousing, tormenting picture of Krista disappeared into a swirl of spots. He wished the same would happen to the real Krista as he crossed the parking lot to the air-conditioned building.

He liked the heat, but sometimes it was better not to get too hot.

Krista unpacked her carton of supplies in her new workroom and immediately set to work. Music, soft rock, filled the room from the small stereo Ruben had carried in earlier.

Years of training and practice had made Krista a reasonably decent artist—but only decent. She lacked the talent of so many of the other designers she knew. But she could turn her decent sketch into a pattern, and the pattern into a completely-finished garment, with amazing ease. It helped her wardrobe. Except for her jeans, courtesy of Lee, Levi's and Wrangler, nearly everything she owned was a Krista McLaren original. She designed clothes for herself, and after years of hard work, other women were starting to like them, too.

The McLaren collection was known for the comfort of its casual clothes and the romance of the dressier ones. Her dresses, skirts and tops were soft and flowing, with ruffles and ribbons and lace, like the outfit she was working on. She studied the skirt pattern she had just completed, then lifted a length of fabric, a lightweight cotton in pure white. She placed it alongside a smaller piece of material, eyelet in a pink so pale that one had to look twice to see the color. She had dyed the fabric herself, before leaving New York, to get the shade she wanted. She added several yards of eyelet lace in the same pink and went to work.

She pinned the pattern to the white cloth, making minor adjustments, then cut out the pieces with dressmaker's shears. The skirt was simple—very full, with an elastic waist for comfort and a twelve-inch-wide ruffled hem. She sewed it together, edged the hem with pink lace, then set the skirt aside and reached for the eyelet.

The camisole top went together as quickly as the skirt. She had made the pattern before leaving New York, and the construction, like the skirt, was simple. The front of the camisole was pink eyelet, lined with the same white cotton that made up the back. Wide eyelet formed the straps. She added elastic at the waist, which made a ruffled hem, meant to cover the waistband of the skirt.

Krista snipped the last thread and rose from the sewing machine. She stripped off her shorts and tank top and pulled on the new outfit. It was a perfect fit, and she turned in front of the triple mirror to admire the new clothes.

Perfect. They were soft, feminine, romantic. This was what she would wear when she seduced Rafael Contreras.

A blush colored her cheeks. Her friends in New York would be astounded if they could see her now, planning the seduction of a man who didn't want her. The Krista they knew spent her time avoiding seduction. Still, she wished she could get some tips from a couple of them—like Angeli, the beautiful Italian model who lived next door and had a different lover every week, or Isabella, a celebrity photographer and princess of some tiny, obscure European country. Her lovers, she admitted, outnumbered her loyal subjects.

They knew men—Angeli and Isabella and the others. They would know how to break through the defenses of a man like Rafael Contreras. Krista knew very little.

There was a knock at the door, followed immediately by Art McLaren's entrance. He looked around the room, and a frown of displeasure crossed his face. "What the hell is this mess?" he demanded.

Krista's hopes had risen with his entrance. It wasn't often that her father sought her company. Now they fell again. "Hello, Dad."

"What have you done to this room?" he demanded, ignoring her greeting as he had so often ignored her. He walked to the center of the room, his big frame dominating the area.

"I need a workroom while I'm here," Krista said. "I just finished this. What do you think?"

His sharp blue eyes skimmed over her, barely noticing the clothes; then he shook his head, his gray-flecked brown hair lifting slightly. "I don't know why you can't buy your damned clothes like everyone else." He turned in a slow circle, again looking at the changes she had made. "Workroom," he scoffed. "What do you know about work? You've never done a day's work in your life. I didn't send you to all those damned schools just so you could sit around and sew all day."

"No, Dad," she agreed, disappointed yet again. You sent me to all those schools to keep me out of your way, she added silently.

"Hell, the least you could do is get married and have some children. Maybe *they* could make me proud. God knows *you've* failed at that."

Krista sat down on the edge of the table. Now was the time to change the subject, before he began listing everything she'd failed at. She knew the list by heart, anyway. "Dad, do you know a man in town named Rafael Contreras?"

Art's alert eyes were drawn back to his daughter. He pulled up a chair and sat down, then lit a cigarette. He muttered, "I just don't understand it—hiring Mexicans to be in charge of the border. Everyone knows how those people stick together. Hell, you put them in charge of the border, you may as well just open it up and let every damned person in Mexico move up here."

His daughter winced. She'd never realized that Art was so prejudiced, though Juana had tried to warn her. But then, she didn't know her father well enough to know how he felt about anything besides her failure as a daughter.

His eyes narrowed suspiciously. "How do you know Contreras?"

There was a time to be honest, and Krista quickly decided that this wasn't it, so she lied. "I don't. I just saw him in town one day."

It wasn't a real lie, she consoled herself. Her brief encounters with the man didn't constitute knowing him.

Art sensed his daughter wasn't being completely honest, and he rose from the chair and strode toward her. He held her chin in one hand and looked down into her face. "If you need a man, there are plenty of good ones in town. Americans. If you've got to have someone to amuse you while you're here, find one of them. Stay away from the damned Mexicans."

Krista pulled free of his grip, coolly replying, "I'll keep that in mind, Dad."

He blew smoke from his cigarette into her face before walking to the door. "We're having company for dinner. People I'm doing business with. Dress pretty and act nice."

"Yes, Dad." She stared at the door as it closed behind her father, and a curse came from her mouth.

Dress pretty and act nice. Get married and have children. Stay out of his way. The only things her father had ever asked of her in her entire twenty-eight years. Art McLaren had never wanted a daughter—just a little wind-up doll who performed on command and stayed in the background the rest of the time.

Krista picked up her shorts and shirt and carried them to her room. One last time before removing her new outfit, she turned in front of the mirror. If Rafael Contreras was no more impressed with her than her father had been, and she suspected he wasn't, she was in trouble. She very well might be anyway.

Dinner was boring; the people her father had invited were boring; the whole night was boring. The three men talked a lot and said nothing. Their chatter and the smoke from their cigarettes, along with the obvious interest the older man displayed in her, combined to make Krista's head hurt. She excused herself after dinner to go into the kitchen. As soon as she helped Juana serve one of her sinfully good desserts, she would slip upstairs to her room, she promised herself, away from that horrible, choking smoke and that horrible, leering man.

The kitchen was empty. Assuming that Juana must have run home for some reason, Krista began putting the dessert plates and forks on a serving tray alongside a rich buttercream cake.

"Need some help?"

Mr. Baker—or was he Smith?—stood in the doorway, still leering. Krista gave him a coldly discouraging look. "No," she said flatly.

The man came closer, and she could smell his very expensive cologne. Everything about him was expensive—his silk suit, his Italian-leather shoes, his gold watch, even his cuff links. He was a physically attractive man, though almost as old as her father, but something about him repulsed her. He reminded her of a snake.

"Let's just forget about that cake, honey, and you can be my dessert," he suggested.

Krista picked up the tray, holding it securely in front of her. "I don't know what your business is with my father, Mr. Baker, but *I'm* not part of it. Now I suggest you get out of my way, or you'll be wearing Juana's best French buttercream cake all over *your* best silk suit."

He looked ready to refuse until the door behind Krista opened and the housekeeper came in. She correctly assessed the situation in an instant and moved to take the tray from Krista. "I'm sorry. My errand took longer than I expected. Please, *señor,* go back and sit down, and I will serve your dessert. You'll be leaving for your appointment, *señorita?*"

Krista seized the opening gratefully. "Yes, Juana, I will. I'll see you tomorrow. Goodbye, Mr. Baker." She fled up the back stairs as Juana politely insisted that the man leave the kitchen.

In the safety of her room, behind locked doors, Krista changed from her dress into jeans and a snug-fitting T-shirt. It was a lovely night, and she was going out into it. She didn't want to remain in the house with her father's lecherous friend, and a drive sounded wonderful.

She drove fast, the top of the dark blue Mustang down. She liked the sense of power, of risk, that high speeds brought; she found it exhilarating. She had to slow down to the speed limit, though, when she reached Nueva Vida. One more speeding ticket, her insurance agent had warned, and she'd find it cheaper to hire a chauffeur than to pay her premiums.

At nine o'clock on a Monday night, activity in Nueva Vida was almost nonexistent. The lone policeman she saw was in the bank parking lot, reading a book by the squad car's interior light. All the stoplights on the main street had been turned to continually blinking yellow, and Krista drove through the entire town without once touching her brakes.

She drove about a half mile farther south, realized she was heading for the border and swung her car into a wide U-turn. Too late she saw the truck approaching from the south, and she jammed the accelerator to the floor, jerking hard on the steering wheel.

Over the squeal of the Mustang's tires came that of the truck's as its driver slammed on its brakes, swerving to the left to avoid plowing over the small car. The Mustang left the road at an alarming speed; then Krista remembered to move her foot from the gas pedal to the brake. The car skidded over sandy dirt, uprooting several small shrubs. Only the seat belt kept her from bouncing out of the open car before it finally shuddered to a stop in a small ditch some fifty feet off the road.

Krista's heart was pounding so loud that for a moment she could hear nothing else. Slowly she became aware of the car's engine, still running, and a song coming from the radio, then the sound of running feet. From out of the night a dark figure reached her car, and Rafael Contreras demanded, "Are you all right?"

Slowly, reluctantly, Krista raised her head to look at him. "Hello," she said in a small voice.

Rafael stared at her, then muttered something in Spanish. She caught the word *Dios,* which she knew meant God, and she assumed he was either damning her or asking God to remove her from the face of the earth. At that moment she wouldn't have objected to a little disappearing act.

"What the hell were you doing? You could have gotten us killed!"

She swallowed hard, trying to think of a proper response, like "I'm sorry." What she'd been doing was obvious—and stupid—and she saw no reason to make it easy for him to point that out. After a moment she said, "You scared me."

Rafael's eyes widened, and he turned his back to her, leaning against the rear fender of the sports car. *He* had scared *her?* She had made a U-turn on a curve—on a *curve,* for God's sake—had forced him to practically burn out his brakes to avoid hitting her, had run herself off the road, and now she said *he* scared *her!*

His heart rate slowing to normal, Rafael turned back, opening the car door. "Get out."

"I... don't think I can."

"Are you hurt?"

She shook her head.

"Then..." His eyes swept over her, and he noticed that both her hands were still gripping the steering wheel tightly. He pried her fingers free, then bent over to unfasten the seat belt. He was slow to straighten again. Her different scents—perfume, shampoo, soap—filled his nostrils, and they all smelled good. He wanted to gather up a handful of her hair to smell, to press his face against the soft flesh between her small breasts and inhale the scent of her.

Damn it, stop, he commanded himself. None too gently, he helped her from the car to stand on wobbly legs, then turned his anger with himself on the woman responsible for it. "I've seen you three times today, *señorita,* and that's three times too many," he said coldly. "When you said we were destined to run into each other, I didn't think you meant it literally."

Krista's own surge of anger chased away her shakiness. "You can't believe I did this on purpose! I could have been killed! I guess you think I have nothing better to do with my time than follow you around and look for ways to get together with you! You flatter yourself, Contreras. I have plenty of more important things to occupy my time!"

All through her outburst Rafael stared down at her, hearing her words but paying no attention to them. He wanted to kiss her. He wanted to see if her lips were as soft as they looked, if her mouth tasted as sweet as he expected it to. He wanted to seduce her with nothing more than a kiss, and he could do it. He knew he could....

Not Art McLaren's daughter, he reminded himself. She reminds you of Rebecca. She has blond hair and blue eyes, and she's McLaren's daughter.

But the rebellious part of his mind was compelled to argue. She's beautiful, and you want her. And she wants you. Rebecca doesn't matter; her father doesn't matter. Take what she's offering. Take what you want.

His hand was halfway to her hair before he realized it and pulled it back. This woman was dangerous. He couldn't allow himself to seduce her. Even one brief night learning the pleasures of her body would affect the rest of his life.

"Do you have a flashlight?" he asked abruptly.

Reluctantly, Krista said no. If he didn't already think she was stupid, he would now. A flashlight was a basic piece of equipment for a car, like a spare tire or a jack. Only an idiot would drive at night without one.

It was apparent that Rafael thought so, too. "I'll get mine," he said grimly, striding across the scarred ground to his Bronco, which was parked on the shoulder of the road.

Instead of waiting for him, Krista decided to go ahead and check the damage to her car. She almost fell into the ditch that her right wheels had slid into, but she caught herself. It was hard to see in the darkness, so she bent to take a closer look.

"Need some help, lady?" an accented voice asked from right behind her.

A cry of fright escaped her, and she popped up to stare at a young Mexican boy. "My God, you scared me!"

He grinned, raising his hands in the air. "I'm not armed or nothing. I was on my way to my uncle's house, and I saw your car. You all right, lady?"

"Yes, I am."

"It's not smart to be out all by yourself this late at night, lady. Someone could hurt you."

"And it's not smart to get so involved looking at pretty ladies that you don't hear someone come up behind you," came Rafael's raspy voice.

The boy was as startled as Krista had been a moment earlier. He peered closely at the man's clothes, noting the jeans and red shirt, then relaxed. "You off duty, Contreras?" he asked cockily.

"Yes, but I can still take you in, Eduardo. I know you don't want that, and I've got enough problems tonight without adding you to the list, so do us both a favor and go home."

"I could walk over that hill and wait until you're gone, then go north," the boy boasted.

"And I'd find out and come looking for you." Rafael switched on the flashlight and played the beam along the side of the car.

Krista crossed her arms over her chest and turned a skeptical look on Eduardo. "On your way to your uncle's house?" she asked dryly.

He laughed, shrugging his slender shoulders. "How was I supposed to know you'd be with Contreras? This your lady, Contreras?"

Rafael stiffened imperceptibly, but neither Krista nor Eduardo noticed. "I'm not, but if it were in his power, I think he'd give me to you," she teased. "He thinks I'm a nuisance."

Eduardo gave a low whistle and wrapped one arm around her waist, pulling her close. "I'd be glad to take you off his hands, lady. I bet you and me could have some real fun together."

Rafael straightened at the front of the car and turned off the light. He told himself it was ridiculous to feel jealous of a sixteen-year-old boy who was holding Krista in a casual embrace, but that didn't make the feelings go away. He issued a sharp command to Eduardo in Spanish, ordering him on his way.

"Got to go, lady," Eduardo said apologetically. "I been caught too many times this month. Maybe I'll see you again."

Krista gave him her prettiest smile. "Maybe so, Eduardo. Be careful."

They watched the boy until he disappeared in the darkness; then Rafael said flatly, "Your radiator is busted, and the left front tire is flat."

"Oh." She smiled brightly. "Then I'll have to ask you to drive me home, won't I?" Even in the moonlight she could see his face settle into stern, uncompromising lines. "Come on, Rafael, surely not even you would leave me out here alone."

No, he couldn't do that. The next person who happened along might not be as friendly as Eduardo. "Get your things."

Krista tried not to look too triumphant as she reached inside the car for her purse, but she was elated by the chance to spend more time alone with him.

She shouldn't have been. He stopped in town to call a tow truck, giving the man the precise location of the car; then he headed the Bronco out of town, never speaking. As they approached the Blue Parrot on the north edge of town

Krista broke the silence. "Feel like stopping for a drink? My treat—as thanks for your help."

"No." He didn't want a drink; he simply wanted to get away from her. Every moment he spent with her weakened his resolve to have nothing more to do with her.

There was no further conversation until he stopped the Bronco in front of the lovely old house. "Thanks," she said.

He stared straight ahead, giving no sign of hearing her.

Krista sighed wearily. "You're never going to give me a break, are you?" She got out of the truck. "I'm sorry about the accident, I hope you're all right, and I'm sorry I put you out by needing a ride home. Thanks a lot and good night."

Chapter 3

She was going to forget him. That was simply all there was to it. For some reason Rafael Contreras had decided he didn't like her. He obviously wanted nothing to do with her and, after all, she did have her pride. She didn't need him for a friend or anything else. Rafael Contreras was nothing special.

Oh, but he *was* special. Krista had never met a man who interested her the way he did. Until now. What a man to fall for.

Without conceit she could easily name a dozen men in New York who would be happy if she showed the slightest interest in them. But not this one. Not strong, silent Rafael Contreras. He would be quite happy, she suspected, if she left town and he never saw her again, and that nagged at her.

Who the hell was he, to brush her off as unimportant? He hadn't even given her a chance before deciding that she wasn't worthy of his attention.

Krista rubbed at her temples to ease the headache trying to start there. She had slept poorly the night before—with her doors locked, because her father's guests had spent the night. Sometime around two o'clock, while she tossed sleeplessly in bed, trying to force one handsome Mexican from her mind, the ever-friendly Mr. Baker had tried the door, softly calling her name several times before he gave up and returned to his own room.

After a few hours of restless sleep she'd gone downstairs to breakfast, only to find the man in the chair next to hers. While he carried on a casual conversation with her father and Mr. Smith, he continued to ogle Krista, making frequent references to the next time he'd see her and how he hoped they'd get better acquainted. Over her dead body, she thought crossly.

As soon as breakfast was over the guests left, and Krista was subjected to a lecture from Art for leaving early the night before. Then she received a call from the garage with an estimate on her car that made her bite her tongue in shock even as she authorized the work. That was followed by more thoughts of Rafael and arguments with herself over her course of action regarding him.

All in all, she thought as the radio announcer proclaimed the time to be twelve-thirty, it hadn't been a good day so far.

Royce Ann Stone was never on time for anything; she was either early or late but never on time. She arrived for their one-o'clock lunch date at twelve thirty-five, providing a much-needed diversion for Krista. "I swear, Krista, you look like death warmed over," the woman said in greeting. "I heard about your accident. Are you sure you're all right?"

Krista reassured her, then casually asked, "How did you hear? I haven't told anyone."

Royce Ann pushed her raven-black hair over her shoulder. "Nueva Vida is a small town. News spreads fast. Everyone knows that Krista McLaren's Mustang was towed in last night and that Rafe Contreras called the tow truck, but no one knows what happened. Care to make me the first?"

With some embarrassment Krista told her about the illegal, dangerous and very stupid U-turn that had caused her wreck.

"So...was he any nicer?" Royce Ann asked; then she laughed. "Nice. What a word to use in reference to Rafe Contreras. I imagine 'nice' for him is not biting your head off."

They were in the workroom upstairs, Krista working and Royce Ann watching from a comfortable chair opposite her. "Rafael is different," Krista said softly, her scissors still. "He's not like any of the men I've known."

"Is that any reason to decide you've got to have him? He's just a man, Krista. Surely he can't compare to the men you date in New York. There's that Frenchman, and the Italian count, and the baseball player, and the actor—all gorgeous and sexy and rich. How could you even consider a man who works for the border control, who probably doesn't make more than a few thousand dollars a year more than Jim? And believe me, that's not a lot. A man who doesn't like people, who's not even—" She stopped suddenly, and color suffused her cheeks.

Krista knew as surely as she knew her own name what Royce Ann had started to say. "It bothers you that he's Mexican, doesn't it?" she asked, solemn but not accusing.

Royce Ann's blush deepened. "I—I...it's not that he's Mexican... Well, maybe it is. You know, Jim spends so much time picking up illegals and shipping them back to Mexico, and sometimes they're armed, and they fight, and they come right back, and they create so much trouble. Yes, I guess I have become a bit prejudiced."

"The problem's with the system, Royce Ann, and with the Mexican government. I know Jim's job isn't the easiest, and he deals with some bad people, but that's no reason to dislike all Mexicans, is it? There are a lot of bad Americans, too. Besides, Mexican or not, Rafael's on Jim's side; he's working *with* him, not *against* him."

Royce Ann shrugged apologetically. "No one ever said prejudices were rationally based."

"Well, it doesn't matter much, does it? He obviously isn't interested in me. I guess I'll just have to find someone I *do* impress."

"The offer to set you up with some of Jim's buddies still stands. Darren's really nice, and he's cute, and I think you'd like him." Suddenly Royce Ann's blue eyes widened. "Wait a minute. Who is he to decide that you're not impressive? How can you let some man treat you like that, Krista?" she asked indignantly. "Doesn't he know how lucky he is that you've even bothered to look at him? Doesn't he know that you've dated actors and counts and *Mike Davis?*"

Krista laughed as she began clearing her work table. "Somehow I don't think Rafael is a baseball fan. I doubt he has any idea who Mike Davis is and couldn't care less. Come on, Juana should be serving lunch in a few minutes."

The table was set in a glass-walled, air-conditioned sitting room that offered a spectacular view of the desert and distant mountains. Royce Ann sprawled in one of two wicker chairs, looking out. "I hate the desert, and I hate the heat," she said flatly. "If Jim had to go into government service, I wish it had been the navy or the marines—someone who knows the meaning of the word 'transfer.'"

Krista sat down across from her after filling their glasses with iced tea. "If he'd joined the marines they'd probably have sent him to Yuma. The navy would've sent him to El Centro."

Royce Ann grimaced at the mention of the two towns, both small and both in the desert. "Yeah, but they wouldn't keep him there indefinitely. We'll *never* get out of Nueva Vida."

Drawing her fingertip down the side of her glass, Krista dislodged the drops of condensation, and they formed a tiny rivulet. "I like the desert," she remarked dreamily. "It's so strong... and quiet... and mysterious. It endures. Whatever happens, it will be here."

Royce Ann stared at her, her glass halfway to her lips. Was her friend talking about the desert—or Rafe Contreras? Contrary to Krista's claims that she would find someone other than Contreras to practice her charms on, Royce Ann was certain in that moment that she would never be convinced to date anyone else in Nueva Vida. Krista had fallen hard for the man least likely to return her affection.

"Have I sprouted horns? Turned purple?"

The questions jolted Royce Ann out of her thoughts. "What?"

"You were staring at me as if you'd never seen me before. Do you find it that hard to believe that someone actually *likes* living out here?"

"Oh...well...it *is* odd. It's pretty when the flowers bloom, but the rest of the year it's always the same. Hot and dry."

"If you hate it so much, you could always move away," Krista quietly stated.

"But Jim's job—"

"Jim doesn't have to go." Her expression was slightly pained. She was remembering the day her lovely, beautiful mother had left because she couldn't stand the desert, the house or "that clinging brat" any longer. For a time the child that Krista had been had hated the desert and the house, and she had hated herself for making her mother leave. It had taken years for her to let go of her guilt, to realize that no one was responsible for Selena's actions except Selena herself.

Krista knew what Royce Ann's response to her suggestion would be: shock that any woman could possibly care more about where she lived than whom she lived with. She was staring at Krista in disbelief. "You mean leave Jim? I couldn't do that. I love him! I'd live in the middle of the Sahara if that was where he was!"

She smiled. "So the desert isn't so bad as long as you're with him. You know, Royce Ann, I think you just like to complain. That's all it is, just a desire to complain about *something.*"

The black-haired woman's defense was stalled by Juana's entrance with their lunch. By the time they finished eating she had forgotten what had been said, and Krista was spared any further thoughts on the subject.

* * *

Three days had gone by with no sign of Krista McLaren. Maybe she'd already lost interest. She undoubtedly wasn't used to being refused anything. She'd probably found someone else in town who would willingly offer the attention and the worship that Rafael had withheld.

The suggestion both relieved and irritated him. He was relieved because he didn't know how much longer he could have kept her at a distance. When he wanted something as badly as he wanted her, it was hard to listen to his mind when it said no. His mind wasn't the part of him that ached to possess her.

He was irritated for the same reason. When he wanted her that badly, the idea of her being with another man wasn't a pleasant one. His mind knew it was best she hadn't come around, but his heart and his body wanted what was best for *them*.

Rafael stretched his legs out in front of him. It was a clear, still night, and he often found himself sitting on the porch steps on nights like this, when it was easy to think, but this evening the night's magic was gone. For a week now it had been gone—since meeting Krista McLaren.

The progression of his thoughts was natural, from Krista to another blonde with blue eyes. Rebecca Halderman. He had loved her with all the passion and intensity that a young man could possess, and she had hurt him as deeply as a young man could be hurt. She had broken his heart, destroyed his faith in women, ruined his sister's life and damn near ended his. All because she was rich and spoiled and used to getting her way.

Had she ever considered the damage she was causing when she seduced him, when she dazzled him with the beauty of her fair skin and her blue eyes, when she offered him her perfect body? Had she ever cared that his family had lost their dreams, that Josefina had paid as high a price as Rafael himself?

No, he was sure she hadn't cared. Rebecca had been wealthy, spoiled and selfish. She cared only for herself, for her amusements, and the consequences be damned. She had gotten what she wanted, and that was all that mattered to women like Rebecca Halderman. Women like Krista McLaren.

It had been twelve years—twelve long, lonely years. Shamed by Rebecca's deceit, guilt-ridden because his family had been forced to return to Mexico and because of Josefina, Rafael had gradually lost touch with his family. His mother still sent occasional letters, pleading with him to return home for this holiday or that birthday, but he refused. He had failed his family. He had been stupid, foolish, careless, and he had brought them grief and pain. After twelve years he still couldn't forgive himself.

The dozen years hadn't been so bad for the Contreras family. Rafael sent them money regularly, and they had been able to buy a small farm to replace the one he had caused them to lose in California. Josefina was now married, the mother of three and very happy, according to their mother's letters.

Everyone had healed except Rafael. He was still alone; he still ached; he still blamed himself. He still needed someone.

That last thought didn't sit well with him. He prided himself on being self-sufficient. He provided everything he needed himself. But in the dark night he could admit that he needed someone—a woman, a lover, a friend. A wife. He wanted children; he wanted not to be alone, as he'd been for the last twelve years, as he would be for the rest of his life.

He could probably marry Constancia. He didn't love her, and he knew she didn't love him, but did that really matter? Maybe marriages without love were best, because if you didn't love, you couldn't be hurt. Maybe he and Constancia could have a good marriage with lots of children . . . a comfortable marriage . . . a dull marriage.

An image of a laughing Krista McLaren flashed before his eyes. Life with *her* would certainly never be dull. She could make him look forward to getting up every morning and coming home every night. She could brighten his life, chase away all the dark shadows that haunted him, and she could give him beautiful children.

And those things made her dangerous. Rafael instinctively knew how easily he could care for Krista and how disastrous that caring would be. She was a shallow, spoiled, rich girl, and there was no way she could possibly be the kind of woman he wanted her to be. Why risk getting hurt again?

No, he'd learned his lesson from Rebecca, and he was far too smart to need a refresher course. Krista McLaren could never be a part of his life. If he ever allowed that, it would destroy him.

Saturday was a very hot day. Krista had been restless that morning, had felt a desire to get out in the desert, into the heat. She tried swimming in the pool behind the big house, but it didn't help, and neither did lying on the tiles in the sun. So she had changed from her swimsuit to light cotton pants of baby blue and a thin, ribbed-knit tank top of white. It clung to her breasts and her midriff and accented her golden tan, and it was cool. She put on a pair of leather sandals that laced around her ankles, then left the house for the stables.

The black stallion, Diablo, was sleek and powerful. Nearly impossible to handle, he lived up to his name, "devil," with everyone but Krista. She had so thoroughly charmed the animal that he docilely let her ride without a saddle, dutifully obeying her slightest whisper.

She gave the horse his head, letting him wander where he wanted. She wasn't very familiar with her father's property, but she trusted Diablo to take her home again when he was ready. She sat astride the stallion, soaking up the sun's heat, letting it relax and soothe her.

They passed through yet another of the gates in the fences that crisscrossed McLaren land, Krista leaning down to close it behind them. Then suddenly Diablo stopped, his ears pricked. He sensed the presence of someone else, and he didn't like it.

"You're trespassing."

Krista nearly fell from the horse's back at the sound of the soft voice behind her. She wheeled Diablo around to face Rafael Contreras. "What?"

"This is my property." He was standing next to an unsaddled palomino whose rich gold color almost matched that of Krista's hair. The horse reacted nervously to the strangers, both woman and stallion, but Rafael calmed him with a hand on his neck.

She shifted uncomfortably. Though she'd had no idea that she was even near his land, after the way she'd popped up three times last Monday she knew he wouldn't believe her.

He was standing there in boots and jeans and nothing else save a red bandanna rolled tight to serve as a headband, and she let her eyes sweep over him, from his wide shoulders to his bronzed chest to narrow hips covered with faded denim. They made the trip back up his body to his head, skimming over the thick mop of black hair, black eyes, the perfect nose, the sexy mustache and the grim, unsmiling mouth.

Her long silent scrutiny instead of her usual blinding smile brought Rafael's eyes to her, and he scowled with open hostility. *Then* that damned smile appeared. "Hello."

It was his turn to look, to study. He already knew her face; it had been etched in his memory since the first time he'd seen her, at the Blue Parrot. He skipped it, moving on to study her body.

It was a body made for a man. Everything about it was absolutely perfect, from her small, high breasts and tiny waist to her slender hips and long legs. But Rebecca's body had been perfect, too, he reminded himself.

Though Krista knew he would prefer not to talk to her ever again, she sat in silence, knowing that eventually he would speak. At last he did. "I don't recall inviting you here."

"I thought that in the friendly Southwest you didn't have to wait for an invitation."

"I'm not friendly."

She grinned. "No kidding."

Turn away from her. Pretend she isn't here. Pray to God to send her away, he told himself. But he continued to look at her for a long moment, until the golden horse nudged his shoulder. He began walking, the palomino at his side. "How did you know where I lived?"

"I didn't. Diablo was doing the navigating. I'm just along for the ride. I'm sorry I bothered you." She tightened her grip on the reins that had been resting lightly in one hand, intending to leave, but Rafael reached up and took them from her. Forgetting his name and reputation, Diablo placidly allowed the stranger to lead them.

They crested the hill, and in the valley below was Rafael's house. He led the two horses to the corral, where another one waited. Broken railings on one side showed how the palomino had gotten out.

When Rafael picked up the hammer resting on the top railing, Krista commented, "It's a bit hot to be working, isn't it?"

"It's a bit hot to be chasing that horse across the desert," came his surly reply. He turned his back on her, cursing himself for bringing her here. Why had he done such a damned foolish thing? Then she swung to the ground and moved to the side, where he could see her from the corner of his eye, and he knew why: it had been five days since he'd seen her, and that was too long.

"Jim said you'd bought the Moreno place, but that isn't the Moreno house, is it?"

He didn't look up from his work. "I tore it down and built that one."

"I like it."

"Yeah, sure." His entire house would probably fit into her bedroom at the beautiful old McLaren home.

She turned back and reached out to steady the board he was nailing into place, raising her voice to be heard over the banging of the hammer. "How long have you lived here?"

"Not long."

"Why did you buy a place so far out of town?"

"I wanted to."

"Do you like the desert?"

"Yes."

His short, gruff answers didn't put her off. At least he was talking to her, she consoled herself. And it had been his idea that she come down to the corral with him.

Rafael drove the last nail into the board and turned around to get another. He was surprised to find himself only inches from Krista; he hadn't realized they'd gotten so close. He took a step forward, and she took one back, but that put her against the rough boards of the corral, and she couldn't move when he came still nearer.

He wasn't going to touch her. He just wanted to be close to her, to smell her scent, to feel her heat. He wasn't going to touch her at all, yet his hands came up to her shoulders and pulled her away from the boards and against him. His entire body responded to her, his muscles tightening, his jaw setting in a taut line.

She was warm and soft, and she felt so good beneath his hands. Blue eyes locked with his as he slowly rubbed his hands along her bare arms, down to her wrists, then up again. A funny feeling settled in Krista's chest, making it hard to breathe. Rafael's hands settled at her waist. She raised hers to his shoulders, then across to rest, fingers spread wide, on his chest.

He couldn't let go of her; he couldn't pull his gaze from hers. He wanted her—oh, God, how he wanted her! He wanted to forget who she was, who he was. He wanted to forget everything and simply make love to her until he could no longer move or feel or think. But that would be a fatal mistake. There was no way he could keep her, and no way he could walk away from her in one piece, unscathed.

Krista felt the tension in him and realized at last that he wanted her. Whatever his reasons for keeping her at arm's length, lack of attraction wasn't one of them.

Let go of her—send her away!

Rafael ignored the frantic commands of his brain and continued to look into her sky-blue eyes, eyes he could drown in. He sensed the danger she held for him, and it made his mouth form a thin, unsmiling line, made his eyes turn hard.

Only inches separated them.

Slowly, unwillingly, his hands left her waist for her hips, sliding around to cup her buttocks. He pulled, closing the distance so that her breasts rubbed his chest and her hips were snug against his and his hardening arousal.

He held her with one arm around her waist and brought his free hand up to cover her breast. Krista's eyes widened; she was frightened by the intensity of the feelings he roused in her. He made her want him in ways she didn't understand. His hand was sending marvelous sensations through her breast, and as his masculine hardness pressed erotically into her belly, she forgot everything. Slowly she twined her arms around his neck and sought his mouth with hers.

She wasn't as skilled as Rafael had expected, but in her kiss there was an eagerness to please, to taste, to explore, that he found exciting. He forgot all the reasons why he couldn't get involved with her, ignored his mind's warnings and took control of the kiss, his mouth ravaging hers. His hands were on her back, pulling her shirt free of the waistband of her slacks, gliding beneath the damp white fabric, along her spine, over soft silken flesh.

Diablo snorted impatiently, but Krista heard nothing, felt nothing but her desire for Rafael. While he continued his intimate exploration of her mouth, she let her hands explore his body. The muscles in his back were taut, well developed, covered with bronzed skin as soft as her own.

Rafael pushed her back and removed her little white shirt, tossing it over the top rail of the corral fence. She was gold, except for the coral-colored peaks of her breasts. A rich gold, like expensive wine, that gleamed in contrast to the darker bronze of his hands on her. He cupped her breasts in his hands, his thumbs rubbing slowly over her aching nipples.

"Rafael," she whispered.

His hands became still at the sound of her voice, and he stared at her for a long moment, appalled by how close he had come to losing control. He took a step back, picked up her shirt and wordlessly handed it to her, hoping that his hand wouldn't tremble or disobey his brain's commands and reach for a small, perfect breast again.

She pulled the shirt on, then searched his eyes for some hint that the intimacy they had just shared had touched him. There was only a brief flicker of something she thought might be regret; then it was gone, and his eyes were empty.

"Go home, *señorita,*" he said quietly. "There's nothing for you here."

"I just want you," she whispered.

He shook his head. "I could make love to you, but it wouldn't be worth the effort. Go home. Stick to your own kind."

Krista stared at him for a long moment, until her fragile hold on her emotions had strengthened; then she forced a smile. "I think, Señor Contreras, that you're afraid to stray from your 'own kind.' Afraid that you won't measure up to my standards?" she speculated.

Rafael neither agreed nor disagreed.

She moved Diablo so she could mount him from the fence. "I'll see you again, Rafael." There was no challenge, no threat, in the soft-spoken words. Just a statement of fact.

"No." He picked up the hammer and a handful of nails and turned his back on her.

Her laugh was as light as the wind. "Goodbye, Rafael." She bent low over the stallion's back and gave a quiet command, and he leaped forward.

Rafael watched her go, his mouth forming a succinct curse. She was gone, but she would be back. He had escaped this time, and maybe he would the next time, but eventually he was going to make love to her, and when he did, he would be lost.

He worked hard the rest of the day, ignoring the heat, the sweat that trickled between his shoulder blades, the unsatisfied ache in his groin.

The sun had set, and the heat had gone. His work was done. Only his desire remained. He stood on the porch, his body still damp from his shower, wearing only a pair of cutoff jeans. He was drinking his last bottle of beer, staring into the darkness, and thinking.

He could drive across the border to San Ignacio and have dinner with Constancia. But Rafael had learned long ago that he couldn't satisfy his desire for one woman by using another, and he respected Constancia too much to try. Years ago he had tried desperately to stop wanting another blond-haired, blue-eyed witch by using every woman he knew, but it hadn't worked. Only time had blunted his desire for Rebecca.

Rebecca. He closed his eyes and called up the picture of the woman he had loved, but the image that appeared wasn't Rebecca's, but Krista's. Lovely, beautiful, sexy Krista, who had been in his arms less than seven hours ago. He was a damned fool for letting her go.

Krista had been pleasantly surprised by Rafael's response to her on Saturday, and she spent the rest of the weekend thinking of ways to see him again. She felt reasonably sure that if it were left up to him, she would never lay eyes on him again. But maybe he wouldn't feel so threatened by her if they were in a group, and so, with Royce Ann's help, she decided on a party, to be held the following weekend at her father's house. She would just keep her fingers crossed that Rafael would bother to show.

She decided to deliver the invitation in person on Tuesday. When Rafael returned from lunch he found her there, perched on the edge of his desk. Royce Ann was with her.

He cursed silently. Each time he saw her, his desire for her grew stronger, and it was harder to remember the reasons why he had to stay away from her. She was getting under his skin, occupying his thoughts and even slipping into his dreams.

"So what time do you want us Friday night?" Nick was asking.

"Seven o'clock." Krista was aware of Rafael, studying the bulletin board near the door. She wondered how long he would try to avoid her by standing there. She put on her most charming smile and called, "What about you, Señor Contreras?"

She had brought the attention of everyone in the room to him, including his boss, Martin Thompson, so he couldn't ignore her. Slowly he raised his head and turned toward her. "What about me, Miss McLaren?" His cool tone of voice held a warning, but she chose to ignore it.

"Royce Ann and I are having a party Friday night to welcome me back to town. I've invited all your co-workers. Will you come?"

Rafael walked to his desk, everyone's eyes on him. While he pointedly waited for her to move, he could smell her perfume, the same musky scent she'd worn last Monday night and again on Saturday. He decided he liked it very much. "I don't go to parties, Miss McLaren," he said flatly.

"There are a lot of things you don't do, aren't there? Your life must be very dull."

No, dull was not the word, Rafael thought, not since this woman had come into his life, determined to—to what? To seduce him? To use him? To be entertained by him while she was bored?

"I like my life," he said, his voice still flat and unemotional.

"Do you?" Krista stood up and brushed past him, intentionally rubbing against him. "Excuse me, *señor*," she teased softly. "I'll put you on the guest list as a definite maybe. You might change your mind between now and Friday. I assure you, it will be worth the effort."

Her reference to the remark he had made on Saturday would have brought a blush if Rafael hadn't held such tight control over his emotions. Would she be worth the effort?

What effort? He snorted. He got hard when he looked at her or thought of her. His body begged to do what his brain refused. The only effort was in holding back.

"See you guys Friday," Krista called as she and Royce Ann left.

The other men were watching Rafael speculatively, all wondering why Krista had singled him out for attention. One who didn't care why was Martin Thompson. "In my office, Contreras."

His jaw set in a stubborn line, Rafael followed the older man into a small, private office.

"I want you to go to that party."

"Why?"

"Because you need any help you can get investigating Art McLaren. His girl seems to have taken an interest in you. Use her."

Rafael's face remained impassive, but inside he winced. He was certain that Krista McLaren couldn't be the kind of person he liked, despite his desire for her, but he didn't want to use her. "There's no evidence that she's involved in her father's dealings. She should be left out of this. Completely."

"She's his daughter. She knows things." Thompson sat down behind his desk and folded his hands over his stomach. "Things she'll tell a man under the right circumstances. Don't be a fool, Contreras. Krista McLaren is interested in you for a little fun. She's probably never slept with a Mexican before. You're hardly the kind of man she'd want anything permanent with. You'd be using each other. You sleep with her and get whatever you can on her old man before she gets bored with you."

In that moment Rafael decided that he despised his boss with every ounce of feeling he possessed. "I won't sleep with anyone for you, or this department, or the DEA, or the President of the United States." He opened the door of the office, then glanced back. "But I'll go to the damned party. Anything else?"

"No." Thompson was grinning smugly. "That's all—for now."

Rafael left the building and went to a pay phone down the street to place a call to New York. It was inconvenient, but since no one in the department knew of the McLaren investigation besides Thompson, it was a necessary precaution. McLaren was a rich man, and he ruled this part of the state. He could easily persuade someone to pass information along to him.

"Houseman."

"Contreras."

"What's up?"

"I need some information on McLaren's daughter."

"Anything in particular?"

Rafael scowled. Sure, tell me she's not like Rebecca. Tell me it's all right to sleep with her. "Everything for the last couple of years."

"Sure," Richard Houseman agreed. "You think she might be involved?"

"No. Just checking."

"All right. Anything else?

"No."

"Has McLaren been doing anything?"

"He had visitors last week. Baker and Smith."

"I know them. They work out of Miami. I wonder if he's planning to expand his business again. Listen, I'll get that information to you as soon as it's ready."

Rafael hung up and headed back to work. Had he asked for that information because it might help their case? Or because the suspect's daughter was fast becoming a personal interest?

He left the question unanswered, because the answer didn't please him. No, it didn't please him one bit.

"Why did you call him *'señor'?*"

"He called me *'señorita.'*"

"No, he didn't. He called you 'Miss McLaren' in a voice that would freeze the desert."

"Well, the last time I saw him, he called me *'señorita.'* Is this going to be another lecture to stay away from him, Royce Ann? Because if it is, I think I've heard all I want to hear, okay?" Krista asked with a sigh. She appreciated her friend's concern, but it was wearying.

"The man has no heart, no warmth and no feelings."

Krista remembered his hands on her body Saturday, his kisses, the response of his body, and she smiled secretively. "No," she softly disagreed. "He's got feelings." And she was going to bring them out if it killed them both.

Chapter 4

Parties were important affairs in Nueva Vida, parties at the McLarens' doubly so. The fact that this one was being hosted by Krista McLaren made Rafael especially reluctant to go. Though the invitation had been for seven o'clock, at seven forty-five he was still at home, still naked after his shower. He was trying to think of an acceptable excuse for not going. Failing at that, he pulled himself off the bed and began dressing.

He wasn't sure how the rest of Krista's guests would be dressed, but he wasn't going to change his style for her. He put on a pair of comfortable blue jeans, a red knit sport shirt and worn sneakers. Unable to delay any longer, he left for the McLaren house.

The backyard was brightly lit with floodlights and lanterns. Tables laden with food extended the length of the yard on one side, and smaller tables were scattered around for dining. The patio had been cleared for dancing, and a corner of the yard was set apart for the younger children. There was music, talk, lots of laughter. The guests were all having a good time. All but Rafael.

He got a bottle of beer from the tub filled with ice and a half dozen brands of beer, both domestic and imported—but not from Mexico. He flipped the cap into an overflowing trash can, then found a dark wall to lean against.

It was easy to find Krista in the crowd. She was smiling that beautiful smile, playing the perfect hostess, making the rest of her guests comfortable and making him damned uncomfortable. His jeans seemed a hell of a lot tighter than they'd been fifteen minutes ago.

She wore a yellow sundress of some clingy fabric that draped over every curve and exposed long, shapely legs. The bodice was loose, hiding her breasts, yet revealing them with every breath she took.

Oh, God, she's beautiful, and I can't have her.

The thought angered him, and he bitterly countered it. I *could* have her. I could make love to her tonight if I let myself... but I won't.

Krista felt his eyes on her, and she slowly turned searching for him. Finally a movement against the house identified him, and she started in his direction, avoiding friends who would want to talk. "Hello."

Rafael glanced at her but didn't speak.

"I'm surprised you came."

"Are you?" he asked dryly. He doubted that.

Krista didn't mind his obvious reluctance to be there. Given enough time she could wear down his resistance, convince him that she was, to use his words, worth the effort. Until that happened, she would use any means to spend time with him. "Are you hungry?"

"No."

"Want to dance?"

"No."

"Want to talk?"

He turned his head to study her. "Yes. Look at your guests. Notice anything odd?"

"No. It's just people from town."

"There must be a hundred people here."

"About that."

"Ninety-nine white people—and me. I'm the only non-white here. 'Just people from town.' A border town that's about fifty percent Hispanic, and you invite one to your party." He gave a snort of disgust. "Of course, there are the servants, the people waiting on your guests, serving their food, baby-sitting their kids, parking their cars—they're all Mexican, aren't they?"

Krista could feel her face turning red, but instead of defending herself, she quietly observed, "You have a real prejudice against white people, don't you?"

Rafael took a swallow of beer. "I don't like people in general."

"And you don't like me in particular."

He heard an odd quiver of emotion in her voice and looked at her, but in the shadow of the house he could see very little.

"It's not fair. You don't know me."

"I don't want to know you."

"Why not?"

He thought of the answers he could give her. Because you *scare me. Because I want you*, and wanting can easily change to needing. And the most important one of all: because I'm one of the men who's going to put your father in jail for the rest of his miserable life. But he couldn't say any of those things, so he answered her question with one of his own. "Why should I?"

She smiled. "Because I'm a nice person."

"Well, I'm not."

She scoffed at that; then a movement in the light caught her eye. It was Royce Ann, heading in their direction. "Let's go inside and talk," she suggested, moving quickly to avoid her friend.

Rafael knew Art McLaren was too smart to leave anything incriminating lying around the house for a nosy border-patrol agent to pick up, but he followed her anyway, because it practically guaranteed privacy. If they were inside the house it would be harder for any of her ninety-nine guests to interrupt and pull her away from him, and he self-ishly wanted her to himself.

They went into the house, unnoticed by anyone but the disapproving Royce Ann. Krista led the way through the kitchen to a broad hallway and entered the third room on the right. Rafael remained at the door until she had turned on a small lamp. Then he closed the door behind him, his fingers turning the lock—to ensure their privacy, of course.

"So talk, *señorita,*" he said in a raspy, gravelly voice that made her shiver.

Krista gestured to the sofa. "Sit down, please." When he had done so, she joined him, sitting close but not threaten-ingly so. "I'm glad you came."

"I bet you are, *señorita,*" he said sarcastically. "Men don't turn you down very often, do they?"

She lifted her shoulders in a delicate shrug. "I don't of-fer very often."

Sitting alone with her in the small library was sheer mad-ness. He must have been crazy to think he could come in here with her, shut off from the other guests and not touch her. Or maybe he *wanted* to touch her, wanted to be reck-less and incautious and seduce her despite all the warnings.

Krista was hoping he would do something, anything, but when it came, she was startled by his directness. One long, brown finger, still cool from the beer bottle he held, hooked beneath a tiny strap and guided it off her shoulder. The ac-tion was repeated with the other strap; then Rafael pushed the bodice of her dress to her waist.

His throat was suddenly dry, and he drained the last of the beer, then leaned forward to set the bottle on the floor. Krista sat motionless, barely breathing, afraid any move-ment on her part might cause another withdrawal like that of last weekend.

Her breasts were perfect. For a long moment he simply looked at them; then he reached out to touch one. His fin-gers stroked lightly over her flesh, and he saw the coral tip stiffen as his fingers came closer to it. Leaving it unsatisfied, he transferred his caresses to the other breast, watching its identical response.

"You wanted to talk, *señorita,*" he reminded her.

"T-talk?" she echoed. She could barely *think; talking* was out of the question.

He rolled one pebble-hard nipple between his fingers, and Krista softly moaned. He watched the pleasure he brought steal across her face while his fingers teased, stroked, learned her breasts intimately. Finally he bent over her, casting his shadow on her, and kissed her mouth. He didn't have to coax her; she was eager to accept him, her mouth parting for his tongue's leisurely explorations.

It was a lovely kiss, and it made Krista greedy. "Again," she whispered, and Rafael obliged her. He nibbled at her full lower lip, evading her attempts to guide his tongue into her mouth again. His left hand came up to play lazily with an aching breast. When she triumphed over him and got his tongue where she wanted it, he gave her a surprise by gliding his hand across her midriff, beneath the elastic waist of her dress and across her abdomen.

She wore tiny panties, only a scrap of lace and a bit of elastic. His fingers eased beneath the garment. They searched through the silken curls and found her, and his mouth pressed hard against hers in time to swallow the moan that trembled through her.

God, how he wanted her! The fact that ninety-nine people, including her father and his boss, were right outside didn't cool his desire one bit. He pushed her down on the cushions and moved over her, one powerful leg thrust between hers, the masculine evidence of his desire burning hot against her thigh. He was going to take her, right there on the sofa, in the middle of her party; he was going to bury himself in her, fill her with his hard need, and consequences be damned.

"Oh, please," she whispered soundlessly, but he understood the words; he felt them. Yes, he would please. He would give her such pleasure that no man would ever satisfy her again. Oh, yes, he would definitely please her.

There was a rap at the locked door. "Krista?" Royce Ann softly called. "Your father wants you now."

She could have cried. Finally Rafael wanted her, and for the first time in years, so did her father. She wanted to remain silent, but already Rafael was drawing away from her. "All right, Royce Ann," she replied, her voice unnaturally low. "I'll be right there."

Rafael moved his weight off her, both grateful for and resentful of the interruption. He silently drew her up and pulled the straps of her dress back in place. He arranged the bodice, his hand lingering over one breast.

"This will just take a minute," she said softly, reaching for his hands. "Please wait, Rafael. Please?"

He didn't answer. Wait, so she could return and finish the scene? So she could seduce him with her eyes, her smile, her mere presence? Wait, so she could destroy him with her charm? With the gift of her body?

Not damned likely. He waited till she was gone, out of the room and out of the house; then he left. He left through the front doors and crossed the lawn to the rows of parked cars.

Her father's demands took only a minute, and Krista hurried back inside. When she found the room empty she knew he was leaving, so she headed outside and toward the cars. "Sneaking off?"

Rafael stopped without turning and waited until she caught up. He delivered the insult in a soft, almost pleasant voice. "No reason to stay."

Krista walked with him to his truck, parked at the end of the line. "There's a name for women who do what you do," she said flippantly. "What happened, Rafael? Did you suddenly remember who I am? Does the thought of making love to me make your skin crawl?"

Rafael's face remained blank. "If you're so determined to have a Mexican lover, there are a lot of them around, and most of them work for your father, so they can't refuse."

She smiled slowly, and he thought it made her beautiful. She should always smile. "I don't want them. I don't want a Mexican. I want *you.* Why can't we be friends, Rafael?"

That notion—that they, with all their differences, could ever be friends—roused his anger, and he turned an icy glare on her. She didn't even know the meaning of the word. Women like her, like Rebecca, thought they could have anything they wanted. Krista had decided she wanted *him*, and in her arrogance she refused to recognize that *he* had a say in the matter. She acted as if it was her right to demand the use of his time, his body and even his heart, but damn it, she couldn't do that!

He grasped her wrist and gritted out cruelly, "I don't want to be your amusement while you're bored, and I sure as hell don't want to be your friend!"

He couldn't have surprised her more if he'd slapped her. His anger was a cold and frightening thing, and it made her quake, but it didn't stop her from asking why. He wasn't the first person to reject her, but he was going to be the first to give a reason. "Why not? What's wrong with me?" she demanded.

"Why me?" he demanded in return. "There are a dozen men out back who would love to be your *friend*." He put all his anger and loathing and disgust into the word, making it sound like something dirty. "Why pick on me?"

"Why did you kiss me like that?"

The soft, unexpected question left him staring until he couldn't meet her gaze any longer; those blue eyes were too trusting, too sincere. His eyes dropped to her mouth, but that was a mistake, too. Her lips were soft and full and made him remember their kisses, made him want more.

"Why did you kiss me that way?" she repeated softly.

His fingers on her wrist gentled and slid down to find hers. "That's the way I kiss," he answered stupidly. He felt thickheaded, off balance, unable to think. Unable to do anything but want.

"Why me?" Krista sensed she was making some headway, and she gently pushed for more. Maybe that ice was starting to thaw.

"You wanted me to."

"And you wanted to."

"And I wanted to," he repeated.

The shock of what he'd said snapped the spell she'd woven around him, and his voice became harsh and mocking. "Why shouldn't I kiss you? You've been throwing yourself at me since we met. Why shouldn't I take advantage of it? I'm sure countless others have."

He was goading her, Krista realized, trying to anger her or maybe hurt her. Otherwise, why *hadn't* he taken advantage? He could have seduced her on that sofa. Instead he had run at the first chance he got.

"Are you afraid of me?"

Rafael caught his breath; then he laughed—a low, ugly sound. "Afraid of you?" he asked sardonically. *Damned right.* He looped his arm around her waist and pulled her up against him. "What's to be afraid of?" He would show her that he simply didn't care. He would make her stay away, make her lose interest in him. "I kissed you. So what? You're not naive enough to think it meant anything, are you?"

And to prove it, he kissed her again. Krista melted against him, giving herself up to the pleasure of his mouth. Maybe it meant nothing to him, but she'd never felt so good, so alive. She wanted to stay in his arms forever.

The blood rushing through his veins was hot, spreading its heat throughout his body. It was hell kissing her, holding her, and knowing that soon he had to let her go. He wouldn't mind being condemned to such hell for a while longer.

He bent her back over his arm. When he lifted his mouth he reached up to fondle her breast. There was a twist to his lips that faintly resembled a smile. "Thanks for the diversion, *señorita*." He pushed her back and swung into the truck.

Her face was pale, but her cheeks burned with the flush of passion or anger; he wasn't sure which. He wanted her angry, angry enough to forget she wanted him and how much he wanted her. He cupped her cheek in one rough palm. "You're not bad. When I get bored again and there's no one better around, I'll come back to finish this."

In a flash of temper Krista shoved his hand away, her fingernails raking over it; then the anger died. "Go home, Rafael," she ordered quietly. There was a wealth of emotion in her voice—disappointment, weariness, hurt.

She watched him drive away, depression settling over her like a physical weight. Was it just her he didn't like, or had something happened that made him distrust everyone? Was she ever going to convince him to give her a chance? And if he refused that chance, how was she ever going to forget him?

For several long minutes Rafael could see her in the rearview mirror, silhouetted by the floodlights. He wanted to go back to her, wanted to take her to his house and make love to her until they were both too weak to move.

But he didn't go back. He kept driving, into Nueva Vida, through the border checkpoint and into San Ignacio. The little house at the end of the street was quiet, lights shining through the front windows. He parked the Bronco behind Constancia's car and went inside.

She wasn't surprised by the reason behind his visit. She'd realized that he was losing interest in her. She suspected that he had met the woman he'd never believed existed—the one who could make him love. It had pleased her to find that she was ready to move forward without him. He had been an important part of her life for a long time, but she'd always known there were emotions in him she couldn't touch, hadn't wanted to touch. She guessed he felt the same about her. The circumstances that had made her happy with their relationship had changed, and now she wanted more. She wanted to find the man who could give it to her, and she knew it wasn't Rafael.

When she pulled his head down and kissed both cheeks, then whispered, "Be happy, my friend," she meant it. And inside she made a silent wish of luck for the woman who had succeeded in touching his heart. Rafael deserved to be happy.

* * *

"I hope I didn't interrupt anything important," Royce Ann said when Krista finally returned to the party, "but I saw you and Rafe go inside, and I figured it would be better for me to find you than for your father to."

"His name is Rafael. Is it too much to ask to be called by your name?" Krista asked darkly.

"Everyone at work calls him Rafe."

"Did they ever ask him if he minded?"

"I don't—"

"Of course not. Why should they care?"

Royce Ann stared at her. "I take it Rafe—Rafael—left sooner than you wanted?" At Krista's glum nod she continued. "I just don't know what to do with you. All the available men in the county are in front of you, and you're pining for the one man who couldn't care less."

Icy blue eyes raked over her. "Thanks a lot, Royce Ann. Are you trying to destroy the small bit of confidence that survived Rafael?"

Royce Ann murmured an apology, then caught her husband's arm as he passed by on the way to get a beer. "Talk some sense into her head before it's too late," she commanded before escaping to chat with another friend.

Jim Stone smiled faintly. "Would you like to talk, Krista?"

"Why not?" she asked crossly. "I've got nothing better to do."

"Care to take a walk?"

"Why not?"

They left the lights and noise of the party behind and headed toward the stables. "So what's up, Krista?"

"Nothing. How about you? Your life all right?"

"Sure." Jim leaned back against the corral fence, resting his arms behind him along the top rail. "How long are you going to stay?"

"Oh . . . I don't know. Maybe a month. Maybe a week. Maybe forever."

"Nice. Well . . . so much for that. What am I supposed to be talking sense to you about?"

Krista turned to lean her chin on the fence. There was one horse in the corral, a mare that trotted over for a little attention. Krista stroked the horse for a moment, then slid her hand beneath her chin to protect it from the rough wood. "You know, Jim, in New York, if I want a date, usually all I have to do is choose someone, and he's willing."

Jim could easily believe that. He'd had a crush on Krista himself years ago, when they'd first met.

"Maybe things got too easy. Maybe that's why this seems so difficult," she mused. "Maybe that's why he seems so different."

"I assume you're talking about Rafe Contreras."

She nodded glumly. "What do you know about him?"

"He's a very private man. He does his job and minds his own business, and he expects us to mind ours. He's good at his work—damned good. I'd rather be out there with him than anyone else."

"Friends?"

"None, as far as I know."

"Family?"

He shook his head. "Not that I know of."

Krista sighed. "You're not a lot of help."

"Sorry." Jim hesitantly touched her arm. "You've really fallen for him, haven't you? I wish I could help you out, Krista, but . . . I don't know how."

She raised her head and turned to look at him. "You could get me a date."

"With Rafe? I don't—"

"Royce Ann says there's a guy named Darren?"

"Darren Carter. He's the tall, thin one."

"If he's interested in a very casual date, I think I would enjoy going out."

"Sure, Krista. I'll talk to him."

Darren's weekend date with Krista was the talk of the office Monday morning. Nick and Mike were envious, Martin Thompson almost triumphant. The look he shot Rafael shouted, "I told you so." In Martin's mind Rafael wasn't the kind of man Krista would want a permanent relationship with; she would inevitably get bored. It had just happened a little sooner than Thompson expected.

Throughout Darren's recitation of his evening with Krista and the others' questions, Rafael's face remained set in its usual impassive lines, but underneath he couldn't stop the jealousy that smoldered into life. He was very careful, though, to show absolutely nothing, because he was being watched closely by Jim Stone for some response.

Who are you trying to fool? he asked himself. You want her, and she knows it. And you *are* jealous. You should be relieved, not wondering if she responded to Carter's kisses the way she responds to yours, not wishing you could break his neck for touching her.

Jim Stone stopped beside Rafael's desk. "You ready to go, Rafe?"

He rose from the desk, reaching for his coffee with his left hand.

"You've got some nasty scratches there," Jim remarked. "You tangle with a tiger?"

"A cat," Rafael corrected him, then amended that. "A wildcat." He swallowed the last of his coffee and tossed the cup in the trash.

Jim followed him out of the building, quietly murmuring, "A blue-eyed wildcat?"

Rafael pretended not to hear him as he swung into the driver's seat of the truck. Normally he didn't mind working with Stone; if he had to have a partner, he preferred Jim, but today he would rather have been alone. He didn't want to spend today with a friend of Krista's.

The usual silence was strained as they patrolled their sector—miles of dusty, dry desert. After a couple of hours Jim thought that if he didn't hear someone's voice he would go mad, so he initiated a conversation—or at least he tried.

"I've known Krista a long time."

Rafael stopped the truck at the top of a hill and switched off the engine. They had a clear view across the border.

"She's a nice woman."

Rafael stared ahead as if his partner hadn't spoken. His eyes were hidden behind the mirrored sunglasses, and they were empty, as usual.

It was hot, but Rafael didn't mind. When Jim turned to get a cold Coke from the small ice chest in back, he offered Rafael one, but it was refused. "Krista's nice, friendly. It's her nature," Jim continued, popping the top of the can.

"Aggressive," Rafael corrected before he could stop himself.

"Not really... well, maybe a little. But what's so bad about that? She's pretty, and she's a good friend, and she's smart."

Slowly Rafael turned his head and Jim felt that piercing stare even though he couldn't see it. It almost made him squirm.

"Why are you telling me this?" Rafael asked in a gravelly voice, his mouth barely moving beneath the neat mustache.

"You know why."

"I'm not interested."

"Have you told her that?"

Repeatedly. He looked back toward the border before answering. "Ask her."

Whatever Rafael had told Krista, he was being chivalrous, Jim thought, in not repeating it. The man was more interested than he wanted to admit.

"She's awfully pretty, isn't she?" Jim took a long drink from the can, then reached into his pocket for his sunglasses. "She and Royce Ann moved here about the same time, and they were best friends in high school. For a long time I had a crush on Krista. It wasn't until just before graduation that I started dating Royce Ann. It almost doesn't seem fair for one woman to be so pretty, does it?"

No, it didn't, Rafael agreed. It didn't seem fair that she had such a strong effect on him. It didn't seem fair that she reminded him so much of Rebecca, or that he was investigating her father. But Rafael had learned at a very young age not to expect fairness. He had to cope with what was given, and what he'd been given was a very strong desire for a woman he couldn't have, shouldn't even want.

He tilted his head from side to side to ease the stiffness in his neck. If he'd been alone he would have sighed hopelessly. Krista McLaren was the only woman he wanted—the only woman who could fill his hunger. How could he cope with that?

Krista L. A. McLaren.

Her name was neatly typed across the top of the folder that Rafael found in his mailbox Friday evening. The manila envelope carried a return address in New York that Rafael knew was Richard Houseman's address. Inside the envelope was the folder, with information on Krista.

Though her career as a clothing designer was just taking off, thanks to family money she lived in an expensive apartment, drove a German-made sports car, went to fabulous parties, wore elegant clothes and dated rich and famous men, among them an Italian count and an American movie star. Her friends were models, designers, actors and people too rich to bother with work. There were no ties to the drug world. If she was part of Art McLaren's deals, the connections were well hidden.

Houseman had included photographs, neatly clipped from newspapers and magazines, the publications and dates penciled in the margins. "Brand Harris at the premiere of his new movie, *Jungle of Death,* with girlfriend Krista McLaren...." "Michel Deveraux made an appearance at the Cannes festival with designer Krista McLaren..." "Krista McLaren to become Lord Andrew Phillips's leading lady?"

Apparently not, for the next photo showed Krista at the wedding reception for Lord Andrew Phillips, one of Britain's most sought-after bachelors, and Krista's close friend Devon Marks. The picture was over a year old, the only decent photo in the folder, and in color. Krista looked absolutely gorgeous, Rafael decided, once his erratic heartbeat had slowed. Next to her the bride and every other woman at the reception paled into nothingness. She was smiling that brilliant smile that did strange things to his breathing and his blood pressure, to say nothing of its effects on other parts of his body.

He stared at the photo for a long time, fantasizing a bit, dreaming of what he would do to her if only he could. But he liked the dream too much, so he pushed it from his mind and went to the next photograph.

The World Series, last fall. "The Dodgers may have lost the Series," the caption read, "but Mike Davis, L.A. first baseman, doesn't seem to mind. He and girlfriend Krista McLaren flew to Paris immediately following the final game, partying away post-Series blues."

That fanned his jealousy, prompting him to look closely at the man. His hair was as blond as Krista's, his eyes a light blue. He wasn't particularly handsome, but apparently he had attracted Krista. Rafael wondered why, then decided he didn't want to know.

There were more photographs and excerpts from gossip columns. Rafael looked at them all, then removed the picture taken at the wedding reception. He locked the folder in his desk drawer and carried the photo into his bedroom. He called himself every insulting name he could think of, but it didn't stop him from putting the picture in his nightstand drawer.

It was cool and dark out, and Rafael needed to cool down, too. He went to the closet and pulled out a belt, threading it through the loops of his jeans. When he reached the center loop in back, he slid a leather holster onto the belt, then pushed the belt through the remaining loops. He placed a .38-caliber Colt revolver in the holster before putting his shirt on; its tails covered the gun.

There was a natural pool about a half mile from his house. It wasn't large, but the water was clear and usually cool enough to be refreshing after the desert heat. He walked east, gradually angling south. The moon was full and very bright, casting deep, black shadows. He listened closely as he walked through the canyons, but the only noises, other than those he made himself, were the natural night sounds.

The pool shimmered in the moonlight, its water still and inviting. Rafael stopped in the black shadow of a boulder as tall as he was and removed his clothes, folding them in a neat pile. His shirt was on top, the .38 hidden beneath it, easy to reach.

He walked naked to the pool, then waded into the cool water. As soon as the water deepened he dived in, slicing through it with powerful strokes. He floated, staring up at the dark sky and seeing Krista's face. If he made love to her once, would it satisfy his desire? Or would one taste of her sweetness make him hunger for more?

The men he worked with would laugh if they knew that cold, unfeeling, inhuman Rafe Contreras was spending most of his hours fantasizing about a woman who dated athletes and actors and noblemen. He was becoming obsessed with a woman who was so far out of his league that they didn't even play the same games.

What would any woman want with Rafael when she could have Brand Harris, the hottest actor to grace the silver screen in years, or Mike Davis, one of the highest-paid athletes in the country? He could never compete with those men. He wasn't rich or famous, and he never would be. He'd never be anything more than what he was right now: a hard-working, low-paid border-patrol agent, ruthless, chilling, cold-blooded. A man to be feared. A man who was going to take away the father she loved, the only family she had. A man who could never offer her anything...except love.

Rafael closed his eyes. Obsession he would accept; he could handle that. But love? After Rebecca, how could he ever love any woman again? Especially one so much like Rebecca?

No, he couldn't allow himself to fall in love with Krista McLaren. That path could only lead to disaster.

Krista lazily swirled her Coke in its glass, watching the ice cubes circle. She wasn't bored, but she feared that her restlessness made her seem so, and she made an extra effort to pretend interest in the conversation around her.

Three weeks had gone by since she'd first seen Rafael Contreras right here in the Blue Parrot. When Darren Carter had invited her here for a drink she had accepted, she was ashamed to admit, only in the hopes that Rafael might once again be there. She should have known better than to even hope. Rafael had made it clear last Friday that he wanted nothing from her. Why couldn't she just accept that and forget about him?

"Sure you don't want a drink? Beer or maybe wine?" Darren asked.

Krista smiled faintly. "I don't drink."

"At all?"

"Not at all." She glanced at her watch. Nine o'clock. "Darren, I hate to ask, but...I need to get home soon. I've got to finish some work in the next couple of days or I'll be in serious trouble."

"No problem. I've got to work tomorrow, too." Darren was relieved at the chance to take her home. Krista was pretty, and nice enough, but her mind was obviously on something—or someone—else, and the hour they'd spent together had been uncomfortable at best. He took her straight home and didn't try to kiss her even once. Krista thanked him politely and went inside the house, avoiding her father in the den and climbing the stairs to her room.

Her restlessness didn't leave her. She tried to watch television, but nothing looked good. She couldn't concentrate on the book she'd started a few days earlier, and she couldn't even think about work, the excuse she'd used for making it an early evening.

A swim. That would be nice, she thought, and she went to the closet to choose a swimsuit.

The pink-and-white camisole and the white skirt she'd made a few weeks ago hung in a prominent spot in the big closet, neatly pressed. Krista reached out to touch the skirt, then quickly began undressing.

She would take her swim, but not in the backyard pool. No, she'd take Diablo and ride to the pool at the old Moreno place. At Rafael Contreras's place. She wouldn't go to his house, wouldn't try to see him; she was just going to take a nice, late-night swim in the pond where she and Royce Ann had spent two pleasant summers. Rafael wouldn't mind, because he wouldn't know, and the ride would soothe her nerves.

On impulse Krista pulled the skirt over head and around her waist. She put on the camisole, then left the closet, walking past shelves of shoes. Barefoot, she left the house for the stables.

Diablo greeted her with a nuzzle before she swung onto his back. It was a beautiful night for a ride, she thought, all moonlight and shadows.

A beautiful night for lovers.

Chapter 5

Rafael left the water and went to sit in the shadow of the rock. He ran his hand through his wet hair, brushing it straight back, then leaned back against the warm rock to stare at the sky again.

He heard the sounds of a horse: the click of shoes against rock; the sliding of pebbles; the whisper of hooves in soft sandy dirt; and he instinctively reached for the gun beneath his shirt.

The night was clear, the full moon gleaming up above. The moonlight made deep shadows, shadows of pure black, like the one that hid Rafael. It was from such a shadow that the horse appeared. Rafael had seen the big animal only once, a few weeks ago, but he recognized it. Each step Diablo took separated him from the blackness and revealed more of his power and beauty. Each step also revealed more of his rider.

She rode without a saddle, needing to be a part of her mount, one with the magnificent stallion. Her feet were bare, as were her legs, gold in the light of the moon. A froth of white skirt covered her hips, bunched up around her thighs, and a pale-colored top covered her breasts leaving her arms bare. Her hair fell down her back, waves of shimmering gold that caught and reflected and absorbed the moon's rays, glowing and glimmering and gleaming.

"Krista."

Rafael said the name in a whisper that had no sound, and his body tightened. His obsession. His fantasy. Even the thought, the saying, of her name could affect him like no other woman ever had.

As Rafael watched and listened and felt, the stallion picked his way over the stone-littered ground, circling the pool toward him. Krista moved naturally with the sway of the horse, a part of him, and Rafael wondered how it would feel if she rode him—if, instead of the powerful stallion, she were sitting astride *him,* legs locked around his hips, moving with the thrusts of his body inside hers.

Unhampered by clothes, his body responded again. What would she think, beautiful, rich Krista, if she could see him now, hard and aching for her? She had won. Their lovemaking was inevitable. It would be tonight.

He laid the gun down, covering it with his shirt. Still in shadow, he watched and waited.

The pool looked inviting, its smooth surface beckoning Krista. Still she sat astride Diablo, her swim forgotten. An ache had started deep inside her when she'd reached the far side of the pool. He was there, in that shadow, the man who made her feel this way. Rafael. She could see nothing, hear nothing, not even his breathing, but he was there, wanting her and making her want him.

The stallion stopped, and Krista slid to the ground. She stood at the edge of the shadow, the moon shining fully on her.

Rafael's breath caught at the sight before him. His hands came up to reach for her, then fell back to his sides. One last time he told himself to leave her alone, but he knew the warning would be unheeded.

Krista took a step toward him, holding out her hands. "Come to me," she invited, her voice soft and husky and sensuous. "Please, Rafael." His feet moved of their own accord, disregarding his brain's command to stop, until he was only two feet in front of her. There was no surprise on her face, only warmth and hunger and need. She had known it would be Rafael; no one other man could make her feel this way.

He raised one hand and traced a path along her jaw. Her skin felt like satin beneath his callus-roughened hand. His fingers moved lower, sliding along her throat, the tip of his index finger coming to rest on the pulse that throbbed there. "You are beautiful."

The whisper made her smile. "And so are you."

"Why are you here?" His voice grated harshly.

"Do you want me to go?"

"Yes." But his other hand came up to cup her breast gently through the soft fabric of her top, his thumb and forefinger finding the hard peak and making it ache.

Krista hurt, longing for his hands and mouth and body to ease her pain. She caught her breath as his fingers glided over the fabric to tease the other pebble-hard nipple. Her breath seemed trapped in her throat, and she had to fight the urge to throw herself into his arms.

He stepped closer, lowering his head to the delicate shape of her ear. He nuzzled her hair back, then touched the tip of his tongue to her ear. When she shuddered, he wrapped his arms around her, pulling her hard against him. "Go home," he whispered.

"I will," she whispered back.

"Now."

"All right."

But he didn't release her. He held her so tightly that freeing herself would have been impossible, and she didn't want to be free.

In a desperate attempt to stop himself, he intentionally conjured up the image of Rebecca. Rebecca, who had used him to achieve her own goals. Rebecca, who had almost destroyed him. But his mind was too overwhelmed with the sensations his body was experiencing, and it couldn't sustain the hazy image. "Why do you want me?"

She touched him voluntarily for the first time, resting her hands on his chest, and she felt his muscles contract. "I want you, Rafael. Isn't that enough?" There was more, but she wouldn't tell him that she felt empty and alone without him. And she couldn't tell him that she thought she was falling in love with him. Her fingers flitted across his hardness before returning to his chest. "Do you want me to beg?"

He stared into her glazed blue eyes. Did he want strong, proud Krista McLaren to beg? Did he want to punish her for being like Rebecca, rich and beautiful and too good for him?

No. He would take what she offered, but he wouldn't take her pride. He closed his eyes. "This is wrong," he murmured, his breath hot and moist in her ear. "Go home before it's too late, Krista."

She wrapped her arms around him. "It's already too late for me. If you send me away tonight, Rafael, I'll die. I'll die without you."

"It's wrong."

"It will be right. We'll make it right."

She smelled so sweet, felt so soft, and he wanted her so much. His body throbbed, he ached to bury himself deep inside her softness, and soon he would. Tonight he would forget all the reasons why it was wrong. Tonight he would enjoy the forbidden pleasures of her body. Tonight he couldn't say no.

Her lips parted eagerly for his kiss, to accept the entry of his tongue. Rafael cautioned himself to move slowly, to make it good for her. He took control, his tongue guiding hers out of the way so he could leisurely explore the dark warmth of her mouth.

His seeking was gentle. Krista sensed a great deal of control in the man who held her, and she wondered if she could entice him into losing that control, into being totally wild and unrestrained and free for even a short time.

His mouth left hers, and his arms released her body. Krista started to protest her abandonment, but he silenced her with a finger on her lips. His hands moved to the ruffled hem of the camisole she wore and pulled it up, across her breasts and over her head. He let the flimsy garment fall to the ground, then began pushing the skirt slowly over her slim hips, taking her panties, too, revealing a silken nest of golden-blond curls and long, muscled thighs. At last the skirt fell to the ground. Rafael saw her naked for the first time, and he knew he was lost.

He needed time to regain his self-control, so he turned away from her. He spread out her full skirt along with his shirt to make a bed for them. When the task was completed he knelt there, his bare legs a dark contrast to the white of her skirt, and waited for her to come to him.

She stood before him on the bed of clothing, and Rafael's arm circled her hips, drawing her to him. His face turned against her belly, and he held her while his free hand caressed her blindly, stroking over her high, perfect breasts, the flatness of her stomach, the gentle curve of her hips. His fingers worshipfully touched her, touched the triangle of golden curls, finding them as soft as silk.

Krista leaned heavily against him, her legs weak and unable to bear her full weight. "Please, Rafael..." Even her whisper was weak.

He wrapped his arms tightly around her and rose to take her nipple in his mouth. He held it between his teeth while his tongue tortured it into an even harder peak. He repeated the action on her other breast, until the torment was unbearable, and she sobbed for relief, for him.

His senses screamed at him to seek his own relief; his muscles ached from their tautness. He eased Krista down to the ground, his hands gently settling her on their bed; then he knelt over her, between her thighs. His manhood rubbed against her, and she moaned his name.

"Guide me inside you," he commanded hoarsely.

She took the hard length of him in her hand and guided him until he was cradled within the moist warmth of her. He moved his hips once, until his entry was complete, then leaned over her, his mouth taking hers possessively.

Krista gave a little sigh of pure satisfaction. "I could stay like this forever."

"*I* couldn't," Rafael growled, his teeth nipping at her lip, his hips beginning to thrust into her. Between kisses he murmured to her in Spanish, knowing she couldn't understand the soft words of encouragement, adoration and intimacy. He carried her with him to heights she had never reached before, until she couldn't breath, couldn't think. Her body responded instinctively, not needing commands from her dazed brain, which could only think that this sweet agony must be heaven.

The bright explosions within her brain made the night seem like daylight and drew a long, tearful cry from her. Rafael's groan rumbled across the tiny valley at the same time, and his lean, hard body shuddered against hers.

Soft, soothing words that held no meaning for her whispered over her, quieting her, and she opened her eyes to look at Rafael. "In English," she murmured with a satisfied smile. "It sounds so nice, but I don't understand."

"You understand," he replied, brushing his lips over her ear.

His mustache tickled, and Krista smiled again before snuggling close to him. "Isn't it a beautiful night?"

"Yes," he replied, but his eyes were on her. Very beautiful. And now he had the answer to the question he'd asked himself earlier: once wasn't enough. A hundred times wouldn't be enough. Not even his hunger for Rebecca had been this strong, this intense.

Krista looked up at his stern, unsmiling face and reached out to touch his jaw. "I want you again, Rafael," she whispered.

Black eyes shifted over her face. "You're greedy."

"Of course I am." She echoed his thoughts. "I'll never get enough of you."

"You'll get bored," he disagreed with a shrug.

Krista's laugh was light. "You can't make me angry tonight, Rafael. I feel too good. I want to make love to you. I want to show you how much I want you."

He drew his hand from her hip to the soft side of her breast, then rubbed over the coral peak and felt it harden. "We can't have an affair, Krista," he said outright, with just a hint of regret.

She quickly countered his resistance. "For the weekend. For the weekend we can be lovers, Rafael."

"We're so different."

"I know. You're so strong and so hard, I'm soft. You're a man, and I'm a woman. You need nothing, and I need you." Her hands were roaming over his body, and she underscored the next point. "You're hard, and I want you. Let me make love to you, Rafael. Let me satisfy you."

With a sigh he let her push him onto his back and take control of his body. He was drugged with sensation, with wanting her as she explored every inch of his body before she moved onto him, taking him deep inside her.

After an exquisite release that left him gasping, seeing stars behind his tightly closed eyes, Rafael let emotion override common sense, and he said, "Come home with me. Just for the weekend."

Krista accepted quickly before he could rethink the invitation.

"Just for the weekend," he stressed. "Sunday night you go home and stay there."

"I understand." But she was smiling happily. She would show Rafael that she wasn't easily dissuaded—nor easily forgotten. After this weekend there would be another, and another, until Rafael couldn't bear the idea of living without her anymore than she could bear the thought of living without him.

He gently pulled away from her and began dressing. After a moment Krista shook out her skirt and pulled it on. Her panties and camisole came next. She watched him pull his boots on and tuck the gun into its holster; then she called the stallion. Diablo looked warily at the man with his mistress. He snorted as Rafael reached out to him; then he inspected the big hand that moved toward his nose. He remembered him from their previous meeting, and he smelled his mistress on him. That was enough for his approval.

Krista watched them with satisfaction. "If Diablo says you're all right, then you must be. He doesn't allow most people to touch him. Ride with me."

He easily swung onto the horse's back and extended his hand to her. She stepped onto his booted foot and let him pull her up, but instead of sitting astride the animal she sat sideways, her legs over Rafael's, her back against his arm. The position afforded her a good look at his face. He always looked so stern, so grim. It made the planes of his face harsh but couldn't hide his dark good looks. "Do you ever smile?" she asked, tracing the straight line of his mouth with a finger.

"No," he replied, and her fingertip slipped inside his mouth. He nibbled at it, sending shivers up her arm and down her spine. "I stopped years ago."

"What happened years ago?"

Hooded dark eyes stared ahead. "I learned that women can't be trusted when they use words like 'want' and 'need' and 'love.'"

She twined her arms around his neck. Then I won't say that I need you, she answered silently. I won't tell you that I love you.

He needed—no, wanted; he couldn't afford to need—to touch her, so he reached beneath her blouse, his hand easily spanning her small golden breast, his fingers capturing her nipple between them.

"You think I'm awful, don't you?"

He thought she was a spoiled rich kid used to getting everything she wanted. Despite his vows to stay away from her, she had succeeded in seducing him, had even extracted the invitation for the weekend. She had wanted him, and now she had him. But how long would she want him? How long before his differences began to bore her?

And how long would it take him to forget her, to control his body's responses to the mere sight of her, to find satisfaction with another woman?

A few hundred yards ahead a light shone yellow in the darkness. They rode to the porch of the small house, and Rafael held Krista's hand, helping her to the ground. He directed Diablo to the corral, where he left him near his own horses. His boots scuffed across the hard ground, quieting suddenly when he climbed the steps. Without breaking stride he looped his arm around Krista's waist and pulled her inside the house.

She found herself standing in the middle of a room that measured twenty by thirty feet and served as living and dining rooms and kitchen combined. It was immaculate, not a thing out of place, not a speck of dust to be seen, not a dirty dish on the counter. Somehow she had expected that, she thought wryly.

There was a television pushed into a corner, a desk in another corner. Newsmagazines were neatly stacked on a shelf of the bookcase—all in order by publication date, she'd bet—and a stereo system occupied a second row of shelves. The furniture was simple, sturdy and masculine. Few pictures hung on the wall, and there were no knickknacks, no plants, nothing to personalize the room. His books were mostly nonfiction, his taste in music mostly country.

All in all the place was about as warm and inviting as the man who lived in it. Rafael noticed that she'd made that observation, though she kept it to herself. He wondered if she knew how much her presence brightened the room. For one weekend, because of her, the house would be friendly.

"It doesn't compare to *la casa grande,* does it?"

She knew enough Spanish—barely—to know that meant "the big house," and she smiled. "It's nice. Your tastes are quite different from my father's."

"And yours?"

She gave him that smile again, as if indulging a bad-tempered child and trying not to laugh at his anger. "My tastes at this moment extend to only one thing: you." She looked around again. "This room needs—"

You, he wanted to break in, but he remained silent.

"—plants. I can bring some over tomorrow."

"I don't have time for plants."

"Five minutes to water them once a week?" She chided him with her frown. "When I pick up some clothes I'll get a couple of ivies. They're easy to take care of."

He arched one brow. "Clothes?"

"You said I can stay until Sunday night. Do you expect me to wear these the whole time?" She grinned slyly. "Or do you prefer that I wear nothing?"

"You can take your horse home in the morning and bring your car back."

Krista went to him and began unbuttoning his shirt. "You're avoiding my question. I know that I prefer *you* naked." She slipped his shirt off his shoulders and drew her fingers across his chest. She splayed her fingers over his skin. "Your skin is such a lovely color. I look sick next to you."

He looked down at her hands. Privately he thought the contrast was very nice. There was something erotic about seeing her lightly tanned skin against his, but, of course, he didn't comment on it. "Call home."

"I'm a big girl, Rafael. I don't need permission to stay out all night." She undid the button of his jeans and reached for the zipper, but he stepped back.

"You left alone at night on a horse with no saddle. You have no money, no keys, no clothes, no purse, no shoes. Call and tell them you're not coming home."

She went to the phone on his desk, dialed the number and waited for her father to answer. Even the desk was immaculate, she noted. When Art answered she informed him that she would be home the next morning. He asked no questions, and she offered no explanations.

Rafael had openly listened to her end of the conversation. When she hung up he asked, "Does your father accept everything you say, no questions asked? Why didn't he want to know where you are?''

For just a moment her smile faltered, and she gave a flat, honest answer. ''Because he doesn't care.''

The response surprised him, and he would have discounted it if not for the very brief, bleak expression that had passed through her eyes. So everything wasn't perfect at *la casa grande*.

''My bedroom is here.''

Krista followed him down a broad hallway, past several closed doors. He pointed out the bathroom as they passed; then he entered the last room. His bedroom looked more comfortable, less sterile, than the rest of the house, as if the weariness of preparing for and the muddle of waking from sleep prevented him from being as perfect.

The bed was a regular double bed, she saw with a smile. Everyone she knew owned king-size beds, big enough to get lost in. With a bed this size she could get as close to Rafael as she wanted and claim lack of space as an excuse if he complained.

Rafael saw her look at the bed with that faint smile, and he misinterpreted it. ''I suppose you're used to a bigger bed. I don't need one. I sleep alone.''

Her smile widened. ''Oh, these beds are made for two. For lovers.'' Her gaze continued around the room, noticing the fireplace of natural stone and a grouping of photographs on one wall, then reaching the mirror above the dresser. There she saw the reflection of Rafael, undressing behind her. He had removed his boots and socks, and now his hands were on the zipper of his jeans. She watched him pull the zipper down, then ease the denim over his hips. He wore nothing beneath the jeans, and in a moment he stood there naked.

Rafael was aware that she was standing motionless, watching. She turned slowly, letting her eyes move caressingly over his body. Out by the pool he had been so much in shadow; now she saw everything she hadn't seen before, and the sight made her breath catch. He was magnificent. His shoulders were broad, his waist slim, his hips narrow. He had the hard muscles of a man who worked hard, not the ugly, bunched muscles that came from time in a gym. His skin was a satiny bronze, its perfection marred here and there by small scars. He was strong and powerful, and he aroused a strong, powerful response in Krista.

Her muscles tightened, and she swallowed with difficulty. "Rafael..." She cleared her throat and tried again. "Make love to me, Rafael."

He moved to her and pulled the camisole over her head, slid the skirt down her hips, and took her to his bed.

The lamp was out, but moonlight illuminated the room. Krista wasn't asleep, though her eyes were closed and her body relaxed. If she was aware of Rafael's brooding stare she gave no sign of it. With a little sigh she moved closer to him.

He would wait until she was asleep; then he would go to the other bedroom to sleep. He couldn't share his bed with anyone, especially a snuggler like Krista; it made him feel cramped and constricted and trapped. He needed an empty bed to rest.

He'd done it. He'd made love, not once, but three times, with the woman who could destroy his life. The only woman who held any power over him. Art McLaren's daughter. Rebecca Halderman's clone. Rich, beautiful Krista.

He knew that something vital inside him had changed. His life would never be quite the same without her. But he couldn't regret one minute of the last two hours. They had been too perfect, too exquisite. He would never regret letting Krista into his life, not even when she was gone and he was alone.

Her breathing changed subtly, indicating that she was asleep. This was the time to ease her out of his arms and go to the room across the hall to sleep. Still, Rafael held her. He turned his head and breathed in the scent of her hair and the musk of her perfume before pressing a kiss to her forehead. She sighed softly and turned onto her side, her arm gliding over his ribs to hold him close. Her leg moved, knee bent, to rest between his legs, and she sighed again and became still.

He would lie here with her just a few minutes longer, hold her just a little longer....

His eyes slowly closed, and his breathing became as deep and even as Krista's. The shadows moved across the room and covered them with a blanket of darkness.

There was a brief moment, when Rafael awoke to a sun-filled room, when he couldn't remember why this person was in his bed. He didn't share his bed with any woman; it made him restless, and he didn't sleep well. Then he realized that he felt very rested, and he recognized the scent of the woman he was lying behind, and he remembered the feel and the taste of the small breast his hand had covered possessively in his sleep. He didn't share his bed with *any* woman, but he could share it with *this* woman.

His fingers moved reflexively over her breast and found its nipple hard. "Are you awake yet?" a soft, sexy, feminine voice asked.

"Yes."

Krista turned to face him, remaining in the circle of his arm. She wasn't sure what to expect from him this morning. Blue eyes probed his face, finding no hint there. At last she bent forward and pressed a gentle kiss to his unshaven cheek. "Good morning."

Is it? he wondered. You shouldn't be here. I'm a damned fool for letting you stay. But he chose to ignore the silent voice. For this weekend he would be a fool.

"What would you like to do today?"

Rafael looked down. Her body was against his, her breasts pressing into his chest, and he almost smiled. What would he like to do? He'd like to keep her in his bed, naked and soft and warm, and feast on her body. He found the idea of making love to Krista all day most appealing.

"First," he began slowly, "you need some clothes."

"All right. And then? What do you usually do on Saturdays?"

"Work."

It was the answer she expected. Hadn't he been working in the intense afternoon heat when she'd come over a few weeks ago? "All right. You work and I'll watch you." She smiled shyly. "I might even help you." She placed a kiss on his chin, then wriggled out of his arms, left the bed and hastily dressed. "I'll be back in an hour."

Rafael rose from the bed and walked to the closet. When he came out he was wearing a pair of cutoffs. "I'll get your horse."

It took her an hour and ten minutes to ride home, pack, shower and drive back in her Mustang. Rafael was sitting on the porch steps, wearing faded jeans and no shirt or shoes, drinking a glass of ice water. He met her at the car, taking the expensive leather suitcase from her.

"Thanks." She leaned toward the floorboard and came up with a box holding three pots. "This is an ivy, and the lacy one is Spanish ivy, and this is a coleus. We can take some cuttings and root them, and you'll have plenty of plants in no time."

Rafael looked at the plants that he'd told her he couldn't take care of and just shook his head. He was beginning to learn that this was typical of Krista: she wouldn't take no for an answer.

"Did you eat breakfast while I was gone?" she asked.

He shook his head, holding the door open for her. He had showered and shaved and sat on the steps, watching for the cloud of dust that signaled her return, and he had watched the time, wondering if she might change her mind and not come back.

"Good. I brought Juana's famous recipe for cinnamon rolls, and just in case you don't have all the ingredients, I brought them, too." She nodded to a paper bag wedged between the pots. "I guarantee they're the best rolls you've ever tasted."

She set the box on the dining table and removed the plants, then carried the sack into the kitchen. Rafael refilled his glass from a pitcher in the refrigerator before sitting down on a bar stool to watch.

"Why are you here?"

She spared only a quick glance from the mass she was stirring in his largest bowl. "Here with you, or here in Nueva Vida?"

"In Nueva Vida."

"I came to visit my dad, though I don't know why, and to see my old friends, and to get out of New York," she said candidly. "I don't like New York much."

"Nueva Vida must be boring after the city."

"No, I definitely haven't been bored. Have you ever lived in a city?"

"San Diego."

"Did you like it?"

"No."

"Why not?"

"Too many people."

"Did you find Nueva Vida boring after you left San Diego?"

"No, but—" She had trapped him before he realized it. "But you're different."

Krista frowned uneasily. "I wish you wouldn't say that."

"It's the truth."

"You don't have to make it sound like an insult. What are the old cliches? 'Variety is the spice of life.' *'Viva la différence.'*" Her easy smile returned. "Let me add a little spice to your life, Rafael."

He couldn't stop the quick grin that turned up the corners of his mouth. "You already have."

Krista looked at him, and kept looking long after the grin was gone. Without commenting she turned her dough into an oiled bowl, covered it with a dish towel and set it outside on the porch. "That will rise in no time in this heat," she explained when she returned. She measured brown sugar, spices and nuts into a bowl, set a pan of butter on the stove to melt and reached for a battered coffeepot. "Want some coffee?"

He nodded. "It's in the freezer."

"That's where I keep mine, too. Have you ever been married?"

Rafael watched her spoon the coffee grounds into the basket. She filled the pot with water, then turned in time to see his scowl. "No."

"Is that look for the institution of marriage or for a close call?" she teased.

"Both."

"I like the idea of marriage. I plan to get married someday. I'm going to have about a dozen kids."

"And hire how many servants to take care of them?"

"None."

He looked skeptical. "What about your parties and your trips and your career?"

Krista shook her head. "You have some strange ideas about me, Señor Contreras. Why would I want to do those things if I had a husband and children to be with instead?" She drew a bar stool close to his and sat down. "I think you have me confused with someone else . . . maybe that woman who made you stop smiling years ago. Am I a lot like her?"

He didn't want to talk about Rebecca, to notice the similarities between her and Krista. He didn't want to do anything but look at her and touch her and make love to her.

"Why do you live in New York if you don't like it?" he asked to distract himself and to lead her away from Rebecca.

"It's as good a place as any, I suppose." She retrieved the dough from outside and began working it, rolling it out, spreading it with melted butter, then with the sugar mixture, shaping it into a tight roll, then slicing it. She arranged the pieces of dough in a pan and set them aside to rise a second time. When she was ready to talk again she moved to a new subject. "Those pictures on your bedroom wall—is that your family?"

"Yes."

"Show them to me, please."

Rafael hesitated, then extended his hand and led her down the hall to his room. There were four photographs. He pointed out his parents, grandparents, brothers and sisters and their families, rattling off names that were melodious and exotic sounding. Krista was intrigued by the names and the numbers.

"There are so many of them!" she exclaimed. She was trying to count, but she couldn't remember which were brothers and sisters and which were in-laws.

"There are twelve. I'm the thirteenth. The unlucky one." The one responsible for the worst time of their lives, he finished in his mind.

Krista glanced at him, but his face gave away nothing. She moved to look at the final picture. "A family reunion?"

"A year ago."

"Why aren't you here?"

"I didn't go."

"Why not?"

Rafael walked out of the room. Back in the kitchen he poured two cups of coffee while Krista put the rolls in the oven. He sat down again on the bar stool. "I haven't seen my family in seven years."

His voice sounded harsh and raspy in the silence of the house. Krista waited for him to continue, but nothing came. "Why not?" He obviously loved them.

Rafael stared into his coffee for a long time. Finally he shook his head, refusing to answer. Krista was familiar enough with guilt to recognize that that was what kept him from his family. He felt he'd done something to hurt them, and his guilt kept him away. *The unlucky one*, he'd said. "Whatever it was," she said softly. "I'm sure they don't blame you. They look too nice, too loving."

Her insight made him withdraw from her. Krista could actually see him pulling into himself, the hard coldness protecting him until the painful memories had been buried again.

"Every summer at the Del Mar fair, north of San Diego, they sell cinnamon rolls that smell almost as good as those." Rafael grasped Krista's wrist and pulled her to him, fitting her between his thighs. His breath was warm and moist when he pressed his mouth to the hollow at the base of her throat. His tongue moved slowly to wet the skin; then it followed a trail up her throat to her ear. "Why are you here, Krista?" he murmured, his mustache brushing over her ear at the same time that his hands unbuttoned her blouse. "Why?"

"Because I want to be," she responded. She gasped when his hands found and covered her breasts.

"I'm glad you are." Rafael ducked his head to suck one hard coral bud into his mouth, and Krista cried out softly, steadying herself with her hands on his shoulders.

The buzzing started softly, then grew into a harsh, discordant noise that was impossible to ignore. Slowly Rafael raised his head, refastened the buttons on her blouse and gently pushed her away. "The rolls," he said.

She went to the oven and shut off the timer before opening the door. The aromas of cinnamon and fresh-baked bread filled the room. They ate on the sofa, coffee cups balanced on their knees, their plates filled with hot, sticky rolls.

"Are they as good as the ones at the Del Mar fair?" Krista asked, fishing for a little flattery.

"Better." He cleared the dishes away. He pulled her to her feet and kissed her, tasting the last bit of syrup on her lips. "I've got to do some work on my truck. You can stay in here where it's cool."

And let him get out of her sight? Not very likely. "I'll come out and watch you and dream erotic dreams," she said with a secretive smile.

With a man like Rafael, was there any other kind?

Chapter 6

"It's hot outside," Rafael warned, his attention concentrated on her mouth. He liked that smile, and he reached up to touch it, to capture it.

Krista turned his right hand to her lips, pressing a kiss to the back of it, then raised his left hand. She stopped suddenly when she saw it.

Silence echoed in her ears as she stared at the four deep scratches that extended from wrist to knuckles. They were scabbed over and healing, but still looked very painful. Sickened by the knowledge that she had done that to him when he left her party, Krista tried to speak, but no words would come out. Rafael followed the line of her gaze. Quietly he assured her, "It doesn't hurt."

"I'm sorry, Rafael." She gave the hand a kiss so fleeting that he barely felt it. "I am so sorry."

"It's all right. Come on." He led her out of the cool house into the stifling heat. His Bronco was parked under the only tree, but it provided little shade. Krista leaned against the trunk and watched him, though he spent most of the time under the truck and all she could see were his jeans-clad legs.

"How long have you lived here?"

"Three years here, two in town."

"It's nice. I like it here." She sighed softly. "It's so quiet."

"Usually."

Krista leaned over the fender and under the open hood, and through the spaces around the engine she could see half of his face. "Are you implying that I make a lot of noise?"

"Are you denying it?"

"No." She smiled ruefully. "I like talking to you. I like hearing your voice. It's sexy."

When he finished with the truck it was after four o'clock. "After I clean up," he said, wiping his hands on a rag, "we'll get some dinner. Do you like Mexican food?"

"Sure. Las Rosas or Maria's?" she asked, referring to the two Mexican restaurants in town.

"La Paloma. Across the border."

"Do I need to change?"

Black eyes skimmed over her tiny shorts and thin cotton shirt. "Maybe you should," he answered, though he certainly approved of the way she looked.

While he was showering she cleaned up and put on a pale blue cotton skirt and a sleeveless knit sweater of a darker shade. She brushed her hair into a ponytail, bent from the waist and braided it, then sprayed on perfume and added some gold jewelry—bangle bracelets, a necklace and earrings. She was sitting on the sofa when Rafael came out wearing blue jeans and a cream-colored shirt. The sleeves were rolled to just below his elbows, exposing strong, dark forearms.

"Is this better?" she asked, standing up so he could see the outfit.

"Nice."

Though Krista was used to more effusive compliments from the men who took her to dinner, his single word meant more, for she was sure compliments didn't come often from this man.

The drive into town and across the border passed in the silence that Krista was learning to accept. Dinner at the small restaurant was also fairly quiet.

La Paloma was plain—rickety tables covered with vinyl cloths and straight-backed chairs—but the food was exceptionally good, and the dining room was crowded. "If I got to eat food like this all the time I'd be so fat," Krista said with a satisfied sigh. "I love Mexican food."

"My mother cooks like this."

"Where do they live?"

"North of Mexico City."

"Are you the only one living in the United States?"

"We all lived here once. In California."

"But they chose to return to Mexico?"

Rafael stared at some point just past her. "No."

"Were they there illegally?"

"No. They were forced to leave. They lost everything they owned."

Krista gently laid her hand over his, but he didn't appear to notice. "Why did you stay when they left?"

"It seemed best." He pulled free of her and rose to his feet. He paid the bill, then, with his hand on her elbow, steered her toward the door.

Their next stop was on the edge of town: a small, dark smoky bar. The music was country, and the patrons were Mexican, mostly men. There were only two women besides Krista. She followed Rafael to a table in the corner. As soon as he seated her, he went to the bar, returning with a Coke for her and a long-necked bottle of beer for himself. "Not your usual hangout, is it?" he asked, moving his chair closer to hers.

"No, it isn't." She smiled knowingly, trailing her fingers lightly over his injured hand. "That's why you brought me here, isn't it? To show me how different we are."

There was a slight twitch around his mouth that for an instant she thought would become a smile; then his face settled in that chill, forbidding mask that was so familiar.

"Maybe it is," he admitted, acknowledging the correctness of her guess with a nod.

She took a long swallow from the can of Coke that wasn't as cold as his beer. "It won't work. This isn't *your* usual hangout, either. I'm a very flexible person, Rafael. If I want something badly enough it doesn't bother me at all if I have to bend a little to get it."

He believed that. What he couldn't figure out was why she wanted *him*. Was he so different from all the men she'd known before? Was that his attraction for her? Rafael didn't kid himself. He knew that very few people he'd met liked him; his somberness, his aloofness, made most people uncomfortable. Once he'd heard the wife of one of his fellow agents describe his presence as "chilling," so why was Krista going to such trouble to get around his refusals?

A sad, mournful tune came on the battered jukebox that stood at the opposite end of the small room. Krista put her drink down and scooted her chair back. "Come and dance with me."

"Why?"

"Because we only have tonight and tomorrow before you send me away, and I want to have one dance with you first. Because you refused to dance with me at my party. Because I want you to hold me in your arms, against your body." Her voice got huskier with each word, until it was a hoarse whisper, and her eyes were heavy with desire.

After that invitation he knew he would never make it through a dance without making his response to her visible to everyone there, but he swallowed the last of his beer and took the trembling hand that she extended, letting her pull him from his chair and onto the dance floor.

The cleared area was small, and the other two women were dancing with a couple of customers, so they were forced to dance closely, though they would have anyway. Rafael held her to him, one hand splayed across her spine, the other drifting from the curve of her hip to her waist, then her shoulder, then back down again, his fingertips grazing the side of her breast. Their bodies were pressed together from shoulder to thigh, Krista's breasts flattened against the hard strength of Rafael's chest, the silver buckle of his belt pushing into her stomach, his thighs brushing against her legs. When she moved her hips against his, she could feel the evidence that their closeness affected him as strongly as it did her.

She couldn't let it end tomorrow, no matter what Rafael said he wanted, no matter what she'd promised. This man with no smiles, this man who was colder and harder and tougher than any man she'd ever known, had affected her in a way that took her breath away. He'd touched the depths of her heart, her soul, without even trying. She wouldn't let him end the most wonderfully fulfilling time she'd ever lived.

Rafael lowered his head the inch or so that separated his mouth from her ear, and his tongue traced the shell-like outline slowly, his breath hot. His teeth caught at the lobe, nibbling gently, his tongue bathing the cool gold of her earring before returning to the ear itself.

Goose bumps had risen on Krista's arms, and she whispered breathlessly, "When you do that I think I'm going to die from the feelings...." Her hands tightened around his neck, and slowly she forced her head up, moving her ear out of his range. Not one to be discouraged, Rafael simply turned his kisses to her throat, sampling the soft, golden skin. The taste was sweet, as every part of her tasted sweet, and also bitter, from the musky perfume she wore. To Rafael, even the bitterness was sweet.

"Rafael, please," she whispered.

He kissed his way back up the long column of her throat while his hands caressed her and their bodies swayed only slightly to the music. "I do," he said, finally reaching her mouth and sucking gently at her full lower lip. "I do please."

"Make love to me, Rafael." Krista opened drugged blue eyes to meet his. "I need you."

"Here?" One black brow rose slightly. "Now?"

"Yes, now. Take me out of here, Rafael. Don't try to pretend that you don't feel it, too, because I know you do," she continued to whisper in that husky, aroused voice. "I can feel how much you want it."

Unmindful of the other customers, he lowered his hands to her buttocks, pulling her firmly against his hips. "It, *querida?* I want *you.*"

The music stopped, and very slowly he released his hold on her. He untangled her hands from around his neck, grasped one and pulled her toward the door. When they reached the Bronco, Krista slid her arms around him, and her mouth sought his. She barely had time to part his teeth with her searching tongue before he put her away. "When we get home," he said.

"Now," she demanded, reaching out again, but he held her wrists easily.

"Later."

"Oh, please, Rafael . . ." When she saw that he was very serious—had she ever seen him when he wasn't?—she gave a sigh of frustration and climbed into the truck.

Rafael got in and backed out of the dirt and gravel lot. "We'll be home in thirty minutes. You can wait that long, can't you?"

"I suppose so—though there's really no reason to wait, is there?"

There it was again, she thought, that little tug that looked as if he might be on the verge of a smile, though in the dim light it was hard to tell. "I've waited all my life for you," he said, his voice flat and disapproving, and she knew she'd been mistaken about a smile. "I can wait another thirty minutes."

Krista crossed her arms over her chest and tried to pout, but in a few minutes she found herself humming the tune they had danced to. "I like that song. Who sings it?"

Of course a rich, sophisticated New Yorker couldn't be expected to recognize one of country's biggest stars. "Willie Nelson."

"I liked it." She laid her head back and looked out the window at the moon. "The sky is so clear. Sometimes, in New York, I forget what it looks like."

"I couldn't live in a city again," he said unexpectedly.

Krista rolled her head to the left, studying his dark profile. "No," she agreed after a moment. "You couldn't. The desert suits you."

She became silent. Into her idle mind came the memory of their other trip along this road, the night she had wrecked the Mustang. They had been silent that night, too, but it had been a tense, uncomfortable silence. Tonight she was relaxed. She was beginning to understand this man a little better, accepting that silence was very much a part of him.

The house sat in darkness, waiting for them. They were home. Krista smiled to herself, liking the sound of that. How upset Rafael would be if he knew that this house felt more like home to her than *la casa grande* ever could.

He was already upset. When he opened the door and Krista entered the house with him, it felt so *right*. As if she belonged here. He was stupid. His time with her was almost over, and he was indulging in little fantasies of keeping her with him, making a place for her in his life. He couldn't let himself care that much!

Krista watched him move restlessly around the room. He stopped at his desk, took a pack of cigarettes and a book of matches from a drawer and headed for the door. The air-conditioning was off, the door open. She watched him light a cigarette and inhale deeply before turning his back to her.

She removed her jewelry and laid it on the coffee table. She pulled the bands from her hair, tossed them on the table, too, and worked her fingers through, separating the braid. Her next move carried her out onto the porch, behind Rafael. Unhesitatingly she put her arms around him, pressing herself against his back.

"I didn't know you smoked."

"I don't." He glanced at the cigarette with disgust before taking another drag. "I used to. I used to smoke, drink and sleep around."

His sarcasm didn't fool Krista. "Did it help?"

He looked over his shoulder at her. "Help what?"

Slowly she moved around to stand in front of him, on the second step down. "Ease the pain."

Damn it, she was supposed to be shallow and self-centered, like Rebecca. Where did this perceptiveness come from? He stared at her, his eyes darker than the night. He didn't want to answer, but the words came anyway. "No. It didn't."

"Do you want to be alone?"

Again he gave an answer he didn't want to give. "No." He exhaled a stream of smoke, careful not to send it in her direction.

Krista continued to gaze up into his eyes while she slowly undid the buttons of his shirt, tugged it free of his jeans and pushed it back. His chest was smooth, practically hairless, and so soft that her fingers glided over it.

She rose on her toes to kiss the base of his throat, then laid her cheek against his chest while her hands continued to explore. As her fingertips traced along the waistband of his jeans his stomach muscles contracted, their hardness a sensual contrast to his velvety skin.

Rafael stared down at a crown of golden hair, the cigarette burning forgotten between his fingers. When he felt its heat he tossed it to the sandy ground a few feet away, where it sparked, then died. He started to raise his hand to touch her hair, but Krista felt the movement and captured his arm, forcing it to his side. Her message was clear: she was in control. She would take her pleasure in touching him and would give him pleasure in receiving her caresses.

Softly, gently, her lips tasted his flesh, sampling, until they found his flat nipple. It hardened at the flick of her tongue. She made Rafael groan when she sucked at it, gently at first, then hungrily. He wanted to drag her to him and make love with her, but through sheer will he forced himself not to move. It was torture letting her tease him like this, but it was the most exquisite torture he'd ever known.

Krista gave equal worship to his other nipple, already hard in anticipation, before she moved behind him. She removed his shirt, her fingernails grazing his skin as she pulled off each sleeve. She learned his back, feeling the bone and muscle, the small scars.

His face was her next goal. Standing beside him, she turned his face toward her with her left hand. Her right hand remained on his shoulder while the other touched his face, tracing his smooth jaw, then his brows, feathering over his eyelids as his eyes fluttered shut. She shaped his nose and the high cheekbones on either side, and one finger combed over the soft wiriness of his mustache before resting on his mouth.

His lips parted slowly, and his tongue came out to moisten her finger. His eyes were open again and never left hers while he bit gently at her finger.

"Do you want me to finish this here or inside?" she asked in a voice made thick with desire.

Rafael continued his erotic kiss for a moment. His entire body was hard and aching with true, physical pain to join with hers, and it didn't care where. Even wanting her so badly, though, he thought it would be better for Krista if they were in a soft bed. He didn't trust his voice to work, so he gave his answer by taking her hand and pulling her inside the house to his bedroom. He paused long enough on the way to lock the door, turn out the lights and kick off his sneakers.

Krista had half hoped he would choose to stay outside. She feared she would lose her advantage if they took time to move. But Rafael was perfectly willing to let her continue her agonizing seduction. She knelt before him, her shirt gracefully swirling around her, and lifted each foot to remove its sock. When she stood again, her hands rubbed along his thighs but ignored his groin in favor of his waist.

She lovingly pressed her lips to his chest while she worked the silver belt buckle loose. The snap of his jeans separated with a pop, and the zipper rasped harshly to its end. She began inching the denim and his briefs down, and she moved down with them until she was kneeling before him again.

Rafael's breathing was heavy and ragged. He had knotted his hands into tight fists at his sides to keep from reaching for her. It was a struggle he couldn't win much longer.

She guided his clothes off first one leg, then the other, and discarded them. His hips were so slim, she marveled, his abdomen so flat. She stroked and caressed and kissed, and when her lips brushed across him, he groaned aloud and jerked her to her feet, crushing her to him. His restraint had snapped, and it showed in the near brutality of his kiss.

He didn't bother to undress her; there wasn't time. He lowered her to the bed, raised her skirt, removed her lacy panties and plunged deep inside her. "Forgive me for this," he murmured in his last sane moment.

He took her with a ferocity, a savagery, that would have frightened Krista in any man but Rafael. It was a great burst of madness that was over quickly and followed by a deep silence except for their breathing.

When he could speak he said in shame, "I'm sorry." He looked at her, expecting to see horror or disgust on her lovely features. Instead her eyes were closed, and she was smiling serenely. Rafael was confused. "I tried not to hurt you . . . I am sorry, Krista."

She opened her eyes and propped herself on one arm, then leaned over to give him a deep kiss. "That was for you," she said, satisfied and smug and teasing. "Now it's my turn."

"I don't understand you," he said later.

Krista yawned. She was totally relaxed, totally drained, after the explosive releases Rafael had brought to her. Her limbs felt leaden. She couldn't have moved away from the intimate warmth of his body if her life had depended on it.

"You wanted that to happen."

"Yes."

"I could have hurt you."

"No, you couldn't have." She patted his chest reassuringly. "It's not in you to cause physical pain. Did you enjoy it?"

"Of course, but—"

"So did I. That's what matters." She raised her head to kiss his chin. "Good night, Rafael."

He answered her softly. She fell asleep almost immediately, but Rafael continued his thoughts. He'd known he would lose control, but he'd never dreamed it would be so brutal. His fingers moved fleetingly down Krista's body as if to reassure himself that there was no damage.

It wasn't something he would want to do often. He liked being in control and, no matter what she said, still feared hurting her like that. But—and a grin came and went—it had been an interesting experience. One *hell* of an experience.

Rafael slept easily that night, undisturbed by the body that pressed against his. His subconscious mind, so used to protesting when anyone disturbed his sleep by coming too close, seemed to accept that Krista was special and welcomed the comfort of her closeness.

When he awoke Sunday morning she was already awake, watching him sleep. Her blue eyes were heavy, evidence that she wasn't quite alert, and her smile was sleepy. "Good morning."

"Good morning." His voice sounded raspy from a night's disuse, like rusted metal scraping against itself.

They simply looked at each other for long, silent moments; then Krista yawned. "I'm still sleepy."

"Go back to sleep."

"If I do, you'll get up. Besides, I'm hungry. Do you have stuff for breakfast?"

"Yes."

"I'll fix it after I've had a shower, all right?"

"I can cook."

"So can I. You make the coffee, and I'll cook." She stretched her arms over her head, then grabbed at the sheet as it fell. Rafael suppressed a smile at her modesty.

"I'll close my eyes if you want," he offered dryly. He'd spent hours with her naked in the last day and a half; he knew her body intimately, but he found her shyness touching.

She escaped to the bathroom while his eyes were closed. When he heard the door down the hall shut, he got out of bed and put on a pair of wheat-colored cutoff jeans. He started the coffee, got a glass of orange juice and went outside to get the Sunday newspaper.

"How do you get the paper delivered out here?" Krista asked, standing in the doorway, wrapping a towel around her wet hair. She was wearing black running shorts of some silky material and a white tank top. To Rafael she looked as nice as she did dressed up. "Dad tried to get delivery, and they said it was too far."

"So he sends Ruben into town every Sunday morning to get a copy." Rafael put the paper down and went into the kitchen with her. "And Ruben leaves a copy on my porch every Sunday morning."

"Neighborly."

The corners of his mouth turned up slightly. "What your father doesn't know doesn't hurt him. Like us."

Krista stopped, a carton of eggs in her hands. "I don't care if my father knows." She knew her father wouldn't approve, but she saw no reason to tell Rafael that. Besides, she didn't think her father would care enough to do anything about it. As long as Rafael kept her busy and out of his way...

Out of his way until tonight. Krista's eyes darkened. Somehow she didn't think Rafael was going to change his mind. When this evening came he would expect her to go home and stay there. She didn't know if she could.

Rafael was taking some bacon from the refrigerator, and he didn't notice her sudden little frown. "If you think your father wouldn't mind that you've spent the last two days here with me, then you don't know him," he was saying.

"Why do you think he'd mind?" she asked cautiously.

"Because Art McLaren hates Mexicans, and he hasn't bothered to keep it a secret. We can work for him and make money for him, but he can't stand us."

Krista felt uncomfortable, because she knew the truth of his statement, so she shrugged and smiled brightly and asked, "Why are we discussing my father? Usually the only time the men I'm with want to talk about Dad is when they're far more interested in his money than his daughter. Does money mean a lot to you?"

Beneath his mustache his mouth twitched again. "If it did, would I be working for the border patrol?"

"What would you do?" Without waiting for his answer she went on, "Do you like your eggs scrambled or fried?"

"Fried."

"Me, too. You'd better do it, and I'll fry the bacon. My fried eggs never come out quite right. So what would you do if you wanted a lot of money?"

Rafael carefully cracked two eggs into a small bowl. While he waited for the oil to heat he looked at Krista to see the effect of his answer. "I don't know. I think I'd become *un contrabandista.* A smuggler."

"And smuggle what?"

"People. Drugs. Whatever paid the best."

She turned a dark frown his way. "That's disgusting. No one should be allowed to profit from all the people who come into the country illegally. They're breaking the law."

"And making a fortune." *Like your father.*

"It's still wrong."

"The people will come anyway. A smuggler can make it easier for them."

"A smuggler can also take them out in the middle of the desert and kill them."

Rafael shrugged. "It happens. And do the drugs bother you, too? Or just all those poor Mexicans coming into your country?"

She arranged long strips of bacon in a skillet. "For the record, I don't drink, and I don't use drugs. I never have, and I don't ever intend to start. I don't approve of either. However, if grown, mature adults want to spend their money on drugs and kill themselves with them, that's their business."

"What about the children who kill themselves with them? You're not naive, Krista. A lot of kids use drugs, too. Is that *their* business?"

Krista was silent for a long moment. Finally she smiled tautly. "Like most people, I prefer to ignore a problem that doesn't directly affect me. No, I don't approve of drugs being made available to children, but what can I do about it? I'm not responsible for it, and I don't know who is. Please, Rafael, let's drop this. We both know you would never do anything illegal, anyway. You're too honest for that."

He agreed, though in his mind he reviewed her answers. The conversation *had* accomplished something: it had convinced him that she knew nothing about her father's sideline. She *did* know the person responsible for supplying those children with drugs, and through him, the problem was going to affect her far more directly than she could imagine. By the time he and Houseman were finished, she was going to lose her father. He wondered what that would do to her.

Krista tapped him on the shoulder. "I like my eggs fried, not baked through."

Rafael looked down at the two eggs in the skillet. The yolks were set, and the edges were beginning to curl. "If that's the best you can do," she teased, "maybe I should cook my own."

He tossed the eggs into the garbage can and broke two more into the hot oil. "I can do better," he assured her, a hint of challenge in his voice.

Krista finished frying the bacon and toasted a half dozen slices of bread while Rafael cooked their eggs. When they sat down at the small table to eat he started a new conversation. He felt guilty for questioning her with ulterior motives, but that didn't stop him. He often felt guilty for things he had to do in the course of his job. "Are you close to your father?"

"The eggs are good. You *can* do better," Krista said, ignoring his question. Then she lifted her shoulders in a fatalistic shrug. "He's my father."

"Meaning?"

"Are you close to your father?"

"We were."

"But you haven't seen him in seven years."

"That's my problem, not my father's."

"No, we're not particularly close. He doesn't want to be. Years ago he lost my mother, and I was a large part of that problem. It's difficult to forget, I guess."

"Lost your mother? Is she dead?" he asked, though he knew she wasn't.

"No, she's living in Paris with her third husband and is, I assume, very happy."

"Any brothers or sisters from her second and third marriages?"

"Heavens, no. Once was more than enough for Selena. She's not a very maternal person."

"You call your mother Selena?" Rafael was thirty-four years old, but that wouldn't stop his mother from smacking him if he called her Isabel.

"What should I call her?" Krista asked with a smile.

"What's wrong with 'Mom?' "

"Rafael, I've seen my mother twice in twenty-two years. Don't you think 'Mom' is a little bit intimate for a complete stranger?"

"Why don't you see her more often?"

"Why don't you see your family more often?"

He stiffened. He was aware that prying into her life gave her an equal right to pry into his, but he still didn't like the idea. "I choose not to see my family."

"Well, my family chooses not to see me. And, as of now, I choose not to talk about them. If you want to talk about your family I'd like to listen. Otherwise, I'd prefer to change the subject."

He nodded somberly. The memories concerning his own family problems were too painful to discuss with anyone, even Krista. He could respect that she felt much the same about her own memories.

She reached across the table to claim his hand. "Do you have to do anything today?"

He shook his head.

"Then let's stay here and be totally lazy. I don't want to do a thing."

"All right." That suited him fine. He didn't want to share her with anyone, anyway. He freed his hand and picked up their plates.

"I said be lazy."

"You be lazy. I'll do the dishes."

Krista heaved an exaggerated sigh. "You're neater than my housekeeper. Maybe you could go to New York with me. My apartment could use a good cleaning." She rinsed and dried the dishes as he washed them, then insisted on dragging him to the couch with her. There they divided the newspaper, settled into a comfortable silence and read. When Krista finished with her half she laid it aside and tucked herself neatly into Rafael's arms. He lifted the paper over her and continued to read. She occasionally glanced up as he turned the pages, but mostly she just breathed in the smell of him and appreciated the strength of his chest and the satiny smoothness of his skin.

On the last page was a photograph of some event in San Ignacio. It included the mayor and several women, one of whom was absolutely gorgeous. "Isn't she pretty?" Krista asked, pointing to her.

Rafael glanced at the photo and, without thinking, commented, "That's Constancia." He felt Krista stiffen, and she raised her hand to steady the paper.

"Constancia Aranas," she read softly. She had never heard the name before, but she knew immediately who the woman was. "She's your lover."

Rafael was silent.

The woman was beautiful, and she looked so innocent and so trusting. In comparison, Krista felt dirty. "How could you do this to her?"

Rafael pulled the paper from her hand and dropped it to the floor. "I'm not doing anything."

"But—"

"We aren't lovers," he said in his rough, gravelly voice. "I'm not being unfaithful to her."

"You broke up? Why?"

Rafael gave her a reproving look. "You're why. Don't worry. She was relieved when it ended. I heard she's started dating Darren Carter."

Krista was still a bit stunned. No wonder Rafael hadn't wanted anything to do with her. In her field, Krista had seen many beautiful women, and Constancia Aranas was one of them. She was gorgeous, with black hair, and eyes and skin as dark as Rafael's.

Rafael sensed her disquiet and understood its cause, and he reassured her in the only way possible at that moment: physically. He pulled her into his arms and tilted her face up for a very gentle kiss, while his hands roamed restlessly over her body. He couldn't use words to tell her how very special she was to him; that wouldn't be fair, when their affair was ending tonight, but he could show her with his body. It was all he could offer.

It was a good day. They did nothing after making love except watch television and occasionally talk. Their silences were comfortable; both understood that words weren't necessary. Besides, what could they talk about? The fact that in a few hours their affair would end by mutual agreement—though Krista felt she had agreed under duress—offered them few topics of conversation.

She wanted to change his mind, but she didn't know how. She had thought that if he enjoyed the weekend he would want to see her again. Though there was no doubt that he'd enjoyed it, he had given her no reason to hope that there would be anything more.

Why did he have to be so stubborn? If he had a legitimate reason for not wanting to see her, why didn't he just tell her what it was? And what reason in the world could be so important that he would deny her—and himself—something that was so right?

Krista sighed deeply. It was five o'clock. Only a few more hours before she had to go. Then what would she do? More importantly, what would Rafael do? Would he someday want to see *her* again or would he go back to the beautiful Constancia Aranas?

"Are you hungry?"

Lunch had been forgotten in the hours since they'd returned to bed. Now Krista nodded.

"Let me up, and I'll cook dinner," he said.

This time she didn't offer to help. She turned around on the sofa, lying so she could watch him as he worked. He was aware of her steady gaze, but he didn't speak to her. He was also aware of her thoughts. Since he couldn't offer any answers, he said nothing.

Dinner was uncomfortable, and so was doing the dishes afterward. When Krista dried her hands and saw Rafael looking at his watch for the tenth time in an hour she clenched her jaw in frustration. "Do you want me to go?"

He was unkindly honest. "Yes." Their weekend was over. The sooner she left, the sooner he could start working at forgetting her. His mouth tightened impatiently. "You agreed to go home tonight and stay there. You asked for a weekend, Krista, and I gave it to you. What more do you want?"

Anything. Anything he could give her. A familiar feeling was stirring in her chest—pain. The pain of rejection. Though he'd enjoyed the weekend with her, he was certainly eager to be rid of her. She was determined not to let her pain show. She went down the hall to his bedroom and quickly packed the small overnight bag she had brought. Rafael waited for her in the living room.

"Thanks, Rafael," she said, and somehow she forced a convincing smile onto a mouth that wanted to frown, into eyes that wanted to cry. "Walk to the car with me?"

At her Mustang she said goodbye silently, eloquently. She twined her arms around his neck and took his mouth with hers in a kiss so hungry it fired Rafael's desire anew. His hands slid down to her buttocks, cupping her close against his hips and the hardness that jutted there.

One more time, he thought, greedy and weak with wanting her. He wanted just one more chance to hide himself away inside her, to find that incredible release within her, to simply be with her, a part of her, before he had to go back to living without her.

One hand had found its way beneath her shirt, and now her breast swelled to fit it. She was like satin or silk; he didn't know which, and didn't care. He just knew she felt good, so damned good. He would never forget the feel of her. Tonight he had to have her. It was insane, but he had to make love with her one more time.

Krista knew she was going to cry, and if she cried Rafael would know how important this time had been to her. He would know that she loved him. But he didn't trust women who claimed to love him, and he would never let her come around again. If he didn't know, maybe, just maybe, she would get another chance. She broke the kiss and brushed her tender lips across his mustache. "Thank you for a lovely weekend, Rafael." She swallowed hard and blinked to clear her eyes. "Maybe I'll see you around." She eased out of his embrace, got in the car and drove away, her tears breaking free as she left him behind.

Chapter 7

Five days had passed since Krista had driven away from Rafael. It hadn't been easy to leave, knowing he wanted her, but the knowledge that her need was stronger than his would ever be had helped her to go. She had gone home and cried herself to sleep, but in the light of morning she'd pushed her fears and pain to the back of her mind and concentrated only on positive things, such as how to make Rafael fall in love with her.

That was difficult. Because she was pretty and friendly and rich, men had been attracted to her automatically. She had no idea how to go about attracting one as elusive as Rafael. She knew he cared nothing about her money; he would probably like her better without it. Being introverted and very much a loner, he was, she suspected, wary of her friendliness. He thought she was pushy and aggressive—and probably shameless and immoral, as well. And he wouldn't like her any less if she were homely; he wasn't a man to be swayed by a pretty face.

All in all, she had nothing to offer that he would value. Just a body that fit so perfectly with his, and a heart that was filled with hopes and dreams of him. No, she had nothing at all to interest him.

Krista accepted Royce Ann's invitation to lunch that day for two reasons: she enjoyed Royce Ann's company and needed to be cheered up, and she knew her friend wouldn't make the long drive into town without going to the border-patrol station to see Jim. Maybe she would see Rafael. As they were paying for their lunch Royce Ann asked, "Do you mind stopping by to see Jim?"

Krista smiled, pleased to be proven right. "Of course not."

Rafael *was* there, studying a map spread out on the table in front of him. His concentration was intense; though he was aware of the arrival of the two women, he paid no attention—at least, not obviously. He knew Krista was with Royce Ann. He could sense her, could smell that musky perfume she always wore, but he didn't look at her. With one long brown finger he traced a trail across the map, picturing the area in his mind. The image was hard to sustain, because of the woman who kept intruding.

"How are you, Krista?" Jim asked after greeting his wife.

She had kept her gaze off Rafael, looking at everything in the room except him. Now she gave Jim a too-bright smile. "I'm fine."

He glanced over his shoulder at Rafael, then smiled gently. "Why don't you go back and say hello?"

She hesitated. Being familiar with rejection didn't mean it became any easier. What if he refused to speak to her? What if he pretended that the weekend had never happened? *And what if he didn't?* She went to the back of the room, moving around the table to stand directly in front of Rafael. "Hello."

He looked up, his eyes unwelcoming. "What do you want?"

She was stung by his attitude. Her mind told her to leave before he could hurt her, but it had been so long since she'd seen him. "How are you?" she asked softly.

"I'd be better if you'd go away."

That hurt, but she stood her ground. "It's hard to believe that you're the same man who made love to me so passionately last weekend." She was rewarded by a slight stiffening of his shoulders.

The muscle in his jaw tightened, and he leaned forward, resting his weight on his hands. "What do you want?" he repeated, his voice low and cold and hostile.

Her hands folded into tight fists, her fingernails biting into her palms. Every cruel word from him increased her pain, but she couldn't leave. She had to keep talking, to keep asking for more. "Do you swim naked at the pool often? If I rode Diablo out there again at night—'

"I wouldn't be there," he said through clenched teeth.

"I think that was the best time," she continued, as if he hadn't spoken. "Of course, every time was marvelous, but that first time, by the pool, that was . . . exquisite."

A quick glance told him no one could hear, but he ordered her to precede him into a small, private office anyway. There he turned a stare on her that intimidated men twice her size. "What game are you playing?"

She didn't flinch one bit; she hurt too much. "I don't play games. I'll leave that to you. You're much better at it."

Anger turned to puzzlement. "What are you talking about, Krista?" He had thought the terms for the weekend had been clearly stated, that they both had understood them.

"You took everything I had to give, then sent me home Sunday night like a good little whore, well paid for her services," she accused.

Rafael was shocked by the hurt in her thick voice. She hadn't seemed at all angry or bitter Sunday night. He had lain awake most of that long, lonely night, aching to have her beside him, in his bed, in his arms. He had relived every moment of the weekend, but he had never imagined for one minute that she'd been hurting when she left.

"Did it amuse you? To have Art McLaren's daughter beg you to use her?"

He reacted as if he'd been slapped. His hands gripping her upper arms, he furiously demanded, "Is that what you believe, Krista? That I was *using* you?"

Her lower lip quivered, and tears blurred her view of him. Finally she shook her head. "No," she admitted, the word a quiet sob. She freed herself from his grasp and went to the window to stare out. "What is it that makes you hate me? Is it because I remind you of that other woman? Because I'm Art McLaren's daughter? Or is it just me?"

He wanted to hold her, to soothe away her fears and pain. Instead he hurt her again. "I can't have an affair with you. Last weekend was a mistake. I never should have touched you. I never should have made love to you, because—"

Krista whirled around, pale and desolate. "No! Don't say that!" *Please don't regret what we did!*

Rafael raised one hand to silence her. "I never should have made love with you," he repeated quietly, "because now I can't forget you, and I have to. Every night I lie in the bed that we shared, hard and wanting you, but I can't have you. I can't make love with you again."

She went to him, stopping a few feet away. "Why not? What's wrong with me?"

He touched her hair, watched it shimmer as it sifted through his fingers. "It isn't you, *querida*. It's me."

But she couldn't believe him, not without reasons, without explanations. "Don't you know this is special? How can you just throw it away?"

"I have to."

Krista took a deep breath. She despised herself for this scene, for crying, for pleading with him. With the tip of her finger she wiped each eye, drying the tears. "I'm sorry," she said when she was sure she could speak clearly again. "The restrictions you placed on last weekend were very clear. I chose to ignore them."

She rubbed her eyes again, and Rafael said quietly, "You look fine."

There was a knock at the door, and a man's voice called, "Contreras, Thompson wants his office. Hurry it up."

Rafael continued to watch Krista, ignoring the interruption. "Are you all right?"

"Yes." She smiled to support the lie. "I'll try not to bother you again. I'll try to stay away, but I doubt that I can. So...if someone shows up at your house late one night without an invitation, don't overreact. It'll just be me." She reached out to gently touch his cheek. "It was a hell of a weekend, Rafael."

"Yes, it was."

She let her hand fall, moved around him, opened the door and left the room.

Rafael didn't move for a long moment. They'd had two days together, less than forty-eight hours, and he'd managed to hurt her. Her smiles, her cheerfulness, didn't fool him now. He'd seen the pain in her eyes, and it was something he would never forget. He cursed himself for ever letting her come near, but he wouldn't give up the memory of those two days for anything in the world.

"Do you want to see me, or do you just like the view in here?"

Rafael glanced briefly at Thompson, who was seating himself behind the desk. Without a word he left the office.

"So," Royce Ann began as she turned the car onto the street, "how's Rafael?"

"Just about perfect," Krista replied absently. Perfect. He didn't need anything, least of all her.

"I don't understand what it is you see in him," Royce Ann said. "He's so serious. He never smiles. Have you noticed that? He *never* smiles."

No, Krista thought, not since some woman, some white woman, betrayed him with words of love. He must have loved her deeply—but, of course, that *would* be the way he'd love: passionately, intensely. How she must have hurt him, to take away his smiles.

Funny how things worked out. That woman had thrown away something that Krista would give her soul for: Rafael's love. It was so funny it made her want to cry again.

"What were you two talking about in Martin Thompson's office?" Royce Ann probed none too subtly.

"Midnight swims. They can be dangerous, you know."

Royce Ann gave her friend a look that said she must be crazy, but Krista didn't notice. She was lost in memories.

Krista fell back on that old standby—work—to keep herself busy over the next two weeks. She managed to resist trying to see Rafael by keeping herself shut up in her workroom, spending long hours making patterns and cutting them out, and longer hours sewing them together. But her work didn't demand enough concentration to keep her thoughts from the silent, dark man.

The first few days she concentrated intensely on the problem: how could she make Rafael Contreras fall in love with her? Despite the fact that he didn't like her, didn't want her, that he wrote her off as a shallow, spoiled, rich kid—despite all those things, surely there was some way to make him want her, to make him love her.

Finally she accepted the fact that there wasn't. No one could make a man as strong and independent as Rafael do anything he didn't want to do, and he didn't want to want her or love her. That gave her a new problem to consider: how could she make herself forget him and get on with her life? No matter how many times she asked the question, she got the same answer every time: she couldn't.

Late Friday afternoon, at the end of the second week, Krista dressed in a loose, flowing skirt of deep purple cotton and a ruffled, fitted camisole to match. Not even bothering with shoes, she took the black stallion from the stables. She didn't pretend she was just out for a ride. She was going to Rafael's house. She didn't plan to approach him; she just wanted to be near, to maybe catch a glimpse of him.

Diablo came to a stop beside the small shed, patient with his mistress. It was another moonlit night, light and shadow. The shadow of the shed covered her, hid her.

Rafael was restless, a condition he knew too well. He told himself it was because his work was tedious and boring, because he was tired, because his life wasn't exactly satisfactory at the moment. He told himself all sorts of lies, and sometimes he even pretended to believe them. Tonight, though, he was in no mood for lies, for pretense. Tonight he could admit the source of his restlessness: Krista. In those two short days she had crawled beneath his skin, into his heart, his very soul. He wanted to see her, talk to her, hold her, kiss her, love her. God, how he wanted her!

He had gone to the phone to call her three, four, five times, but each time reason stopped him. She was out of his league. He was taking part in an investigation into her father's activities. She was too easily hurt, and he would hurt her. She deserved better than him.

They were all good reasons to stay away from her, and they kept him away from the phone. But they did nothing to ease the ache in his body or the one in his heart.

He went out onto the porch and leaned against a post, staring into the night. Moonlight and shadow—like the first night they'd made love. He remembered every detail of that night: how the moonlight had gleamed in her hair and on her golden body; how she had ridden from the shadows on the stallion as black as night. He even remembered the soft whuffling noise the horse had made.

He wasn't remembering it; he was hearing it again—now. He pushed himself away from the post, his eyes searching the night. There, by the shed. A hint of dull gold.

Krista realized she had stopped breathing, and she filled her lungs with air. He was standing so still on the porch, backlit by the living-room lights that shone through the open door. He looked magnificent in jeans that hugged his body, clinging to his low waist, his slim hips. His chest was bare, and she remembered how smooth it felt beneath her hands, against her breasts.

Tears demanding to be shed closed her throat. He was so damned handsome, so strong and masculine. He was all she ever wanted from life, but he didn't want her. He stood less than twenty yards away from her, but she couldn't bridge the gap that separated them, because he didn't want her.

Rafael moved down the steps and started toward her, his gait smooth and graceful despite the fact that the ground was hard and his feet were bare. She couldn't leave, and so she waited, wondering if he would be angry, and not caring.

He stopped beside the stallion, reached up and lifted Krista off. Still holding her, he slid down the wall of the shed until he was sitting on the ground, and he settled her across his hips. He kissed her, his tongue pushing into her mouth, and she hungrily accepted its entry. His mouth was greedy, demanding, trying to satisfy a lifetime of hunger with one kiss.

He slid his hands along her thighs and discovered only her tiny panties beneath the skirt. The silky fabric tore beneath his strength, and there was only her warm flesh against his hands. A groan escaped his throat, only to be swallowed by her mouth.

"Touch me," he demanded against her lips, "Feel what you do to me." When she hesitated an instant he guided her hand, pressing her fingers against him. "Feel how much I want you, *pequeña*."

"I want you, too," she whimpered, touching him as he touched her. "Please, Rafael . . ."

She undid his jeans, and he slid farther down and lifted her onto him, groaning as she took him inside her. His hands gripped her thighs, holding her, guiding her. Their breath came fast, uneven, ragged. Krista's pleas were soft, Rafael's hoarse, but both were frantic, both a little bit desperate. Krista cried out, with pleasure and with pain. She thought she would lose consciousness under the power of the release that shook her. She clung to Rafael, knowing he was enduring his own agonizing climax, yet still she held him, as if he might prevent her from dying from the ecstasy.

* * *

The ground was hard and cold, the body beside her soft and warm. Krista opened her eyes and, in the shadows, saw Rafael's eyes only inches away. "I tried to stay away."

He touched a finger to her mouth to stop any more words.

"I didn't mean—"

He stopped her again and loosened her arms from his shoulders. He stood up and pulled his jeans to his waist, zipping them.

She thought he was going to leave without a word, but he carefully lifted her into his arms and started toward the house. He set her down on the steps. "I still can't offer you anything," he said quietly, "but the temporary use of my body, and pain. Another weekend with nothing to follow. If that's not enough, if you don't want that, then leave now, please. If you can accept that, if you can accept a cold bastard who can't give you more but is too weak to say no . . . stay. Spend the weekend with me."

It wasn't enough. One weekend would never be enough, but it was better than nothing, and she told him softly that she would like to stay. He took her into the house and offered her first a drink, which she refused, then himself, which of course she accepted.

The house was quiet for the next hour. At last Krista sighed. "It gets better every time."

She lay in his arms, her hand gripped in his and resting on his chest. The moonlight glinted off her golden hair, bathed her skin in its beams. She was beautiful, and he would want her until the day he died. He accepted that, just as he accepted that he couldn't have her.

Krista turned her head to the side, her eyes drinking him in. She saw only the left side of his face, a perfect profile, and she thought he was without doubt the sexiest man she had ever seen. Despite the harsh planes of his face and the stern set of his mouth, he was handsome and sensual. She traced an imaginary line down his forehead, between his eyes, over his nose and mustache to his mouth. It moved beneath her fingertip in a brief kiss.

"Tell me about her, Rafael."

In the night, his arms holding her tight, he didn't need to ask who. There was no reason to pretend ignorance. He could be honest about that, at least. He could tell her the story that might help her understand why he was what he was.

"I was born in Mexico, in a small farm town. We were very poor. I had to quit school when I was eleven and go to work to help support my family. When I got a little older I began crossing into the United States illegally to work. Eventually I got caught near San Diego. I was sick, half-starved. The agent who caught me took me to his home, took care of me, and when I was better he took me back to my family. Later he helped us come into the country legally, to live. He even helped me become a citizen."

He stared up at the ceiling, his gaze never wavering, his voice never changing, but emotion showed in the tightening of his mouth, the tautness of his body. These were bad memories, and Krista regretted disturbing them.

"My father had always wanted a farm, and eventually, with all of us working, we were able to buy a small one. Right down the road from us was one of the biggest farms in the state. Her father owned it. She used to find excuses to come to our place. She'd watch me work."

Slowly his eyes closed in remembrance. "She was beautiful, like an angel." His voice got softer. "Golden hair, blue eyes, a smile that could light the darkest night. She was a beauty."

He stopped then, and Krista was glad. Jealousy of this unknown woman was twisting her heart. The reverence in his voice when he spoke of her . . . ! He could never feel that way about her, she was sure, and it broke her heart.

"We became lovers—secretly, of course. Her father would have killed any man who dared to touch Rebecca without his permission. We had to sneak around to see each other, but it wasn't hard, because her brother, Brian, was seeing my sister, Josefina, so we covered for each other. I loved Rebecca, and she said she loved me, too. She said we could run away and be married. We made arrangements to meet at a motel fifty miles away. When I got there Rebecca was waiting. She wanted to make love before we went to get the license. Her father and some of his workers found us, and she told him that I had forced her to go. She said I had raped her. They beat me until I was more dead than alive. Later he forced my family off their land. They lost everything and had to return to Mexico. When he found out about his son and Josefina, he sent him away, even though Brian told him that he loved her and that she was pregnant. She never heard from Brian again. Not when she wrote to him from Mexico about the baby's birth. Not even when she wrote to him two months later about the baby's death. Losing Brian, then their daughter, almost killed her."

He heard Krista's gasp, and his fingers tightened around her hand. "Rebecca came to see me once in the hospital, to tell me that she was getting married to some rich white man. She'd wanted to marry him all along, but her father didn't like the man's family, so he'd refused to give his permission. She'd known how he hated Mexicans, and she'd been certain that if her father knew she was having an affair with one, he would marry her to the white boyfriend in no time. I just happened to be the first one she came across who was gullible enough to believe that she'd want him, stupid enough to believe she loved him."

He shifted to draw her even closer, stroking her hair as he talked. "Rebecca had instructed the housekeeper to tell her father where we were. She had timed it so we would be in bed when they came. It was too bad Josefina and Brian got hurt, she said, but everything had worked out perfectly." He swallowed hard and took a few breaths to cleanse his mind. "That was the last time I saw her."

Krista was crying. There was no sound, but he felt the hot tears on his chest, trickling across his skin.

"Why do you cry?" he asked wearily.

"She wasn't worth your smiles," she whispered. "Oh, God, I'm sorry, Rafael."

His eyes closed to narrow slits, and he exhaled an empty sigh. "So am I, *querida.*"

"Do you think I'd use you like that? Because my skin is white, my hair gold, my eyes blue?"

He thought she already *was* using him. He knew she believed that her feelings were sincere, but he also knew he was a novelty, a diversion. But he didn't say so, because he knew the reply would hurt her, and he couldn't bear to hurt her, not tonight. "I think I'm tired, *querida,*" he evaded. "And I think I'd like to sleep tonight, holding your body against mine. And I think, *pequeña,* little one, that I'd like to wake with you in the morning and make love with you again before we get out of bed."

She let that satisfy her, let him snuggle her closer, let the warmth and security of his presence lull her to sleep. But she remembered, even as she drifted off, that he hadn't answered her question. His refusal to answer was an answer in itself.

You, he thought she would use him. He thought she couldn't be trusted, because she reminded him of Rebecca. She wanted to protest but didn't have the energy.

"I wouldn't hurt you . . . ." The rest of the denial was lost in sleep, but Rafael understood. His mouth almost made it to a smile before falling into its usual lines. *This* was a woman who was probably worth his smiles. Unfortunately, he had no smiles to give. He had nothing to give but the two things he'd offered earlier: his body, and pain.

God help them, she had accepted both.

"Why can't there be more than just another weekend with nothing to follow?"

Rafael had gotten his wish: he had awakened that morning to find Krista's hands and mouth gentle on his body. They'd made love, each giving until there was nothing left to give, taking until it had all been taken. Now they were dressed, Krista in a long chambray shirt of his, Rafael in jeans, and they were sitting at the small dining table, the remains of their breakfast in front of them.

He considered her question for a long moment, his eyes dropping to stare into his coffee. At last he said, "Just understand that there can't be."

"Why not? Don't you think it would be worth the effort?" Her voice was sharp, close to demanding.

He tensed. "Don't use that tone of voice with me," he warned. "I may be too weak to send you away, but you're not too weak to go. If you don't like what I'm offering, leave."

"I like it. But I want more."

Though he'd had a good night's sleep, Rafael felt tired again, emotionally tired. "So do I," came his dry, empty reply, "but there isn't any 'more.' This is all I can give—today and tomorrow. When you take it, there won't be anything left."

"Is it because of Rebecca? I remind you of her, don't I?"

He started to deny it, to assure her that no other woman occupied his heart. Instead he remained silent—guiltily silent.

Krista felt as if the wind had been knocked from her. She felt hurt, betrayed, cheated. Even if he still loved Rebecca, he must also despise her for what she'd done to him, and Krista reminded him of her. "Do you want me to go home now?"

He had been watching the effect of his nonreply on her. It had been an easy lie; he hadn't even needed words for it. But he was sick of lies, sick of hurting, and he pulled her around the table into his arms and said, "No, *pequeña,* I want you to stay. This weekend is ours, yours and mine. There is no one else. No one, Krista, including Rebecca."

She smiled slowly. "Yours and mine," she echoed. "I wish it could last a million days."

"Two days, Krista. It isn't much, is it?"

She hugged his head to her breast. "Two days with you is worth more than two years with any other man. What shall we do with them? I need beautiful memories to hold on to."

His mouth found her flat nipple beneath the fabric of his shirt and nuzzled it into a peak that was hard with longing. "I can think of one thing we can do, *querida,* that is always *muy hermosa,* very beautiful. Like you."

When his fingers pushed the shirt away she arched her back, offering his lips access to her breast. "Oh, yes," she murmured when he nursed the hard, tingling nub. "Make love to me, Rafael. Make love to me in Spanish."

He carried her down the hall to his bedroom, where he did as she requested. He worshiped her body from head to toe, bathing her soft golden flesh with kisses and caresses meant to drive her wild, and every word he whispered, every plea, every command, every word of adoration, was whispered in Spanish. Though she spoke no Spanish she understood everything, each softly uttered phrase, for they were words a man whispered to his lover, and she needed no further translation.

"What would you think if I said I loved you?"

Rafael looked sharply at Krista, feeling a prick of fear inside. Was she hinting for a response before making the announcement? Or was it just a hypothetical question? He hoped desperately for the latter, but he feared the former. What would he think? He would think it was a whim that would pass before long. He would think that the rich, spoiled daughter of Art McLaren was too shallow to understand what love really was. He would think that the novelty of a once-poor Mexican lover would disappear as quickly as it had come. And he would think he was the luckiest man in the world, to have her pretend love for even a short time.

"I don't know, so don't say it to me," he replied, a little more harshly than he'd intended. "Wait until you find the right man, then tell him."

Krista tilted her head slightly, looking at him with her lips pursed. "And what kind of Mr. Right should I be looking for?"

"Someone with money. Someone who can give you prestige and blue-eyed, blond-haired children."

Those were Rebecca's words; Krista was sure of it. Rafael was just repeating them. "I'm not interested in prestige, and I don't care if my children have blue eyes or black, or blond hair or black."

He said nothing.

Krista pulled herself out of his arms and sat up in bed. "I don't judge people based on their bank balances and their social standing! I don't want your idea of Mr. Right, Rafael, I want *you!*" She wiped angrily at the tears clouding her eyes. "Damn it, Rafael. Damn it, don't let me cry!"

He pulled her down on top of him and rolled with her until she was on her back. Using his body to hold hers still, he tickled his fingers over her ribs, finding the places where she was most sensitive, and her tears were forgotten in peals of laughter. She writhed beneath him, trying to avoid his torturing hands, until she felt the sudden response of his body.

"Oh, Rafael," she breathed. "Again, please..."

"No." He rolled off her and reached for the clothes he had shed only an hour ago. "You'll get sore, and we won't be able to make love tonight. Get dressed."

She watched him pull his jeans on and zip them. His hands buckled the belt quickly, easily; then he padded barefoot to his closet for a white cotton-knit shirt.

"All I have is the skirt and blouse I wore last night."

He pulled the shirt over his head, then gave her a long look. "Then you'd better go home and get some clothes. Jeans."

She stepped into her skirt, pulled her camisole on and sat on the bed, watching him with great interest. He reached down to tuck his shirt in, realized he'd already buckled his belt and grimaced. She had him so mixed up he couldn't even dress properly. He remedied that, tucking the shirt neatly into his jeans, then went to her, spanning her waist almost completely with his hands. "Get going."

"Rafael, let's stay here today." Her suggestion was delivered in a voice heavy with desire.

"You're greedy."

"So you say."

"Take your horse home. I'll pick you up in half an hour."

She let him pull her off the bed and out of the room. "Where are we going?"

"For a drive."

He left her on the porch and led the stallion to the steps. He cupped his hands, giving Krista a step up; then his hands glided along her calf. "Bring a dress for tomorrow," he ordered. "We'll go out."

Krista looked down at him, searching his dark, impassive face for some sign of emotion, but she found nothing. How could he be so passionate in bed and so restrained out of it? Last night he had called himself weak, but she knew he wasn't; he had an iron control on himself at all times. He wouldn't allow himself to be weak.

Diablo was eager to get going, and he snorted impatiently, tossing his head. Rafael quieted him with a hand on his neck. "Go."

She obeyed, resisting the urge to look back as she rode away. It wouldn't be long until he was sending her away for good. When this weekend ended she was certain that not even a late-night visit like last night's would help her. Rafael was determined to rid himself of her, and she couldn't change his mind. She should be grateful that he was giving her these two days.

Krista had been rejected with depressing regularity in her life, first by her mother, then repeatedly by her father. The feeling was nothing new, but the intensity of the pain was. It was just her luck, she thought, always to want the attention and love of people who didn't want to give it—not to her, at least.

"Out for an early ride?" her father asked when they met between the house and the stables.

"Yes, Dad."

"Where were you last night?"

"Out."

He didn't even ask her with whom. "Let Juana know if you'll be home for dinner." He began walking again, and Krista turned to watch him go. She saw him greet his foreman with more warmth than he'd ever shown her, and her mouth tightened into a thin line, so like Rafael's.

"Does it matter to *you,* Dad, if I'll be home for dinner?" she asked softly.

The silence was her reply.

She went to her room and changed into jeans, a T-shirt and tennis shoes. She pulled her hair into a ponytail and braided it, then gathered the things she needed to pack.

A dress, he'd said. She had plenty, but she couldn't make up her mind until she glanced out the window and saw a cloud of dust that meant company. Hastily she pulled a simple pale blue skirt and matching blouse from their hangers, carefully folded them and added them to the growing pile. Another glance out the window showed Rafael's black Bronco in sight now, and she returned to the closet to get a pair of leather sandals.

"I won't be here tonight or tomorrow," she called to the housekeeper as she swept down the stairs. She picked up her purse and opened the door as the Bronco came to a stop on the circular drive.

"Why the rush? Trying to get out before your father sees me?" Rafael asked as she swung into the seat.

"Trying to get out before my father sees *me* again," she replied. She fastened the seat belt snugly over her hips, then flashed a smile at him. "If you'd like, we could find him, and I'll introduce you. Then maybe you could remind him that he has a daughter."

Dark, brooding eyes rested on her face. Sometimes she made remarks like that, hinting at a less-than-satisfactory relationship with her father, but Rafael didn't put much stock in them. Women like Krista—like Rebecca—had been given everything they ever wanted, and it made them greedy. They were never satisfied with what they got; they always wanted more. Krista could drain him of all energy and strength in one lovemaking session and five minutes later demand that he take her again. Like Rebecca.

Funny. That odd little pain in his chest when he thought about his former lover was gone. He had sometimes feared he would never completely stop loving her, stop hurting for her, but it was gone, as if telling Krista about her had been a catharsis of some sort.

He knew *why* it was gone. He had exchanged old memories and hurts for new ones. There was no room in his heart, his soul, for any woman but Krista. He warned himself that learning to live without Rebecca had been easy compared to the problems he was going to have without Krista.

"Where are we going?"

He gave her the same answer he'd given earlier. "For a drive."

Krista shifted to toss her small bag into the back seat. A gray nylon backpack was already there.

They drove north, the miles rushing by once they reached the paved highway. Rafael was a good driver, comfortable with the Bronco. His left hand rested on the steering wheel; his right hand was on his thigh. Krista wished she had the nerve to put hers there.

"When are you going back?"

Krista moved her gaze from his hand to his face. Mirrored sunglasses hid his eyes. His expression was stern, forbidding, sensual. "Back where?"

"New York."

"I don't know. Maybe I won't." She saw the almost imperceptible tightening of a muscle in his jaw and knew her answer displeased him.

"You can't stay here."

"I can do whatever I want."

"It isn't in you. You need the city, the people, the parties, the worship."

"The *worship?*" she echoed, disbelief widening her eyes. "I'm just a normal woman who works for a living, like any other woman. I'm not some princess whose job is to be admired."

He cast a cynical look her way. "You work."

"Yes. I..." She was almost embarrassed to tell him. "I design clothing for several chains of large department stores."

"So your work is looking good."

"My work is making other people look good," she corrected him. She was hurt that he scoffed at her job, at something she worked hard at. "You're a snob, Rafael. You were born poor, and you worked hard for everything you have, and you think that gives you the right to look down on me, because I had advantages that you didn't. My father's money doesn't make me a bad person, and I'm *not*, no matter how hard you try to make me feel I am."

He felt like a fool, but he didn't offer an apology. He kept his jaw clamped shut.

Krista sighed softly as he slowed to make a left turn onto a dirt road. A few yards ahead a pale green truck, belonging to the border patrol, was parked on the shoulder, and Mike Hughes and Darren Carter, along with four Mexican boys, stood beside it. Both men waved, and Rafael raised his hand in salute but didn't slow down.

"That second boy, the short one, his name is Juan. I've picked him up four times in the last month—twice in one day. The one next to him was your friend Eduardo. He's a regular, too."

"Why don't they stay in Mexico, where they belong?" As soon as the words were out Krista realized how awful they sounded, but she couldn't call them back.

Rafael looked at her for a moment, and he almost smiled. Her question seemed to satisfy some need inside him, to convince himself that she *was* like Rebecca. It would be so much easier to get over her if she were really like Rebecca. "You're no different from the other people around here, are you? You don't like Mexicans any more than most whites along the border. If you can't make a profit from them, you'd prefer to keep them out of the country."

Her face had flushed a most attractive red. "I have nothing against Mexicans," she protested.

He challenged that. "How many have you known?"

"Juana, our housekeeper, and most of my father's employees, and you."

"Servants and employees and a border-patrol agent. How many have you *known?* The others wait on you, and I sleep with you, but have you *known* any of us?"

She shook her head. "No, Rafael, I haven't. I rarely see the others, and you're determined not to let me know you. If all we do is have sex, it's because that's all you want from me. So I don't know many Mexicans; that doesn't make me prejudiced against them. *You're* not perfect, Rafael. Why do you think it's so wrong of me to have faults?"

"I don't." He turned north again onto a narrow road that climbed steeply. The Bronco balked on an occasional sharp turn, the wheels skidding, but the truck was built for roads like this, and Rafael was used to driving on them.

The road ended abruptly near the top of the mountain, and Rafael cut the engine. He swung the backpack over one shoulder, reached for a blanket in the back, then gestured for Krista to follow him.

There was a poorly marked trail that went up, and he led the way. After a moment she called, "Hey, come on, wait a minute."

He glanced over his shoulder, saw she was trailing behind and stopped to let her catch up.

"You may be used to chasing kids like Juan and Eduardo, but I do nothing more strenuous than take an occasional walk," she said when she caught up.

He slipped his arm around her shoulders and fell in step beside her, shortening his stride to match hers. "Making love with you is far more strenuous than chasing the kids."

"You make it sound like a chore."

He chuckled softly. "Anything but."

It was the first time she'd heard him laugh. Her smile was brilliant. "That's nice."

"What?"

"That laugh. Maybe someday you'll learn to do it more often." She raised her hand to twine her fingers through his. "Do you still love her, Rafael?"

There was a brief flare of tension that disappeared as soon as Krista felt it. He was a long time answering. Did he still love Rebecca? he wondered. Maybe he never had. Maybe he had mistaken lust and desire for love, because what he felt for Krista eclipsed his "love" for Rebecca. "No. I don't love Rebecca."

He sounded so certain, but Krista wasn't convinced. His feelings for the other woman must have been very strong. Besides, that didn't mean that he could ever love *her*.

He stopped near a stand of trees, and they spread the blanket. Krista dropped onto it, sprawling on her back, her breathing exaggerated.

One corner of Rafael's mouth turned up. "If you don't quit panting, how can I kiss you?"

She quickly swallowed the gulp of air she'd taken in and rolled onto her side to face him. "Better?"

His reply was his kiss. His mouth tasted fresh and clean; his lips were soft, persuasive. His tongue slipped between her parted lips to rub across her teeth, then moved inside to the warmth that awaited him, searching, exploring, tasting. His hand moved to rest on her throat, gently massaging, and the fingers of his other hand tangled in her hair.

The kiss went on forever, and their bodies responded, but neither of them made an effort to move closer, to go further. For the moment they were satisfied with the kiss.

Rafael ended it, and he rolled onto his back, releasing Krista as he moved. "I'm sorry," he said quietly.

"For what?" she asked, sitting up.

"Putting down your job. Trying to make you feel bad. You were right: reverse snobbery."

Far below in the valley the border-patrol truck was still visible, and Krista stared at it for a long time. He'd known he had offended her, and he had apologized. That meant a lot to her.

Who was she kidding? she asked herself cynically. Everything he did meant a lot to her. She just wished he felt the same about her.

Chapter 8

"Why do they do it?" Krista raised a hand toward the valley below.

Rafael sat up beside her and turned an empty stare onto the valley. "For hope, opportunity, a better life. Most people in my country are poor, trying to support a family of eight or ten on thirty or forty dollars a week. Life is better here. They can hope."

"Is that why you crossed over?"

"I was desperate. We were starving on what my mother and father and I earned. But I didn't come to stay. I'd work at whatever jobs were available and send money back home. When the jobs ran out I'd go back to Mexico for a while."

"Thirteen children." She shook her head in wonder. "So many mouths to feed. Why did they have so many if they couldn't take care of them?"

He turned his head slowly to look at her. Though he said nothing, she saw the derision he felt for her question in his expression, and she hung her head in shame. "You must think I'm stupid," she murmured.

"No." He looked away again. "My parents loved every one of us. We may have been poor and hungry, but there was always enough love."

"You're very lucky. My parents could easily have clothed and fed a dozen children, but they couldn't love even one. I was never poor, never hungry, and never loved. You *are* lucky."

Rafael reached for her hand. "Your father must love you very much," he said, his voice quiet and strong.

"All my life I've tried to make him just *care* about me. I wouldn't ask him to love me, just to give a damn about me ... but he doesn't."

"He loves you, Krista," he insisted. How could anyone *not* love her? "Maybe he has difficulties showing it, but—"

She interrupted him to say, "My parents divorced when I was six. They fought over who had to take custody of me, and my mother won—meaning she didn't have to take me. I've only seen her twice since then. My father put me in a boarding school, and I saw him once in the next two years. The only interest he ever took in me was to make sure I stayed out of his way. *She* didn't want me, and *he* didn't want me, and now ... you don't want me either."

A fat tear quivered on her eyelashes before it fell to her cheek. "I'm not a bad person, Rafael, am I?"

He pulled on her hand, drawing her into his embrace. "No, *pequeña*, you're not bad," he replied softly, regretfully. "We're both fools, your father and I. There's only one difference: he doesn't realize what he's giving up. I do."

"That doesn't mean you'll reconsider, does it?"

With a slender finger he wiped the moisture from her cheek. "No, Krista, I can't."

She smiled wanly. "I'll give you this much: you've got rejection down to a fine art. I don't know too many guys who could get away with holding a woman like this while telling her they want nothing to do with her."

"Krista ..."

"It's all right. I'm used to it. Handling rejection is the only thing in life I'm good at." She laid her cheek against his shirt, feeling the steady beat of his heart. "I wish I'd met you before Rebecca. Would things have been different twelve years ago?"

"I was twenty-two, and you were sixteen. Your father would have killed me for seducing his virginal daughter." He nuzzled her hair away from her ear and touched her skin with his tongue. "I wouldn't have been able to resist you, even if you were a child."

"What were you like?"

"I was very serious. Quiet. I began working in the fields when I was eleven. I knew it would take a miracle to get anything better, and I didn't believe in miracles. I thought I would die in those fields." He settled her more comfortably against him, spreading her hand across his chest, positioning each finger, then laying his hand over hers to hold it there. "We're very different, little one, like day and night. You're the sunlight, and I'm the shadows. You're warm and loving and everything good, and I'm cold, chilling, ruthless."

She doubted the accuracy of his self-description. No matter how hard he tried to appear cold and ruthless, he cared. He cared very much.

"Do you ever feel guilty, Rafael?" she asked, glancing toward the valley. "About your job? When you catch kids like Eduardo, are you ever tempted to let them go?"

"Because I know what it's like? What they're trying to escape? Sometimes it's hard, but it's my job. Besides, what would a boy like Eduardo do on his own in the city? He's only sixteen years old. Who would help him? Protect him? He'll have a better chance when he's older."

"Not if you're around. You're good at your job, aren't you?"

"I do the best I can." He lay back, drawing her down with him. "Let's talk about you. What were you like at sixteen?"

She pursed her lips, thinking back to twelve years ago. "Immature," she finally described. "I thought I was sophisticated and worldly, because I'd been in boarding schools in France and Switzerland, but I was very immature. And not very happy. And a virgin." She rolled onto her stomach to look at him. "I wish I *had* met you then. I wish you had been my first lover."

He touched her hair lightly. "I wish I could be your *last* lover."

"That's entirely possible." Quickly she sat up again. "Forget I said that. I don't want you to remind me again that it's got to end tomorrow. Now...this place is gorgeous, Rafael, but I'm hungry, and I don't see a restaurant for miles."

"Lunch is in the backpack."

After eating they stretched out again on the blanket. "This place doesn't compare to France and Switzerland, does it?" Rafael asked quietly. Just his luck—a poor, barely educated boy from Mexico in love with a rich girl who had lived in places he'd only read about. Their lives had been so different; they might as well be from separate planets.

"The desert is beautiful. So are you."

"I don't understand you, Krista. Why are you interested in me?"

She wanted to cry. He didn't trust her motives, didn't trust *her*. He thought she was all pretense, that she didn't understand real feelings, real emotion. He thought she was using him, amusing herself with the lowly border-patrol agent. "I'm very easy to understand, Rafael, but you're looking for things to complicate the issue. You have this image of me as being easily amused and easily bored. You think I'm fickle and frivolous. You think I don't have real feelings, that everything's just a whim, a game. Yes, we're different, but we have to be. People's personalities don't have to match, Rafael. They have to complement each other. Forget that you were poor and I am rich. That doesn't matter. You're strong and dependable. You're a man I could rely on. You're serious and quiet, and you have a calming effect on me. I'm usually pretty cheerful; if we had time, maybe I could make you smile a little more often.''

"Smiles don't mean a whole lot, do they? They don't mean you're happy. You smile a lot, but you're not very happy. You hide behind your smiles.''

"I know. I found out years ago that it was easier to smile than to admit to anyone how unhappy I was. It's a defense mechanism. You hide behind that wall of ice, and I smile. But for now, Rafael, the smiles are real. I *am* happy.'' She moved over next to him, using his arm as a pillow for her head. "I could probably fall asleep right here,'' she said with a yawn.

"Go ahead. I'll wake you when it's time to go.'' And until then he would watch her, commit everything about her to memory, so that in the empty nights ahead he could close his eyes and remember.

She did sleep, her lashes casting shadows on her cheeks in the late-afternoon sun. Rafael pulled her closer, then checked to make sure the backpack was within reach. Inside it was the trash from their lunch, and in a zippered pouch was a compact Colt .38. He was a cautious man.

A cautious man. His innate sense of caution had saved his life more than once. He could tell when things weren't right, could feel it, and was smart enough to pay attention to his intuition. So why had he ignored it with Krista? There had been warning signs all around her, and he had ignored them. He had seen her, considered the consequences of having her, recognized the futility of loving her, then proceeded as if there were no obstacles.

There was no doubt that he would have to pay the price for reaching for the unattainable, but he couldn't regret it. The hours he'd spent with Krista were too precious to regret.

It was odd how different they were. In her typically confident way Krista considered their mutual attraction the most important thing. She saw no reason to let backgrounds interfere; those were no problem. Rafael, though, put far more importance on those backgrounds, on the differences that could separate them, rather than on the attraction that could bring them together.

Never having been refused anything by her wealthy father, except his love, Krista saw no reason why she shouldn't take what she wanted. Having been deprived of many of life's basic necessities, Rafael was naturally reluctant to take what was offered. He saw no way their relationship could succeed, and the investigation he was conducting made a hopeless situation impossible. He had so little time with her. So little time.

The investigation. Rafael scowled as it pushed its way to the front of his mind. Damn Art McLaren. Why hadn't he been contented with the money he made from the oil wells, the cattle, the farming? Why did he have to start smuggling? Even under the best of circumstances a relationship with Krista would have been difficult, because they were so different. Thanks to Art it was damned near impossible.

Two months ago, when Martin Thompson had introduced Rafael to Richard Houseman and told him that he would be working with the DEA agent, Rafael had seen it as just another job. The object of the investigation then had been Jack Marshall, McLaren's foreman, but it hadn't taken long to learn that Marshall was reporting to McLaren, though they had no proof.

Art was smart. He was also so arrogant that his people conducted business openly, sometimes sending small loads of drugs through the local shipping office, sometimes bringing them into the country through the border checkpoint. But two months later the DEA still had no proof to connect Art directly to the drugs. And Rafael's job had been greatly complicated by Krista's arrival. By her beauty and her smile and her love, and most of all by his own love.

"Krista."

She snuggled closer to him.

"Wake up, *cariña*. It's time to go."

"Hold me just a little longer."

"I will, when we go home. It's getting dark, and we need to go."

She let him pull her to her feet, then sleepily watched him shake out the blanket. "You told me not to tell you this," she said when he finished folding the blanket, "and I realize it really doesn't matter much, but I *do* love you, Rafael."

Black eyes stared into hers. "How can you say it doesn't matter?" he asked, his voice pitched low in disbelief.

"Well, of course it matters; it matters like hell to me. But it can't change things. You still can't get involved with me, and my loving you can't change that. I just... I wanted you to know."

He stroked her face with infinite tenderness. "If things could be different... I will cherish your love, Krista, as I cherish you." He very gently kissed her lips. "Maybe someday..." he murmured to himself. After she'd learned how he had used her, after he'd helped destroy her father, when he was free to return her love—she would hate him. She would probably hate him for the rest of her life.

The weekend was heavenly. Krista wished that it could last forever, but Rafael was adamant that it had to end, and she could do nothing to change his mind. Her attempts to do so only created stress between them, so she reluctantly accepted that this was the last time he would let her be with him. But not even that knowledge could dampen her pleasure in the hours they were together. They made love Saturday night, spent Sunday morning lazing in bed, and Sunday evening Rafael took her to dinner, again in San Ignacio.

They both avoided mentioning the goodbye that was inevitable until they returned to Rafael's house after dinner. She picked up her car on the way home, parking it next to the Bronco. By mutual consent and without words, they went inside and directly to the bedroom, where they made love for the last time. It was wonderful, as usual, though tinged with a bittersweet pain that brought tears to Krista's eyes. She snuggled in Rafael's embrace for a few minutes when it was over then withdrew and began dressing. Her fingers fumbled over the zipper of her skirt and the buttons of her blouse; at last he pushed her hands out of the way and fastened the buttons for her.

"You can stay in bed," she said, trying desperately to control the quaver in her voice.

"I'll walk you to the car." He slipped into his jeans and thrust his bare feet into his tennis shoes while Krista gathered her things.

"I'm sorry," he said in a low, sad voice when they reached the Mustang.

"So am I." She wiped at a tear that seeped from the corner of one eye. "I'm very glad I met you, Rafael Contreras."

He wished he could tell her that in a few months he would be free to come to her, free to return her love. But in a few months she probably wouldn't want him. The event that would free him would cost him her love. So he remained silent and gathered Krista in his arms, holding her to his chest, stroking her hair, leaving light kisses on her forehead.

"I won't ask you why." She raised her eyes to meet his, and he saw the moistness that gleamed there. She was unable to mask the pain. "I know you care for me, so you must have a good reason. I won't ask you what it is, Rafael, but I just want to tell you that it isn't fair. It isn't fair at all."

"No, Krista, it isn't." His eyes were as empty as the night around them. "I never wanted to hurt you."

"I know."

"I will cherish the memories of these days, *querida*." His voice was thick and raspy, full of longing and desire and his own pain.

She pressed her cheek to his bare chest, and he felt the trickle of tears. "I love you, Rafael," she whispered. "I'll always love you." His arms tightened around her, and she savored the feel of them for the last time, then stepped back. Gently she kissed him, tasting his mouth, silently saying goodbye. Then she moved to get into her car.

"Goodbye, *cariña*."

"Not goodbye, Rafael. I won't say goodbye." She looked up at him once more, then started the engine and managed somehow to smile sweetly in spite of her tears. "Maybe someday..."

They were the words he had muttered yesterday, before they left the mountain. The only hope left to either of them. *Maybe someday...*

"McLaren's daughter's been sending regular shipments to New York since she got here. Any idea what they are?"

Martin Thompson shrugged, and Rafael remained silent. Richard Houseman waited a moment, then directed the question specifically to Rafael. "Contreras?"

"I don't know. She designs clothes; her work is in New York. But she isn't involved with her father's business."

"How do you know?"

"I know her."

"And just how well did you get to know her during the half hour you were at her party?" Thompson jeered. "Maybe we ought to get Darren Carter in here. He dated her. He *really* knows her."

Houseman took the man seriously; he missed the undertone that signified that Thompson was needling Rafael. "We've got enough people involved in this as it is. I'd rather not bring anyone else in."

Rafael ignored his boss and turned his cold gaze on the DEA agent. "Krista has little to do with her father. McLaren might use her, but it would be without her knowledge."

"I'll find out about those shipments she's made. She could be working with Art on this. From everything we've heard in the city, she's almost too good to be true. She doesn't drink, doesn't smoke, doesn't use drugs, doesn't even sleep around. No one would suspect her of being involved." Except Houseman himself. "How did Art McLaren raise a daughter like that?"

"He had very little to do with it." Rafael rose to his feet and went to stare out the window. Over a week had passed since Krista had left his house. Over a week, and he missed her as much as, even more than, the night when she drove away. A couple of times, usually late at night when he couldn't sleep because his bed felt so empty, he had considered what he would have to do to get her back in his life. It wouldn't take much—quit his job, tell her father about the investigation into his smuggling, go against everything he believed in. Sometimes it didn't seem like too much to ask.

Then his common sense would reassert itself. How could he live with himself if he threw away his ethics and beliefs and saved Art McLaren just so he could have Krista? And his heart would always answer: how could he live without her? Ethics and beliefs did nothing to ease the pain inside him or to fill the emptiness of his life.

"Let's have lunch, Rafe," Houseman suggested. He didn't bother to invite Martin Thompson; the older man would make it more difficult for him to talk to Contreras. He sensed a definite dislike between the two men, and it made him uneasy. Jobs like this always went off better when the people involved got along and worked well together. But whatever Thompson's dislike for the younger man, he had recommended Rafael as the "best damned agent" he'd ever worked with. Thompson might not like the man, but he respected his abilities, and that was certainly worth something.

Rafael reluctantly agreed to the invitation. They went to the Blue Parrot, where a loud lunch crowd of oil-field and construction workers made it possible to carry on a conversation without fear of being overheard. As soon as they had been served, Houseman bluntly asked, "How well do you know Krista?"

Rafael stared at the roast-beef sandwich in front of him. He didn't want to answer; he resented any prying into his personal life, and Krista was a very personal part of his life. But he knew he had to answer, so he did, coldly. "Well."

Richard Houseman used eating as an excuse to think before he went on. He didn't want to offend the obviously an-

gry man across from him, but he needed to know more.
"How well?"

He got no answer.

"Well enough to say for certain that she couldn't be involved with Art's schemes? Well enough to want to believe
anything she tells you without looking for the truth? Well
enough to lie to protect her, or to sabotage this investigation so she won't be hurt?"

Rafael raised his head and looked at him. Beneath the
bronze of his cheeks was a dull red signifying that Houseman had gone too far. No one had ever accused Rafael of
being dishonest or corrupt. "I know her better than I know
anyone in this town, this state or this country. What I want
to believe has nothing to do with it. She has no idea what her
father does to earn all that money."

"Would she care?"

Again Rafael chose not to reply; the answer seemed obvious enough to him.

"What if she *is* involved, Rafe? What are you going to do
about it?"

"It isn't going to happen."

"But what if she is?"

Rafael was stubborn. "She isn't."

Houseman lost his temper. "What makes you so damned
sure?" he demanded, leaning forward to snap the question.

"I am."

Rafael's calm, arrogant answer grated on Houseman's
nerves, but he decided to accept it for now. The man just
might know what he was talking about. "Is she staying at
her dad's place?"

"Yes."

"What kind of relationship does she have with the old
man?"

"A lousy one."

Houseman's blue eyes gleamed at that information.
"Lousy enough that she might help us?"

"No." Rafael had eaten as much of the sandwich as his stomach could handle; his anger had destroyed his hunger. "Leave her out of this. She's done nothing to interest you. She knows nothing about her father. You're not going to drag her into it, Houseman. You're not going to ask her to help destroy the only family she's got."

That was the most Rafael had ever said at one time to Richard. He was impressed. He was also certain that there was more to Rafael's relationship than he was letting on to anyone. He knew her far better than Thompson, or even Richard himself, had suspected. That could be a big help in the future.

Rafael returned to headquarters to pick up his truck, then went out into the desert to patrol. Richard went to the small shipping office, hoping to pry from the clerk a little information about the frequent packages Krista was sending to New York. His luck was better than he expected. In line in front of him, the only other customer in the place was Krista McLaren, in the flesh.

And what luscious flesh it was, he thought with a sly grin. No wonder Contreras was so protective of the woman; she was one of the prettiest Richard had seen in a long time.

"That'll be thirteen dollars and fifty-five cents, Miss McLaren," the clerk said, completing the usual paperwork. "Our business has certainly improved since you came here."

Paying the man, she laughed pleasantly. "As long as I'm here and my job's in New York, I'll be relying on you to help me out."

Richard leaned on the counter, barely able to read the name and address on the box. "Miss McLaren," he said with a warm, friendly smile. "You must be Krista McLaren."

She glanced up, and her smile faltered. "Yes, I am."

"I'm Richard Houseman."

"Nice to meet you." She turned back to the clerk as he counted out her change. While she was occupied, Richard speculatively studied the box she was sending off. It was large, taped securely, looked innocent enough—and probably was, he admitted. The shipping rates were set by weight, and at only thirteen fifty-five the box wasn't heavy enough to be of interest to him. It probably just held patterns or drawings or fabric—whatever designers needed for designing, he decided with a measure of disappointment.

Krista left the office, and Houseman muttered some excuse to the clerk before following her out. "Ever since I got into town I've been hearing about you. I was beginning to think I'd never meet you."

She stopped beside the Mustang, wondering how to get rid of him politely. "I stay busy."

Busy with what? he wondered. Her job? Rafe Contreras? Or her father's illicit operations? "I understand you're from New York. That's where I'm permanently assigned."

Krista's attention was caught by the word "assigned." "Are you with the border patrol?"

"Yeah," he lied. "Just temporarily."

"I have a few friends who work there—Jim Stone and Darren Carter."

Richard noticed that she didn't mention Contreras. He wondered why. "I haven't really gotten to know any of them yet, besides Thompson and Rafe."

"Rafael," she corrected him quickly, then blushed. She hadn't intended to say his name. Funny—it had been over a week, but there was still a sharp pain in her stomach when she even spoke his name. She couldn't imagine what seeing him would do to her.

He watched the nameless expression that fluttered across her features, then was gone. He'd been right in believing Contreras, even though Thompson doubted him. It hadn't just been talk. The man knew Krista McLaren very well. Houseman was certain that they were lovers.

"I'm sorry," she said. "I shouldn't correct people about what they call other people. If he doesn't want to be called Rafe, he'll tell you himself, I guess."

He accepted her explanation, not pushing for more information. "Are you one of those people who dislike nicknames, Krista?" he asked with a genuinely warm smile. "I've always had to deal with people who want to call me Rick or Rich or, worse, Dick."

"I've never had that problem." She glanced pointedly at her watch. "I've got to get going. It was nice meeting you."

"Nice meeting you, too." Eyes narrowed suspiciously, he watched her drive away. Contreras was convinced that Krista was innocent, ignorant of Art's smuggling.

Richard wasn't.

When she was out of sight he went to a nearby phone booth and placed a call to New York City. He gave the name and address of the woman Krista's package had gone to, with orders to find out all they could about her.

Krista's fingers curled tightly around the steering wheel as she drove away. She'd had to bite her tongue to keep from asking Richard Houseman about Rafael. She was hungry for news of her lover—her ex lover, she corrected herself cynically.

Sometimes she was angry with him. What could be so damned important that he had to end their affair? But she trusted Rafael as much as she loved him. She had to believe that he was doing what he had to do.

She slowed the Mustang as she approached the turnoff to her father's house and also to Rafael's. If she went right she would be home in twenty minutes. Home to a house that was empty except for Juana. If she went left she could be at Royce Ann Stone's house in ten minutes. The idea of a few hours with her friend sounded very appealing, just the thing to cheer her up.

A mile off the highway she came upon two border-patrol trucks parked on the shoulder of the dirt road. The two agents, in their dark green uniforms, leaned against the front fender of the rear truck. One was Jim Stone, who raised his hand in a wave, gesturing for Krista to stop as she drew abreast. Reluctantly she did so—reluctantly because the other was Rafael.

"Are you on your way to my house?" Jim asked.

"Yes, I am. I'd like to spend a little time with Royce Ann." Slowly, hesitantly, her gaze moved to Rafael. Jim had come to stand beside the car, but Rafael had remained where he was, mirrored sunglasses in place. Still, she felt his eyes moving slowly over her, and her cheeks colored slightly in spite of her efforts to be cool. "Hello, Rafael."

He nodded once.

"What have you been up to, Krista?" Jim asked, unaware of the tension spreading through her.

"Just work. There's not much else to do around here, is there?" Especially since she could no longer spend time with Rafael.

"Have you decided yet how long you'll be staying?"

Rafael straightened then. He couldn't trust himself to stand there and listen to them chat without doing something stupid, like dragging Krista into his arms and kissing her long and hard. "I'm going on out," he said quickly, before Krista could answer the question. He sent another curt nod in her direction, then got in the truck and left, his wheels throwing up a cloud of dust. That would ensure him a head start. Krista couldn't drive the Mustang with its top down until the thick dust had settled.

Jim watched her watch Rafael leave. "You lose interest?"

She gave a shake of her head. "I've lost hope, Jim."

"I've never known you to give up on something you really wanted."

"I've never wanted anything that was so totally hopeless." Her sad sigh grew into a smile. She had memories. Whatever happened, even if "someday" never came, she would always have beautiful memories of the time she'd spent with Rafael. She counted herself lucky for that. Some people never even had that much.

"I'll never understand Rafe. How any normal man with blood in his veins could turn his back on you..." Jim shook his head in dismay. "Royce Ann always says he's inhuman. She just may be right."

Krista shook her head, too. "Don't bet on it, Jim. You'd lose. Listen, I'll see you later, all right? You take care of yourself out here."

"Sure will. So long, Krista."

She found Royce Ann stretched out on the sofa in the Stones' air-conditioned living room, the television turned to some soap opera or other. She turned the sound down and invited Krista to take a seat. "I thought maybe you'd forgotten about me," she said in her heavy drawl. "How have you been?"

"Busy. I've been working." She omitted the rest of what she'd been doing: moping over Rafael.

"Friday's the Fourth, you know." Royce Ann went into the kitchen and returned with two glasses of iced tea and a plate of brownies. "The town still celebrates at the park all day and has fireworks that night. Want to go with Jim and me?"

Krista wasn't really in the mood for a celebration of any kind, but no one skipped the Fourth of July, not in Nueva Vida. Besides, if she stayed home alone she would get lonely and feel sorry for herself, and she'd been doing enough of that as it was, so she accepted the invitation.

"We'll be having a picnic lunch, and for dinner there's a town barbecue that's always really good. Juana helps with the cooking, and you know how good her food is."

The talk turned from the Fourth to clothes and Krista's work; then, after several hours, she got ready to leave. Her failure to mention Rafael even once all afternoon roused Royce Ann's curiosity, and she wanted to ask if Krista had finally taken her advice and forgotten the man, but she didn't. The last time they had discussed him, Krista had made it clear that she wanted no warnings and no advice. He was a subject, Royce Ann decided, that was better left unmentioned.

Krista left her friend, promising to see her at eleven Friday morning, and headed toward her father's house.

* * *

"After I left you Monday I went by the shipping office to snoop around, and Krista McLaren was there, sending a package."

Rafael turned his head slowly to look at Richard Houseman. "And?"

"It went to Tracy Lord, who happens to be Tracy Lord Smith. Steve Smith's wife."

Rafael knew nothing about Tracy Lord, but Steve Smith was a name that meant something. Smith was a good friend of Jack Marshall, Art McLaren's foreman, and he'd been on McLaren's payroll himself for about fifteen years. He'd moved to New York a few years ago to run that end of the drug business.

Rafael picked up the bottle of beer that had been sitting untouched in front of him for ten minutes and took a deep drink. He decided to stifle his defense of Krista until he heard what Houseman had to say.

"Smith couldn't run an operation like that without his wife finding out. She's probably as much a part of it as he is. Now, her friendship with Krista could be entirely innocent. Still . . ." He stopped, then said flatly, "We can't risk her being involved, too. Someone's got to keep an eye on her."

If Houseman volunteered for the job himself, Rafael vowed he would punch him. He'd be damned if he'd let someone as devious as Houseman entangle Krista in the mess her father had created.

So deep in his dark thoughts was he that Rafael was certain he couldn't have understood Houseman's next words. He raised black eyes that showed a flicker of surprise to the blond man's face and quietly, very quietly, asked, "You want to repeat that?"

Richard didn't mind at all. "I want you to start seeing her again."

"Start seeing . . . Krista . . . again?"

"Obviously you and she had something going. I want you to start it again."

"Obviously?" It seemed all he was capable of doing was repeating the other man's words. His brain was too stunned to put any of his own together.

"What happened? You quit seeing her because of this investigation? Conflict of interest and all that crap?"

Rafael's daze was beginning to wear off. His eyes hardened like black ice, and his voice chilled to match them. "My personal life is none of your business, Houseman."

"When your personal life involves someone under investigation, it becomes my business." Then Richard backed down a little under Rafael's frigid glare. "All right. I don't care what happened in the past. Just get back together with her. Get her to tell you about her business and her connection to Tracy Lord, and about her father." He rose from his seat, aware that Rafael would probably like to break his neck, but confident that he would agree to the task. "Look at it this way: if she's involved, you've got a chance to get her out of it. If she's not, you can protect her from the fallout. When it's all over and we've got McLaren and the others, we'll take your word regarding her. It's up to you."

Rafael felt sick. One part of him wanted to rejoice: he was being told to renew his relationship with Krista, to spend as much time with her as he wanted, to be free to talk to her and be with her and make love with her. His heart rate accelerated at the mere thought. But his brain knew it wasn't that simple. He was being told to use the woman who said she loved him, the woman who meant more to him than any other person in the world. He was supposed to take advantage of her love for him and use it to further their investigation, to help trap her father. Krista, who had been rejected so often that she claimed it was the one thing she was good at, would never forgive him for using her like that. She would never believe his love for her was sincere in spite of his manipulations.

He could refuse. But if he did Houseman would simply find some other way to "keep an eye on her." How? By bringing in someone who would be willing to take advantage of her affections, someone who might not give a damn how much she was hurt in the process? At least Rafael cared. He cared too damn much.

He would have to convince them to leave her out of the whole mess. They would have to see that she had nothing to do with Art's smuggling, that involving her would just complicate an already complicated case. They would have to understand that Rafael wouldn't do what they were asking. He couldn't do it.

But they would insist. Martin Thompson couldn't care less about Krista or whether she got hurt. Richard Houseman wasn't as cold as Thompson, but he wanted one thing: Art McLaren. If someone who was innocent got hurt in the process, well, that was too bad, but those things happened, and as long as he got McLaren, nothing else mattered.

Rafael allowed himself a bitter smile. He had often compared Krista to Rebecca Halderman. Now he was ready to concede that he'd been wrong; other than their physical resemblance, Krista was nothing like Rebecca. Richard Houseman, on the other hand...

He would have to do it. He had no choice. If he handled things right, if he was careful, if he made no mistakes, maybe, just maybe, Krista would someday forgive him.

That was a thought he would keep with him in the days to come.

Friday was a typically hot July day. Rafael sat on the tiny back porch of his house and watched the sunrise. It was the Fourth of July. Independence Day. There was going to be a celebration in town—picnics, games, contests, an evening barbecue and a fireworks display. Rafael had never been to the festivities, not once in the five years he'd lived in Nueva Vida. But today he was going. Whenever he got the courage, he would drive into town and search for Krista.

He was sure she would be there; practically everyone in town except him made it a point to show up. She would go, and she would charm everyone she got close to. She would probably be surrounded by admirers as soon as she arrived, but somehow Rafael had to get close to her. Somehow he would have to separate her from her friends and talk to her, convince her that he couldn't continue this way any longer, that he needed and wanted her with him.

He felt ill again. What he was about to do went against everything he believed in, made a mockery of the honor and integrity that had been instilled in him at a very young age.

But he would do his job, and he'd get close to Krista again. He'd get to hold her again, to touch her and kiss her and talk to her. With any luck he'd get to make love with her that very night.

He would get to make her happy again, for a short time. Until he helped destroy her life.

Chapter 9

She was easy to find, even though it seemed as if all nine thousand of Nueva Vida's residents had shown up for the celebration. None, though, had hair that seemed to reflect the sun's light; none had a laugh that tinkled like chimes caught in a strong wind; none drew Rafael as surely and inescapably as she did. She had come with Jim and Royce Ann Stone, and she was surrounded by every unmarried man in the county, or so it seemed. She was having a good time.

Rafael kept his distance, staying out of sight and watching her. He felt foolish, worshiping her from afar—or was he spying on her? He knew he could approach her, knew that she would immediately leave all those fawning, adoring men if he asked her to. Still, he stayed away from her throughout the afternoon, until the sun had set and they were settling down to wait for the fireworks. That was the first time he saw her alone.

Rafael followed her at a discreet distance, drawing no attention to himself, to the long line at the concession stand near the park entrance.

Krista felt someone move into line behind her and knew it was a man from his scent—clean and strong and masculine. He stood very close, closer than was appropriate, so she took a step ahead. So did he.

The little hairs on her neck stood on end. She felt cornered, unable to step forward because of the boy in front of her, and uncomfortable with the proximity of the man behind. She hoped he would keep his distance when the line moved forward.

Again he moved too close, and Krista shivered involuntarily. "Do I make you uncomfortable, *señorita?*" a raspy voice murmured only inches from her ear.

She whirled around. "Rafael!" she exclaimed, delighted by his appearance. Her eyes swept over him; then her smile faded a bit. "It's been a while."

"Twelve days." He didn't count the few minutes when he'd seen her earlier that week. He held her gaze for a long moment before reaching out to touch her cheek gently. "I've missed you, Krista," he murmured. "Come and walk with me. Please."

She stepped out of line, her thirst forgotten, and walked away at Rafael's side. "How have you been?"

He raised his shoulders in a shrug. "Lonely." He steered her toward the end of the park, more heavily wooded than the rest. There, away from prying eyes, he leaned a shoulder against a broad tree trunk. "How have *you* been?"

Krista moved to lean back against the trunk beside him. With a soft laugh she gave the same answer. "Lonely." She continued to study him in the dim light, as if looking upon a sight she had thought never to see again. "Lonely" didn't even begin to explain how miserable she'd been in the last twelve days. It had only been Rafael's determination to end their romance that had kept her from him, that had stopped her from begging him to give her another chance.

"You've had plenty of company today."

"But they don't matter. You know that, Rafael." A ghost of a smile crossed her lips. "How long have you been here?"

"Since three o'clock."

"I didn't see you."

"But I saw you. With every single man in the county."

"Not every one. Not the one I wanted to be with."

For a long moment they simply stared at each other, neither sure of what to say next. It was Rafael who broke the silence. "Can I kiss you?"

"I'd like that."

Even with her consent, he didn't kiss her right away. His hand came up to stroke her face, to learn its lines and shape and texture by touch, the way a blind person might. Her lips were soft, slightly parted, waiting for his mouth to claim them. When at last it did she gave a little gasp. Her legs went weak, making her grateful for the support of the tree behind her.

The kiss was gentle and sweet, and she longed for more. She reached out blindly to catch Rafael's arms and pulled him to her, her body fitting neatly against his.

Hard with a desire that he knew would never lessen, Rafael raised his head. "You have the sweetest mouth," he whispered.

"Kiss me again, Rafael, with your tongue."

He covered her lips again, his tongue slowly moving into the warmth of her mouth. Sensuously it explored every intimate corner, mating with her tongue, his teeth nibbling at it. His hand found her breast, rubbing over it through the thin cotton of her blouse. Her nipple responded instantly, just as she responded to his kiss.

"Rafael, I want you."

"I need you." He cupped her cheek in one hand, the other continuing to caress her breast. "Krista, *querida,* do you love me?" he asked urgently.

Damn, he hadn't meant to be so blunt about it, but the question was out, and he couldn't call it back without making a bigger fool of himself.

"Yes, I do," she replied dreamily, not noticing his bluntness, or caring.

"Then I'll be yours as long as you want me. The days we spent together were the best of my life. Without you my life is empty. As long as you want me, I'll be here."

Krista's heart soared in her breast, and tears welled in her eyes. That was probably as close to a declaration of love as Rafael could give, and she would treasure it until she died. "I *do* love you, Rafael, and I will always, always want you."

He embraced her tightly, his face pressed against her hair. An unpleasant twinge of guilt tried to ruin his happiness, but he refused to let it. Yes, he was using Krista, but he could make her happy. Yes, she was way out of his league, but he adored her, cherished her, loved her. Yes, he was helping to trap her father, but he was going to protect her, keep her safe, see that she was untouched by Art's crimes. He would do his job, and he would love her, and when she learned of his duplicity, he hoped that she would trust enough in his love to forgive him. He hoped. He was betting his heart, his future and his life on that hope.

"Let's go home, Rafael."

He gently disentangled himself. Allowing himself a small smile, he asked, "And miss the fireworks?"

"I thought they started when you kissed me."

"Be patient," he replied, "and I'll make it worth your while. I'll kiss you in places I've hardly even touched."

Krista shivered with anticipation. "All right, I'll be patient. You want to see the fireworks?"

"Yes. Do you mind being seen in public with me?"

"Of course not."

"Do you mind being touched in public by me?" He wasn't sure he could keep his hands off her for even a minute.

"Of *course* not."

"Let's find a place to sit, *querida;* it's almost time. Then we'll go home," he said with a smile.

Hand in hand they moved through the trees, stopping just at the edge of the clearing. "There are Jim and Royce Ann," Krista said. "I was sitting with them. Do you want to go over?"

Rafael was hesitant to join her friends. On the ground next to them were Nick Morris and his wife, and Mike Hughes and his girlfriend. But he nodded his agreement anyway, then pulled Krista against his body for a long, hungry kiss.

From the quilt a few yards away Royce Ann saw a movement in the trees and looked over. After a few stunned seconds she elbowed her husband and gestured. She didn't want to speak out loud and draw the attention of the other P.A.s to the couple in the trees.

"Is that Krista?" Jim whispered in Royce Ann's ear.

"Yes."

"And Rafe?"

"Yes."

"I'll be damned."

The fact that they were holding hands when they walked over to the quilt escaped no one's notice. Six pairs of curious eyes watched them sit down, watched Rafael lay his hand possessively over Krista's, watched her glance up at him and smile. Six pairs of astonished eyes watched him smile in return—a quick upturning of his lips that lasted only seconds but was definitely a smile.

"We, uh, thought you'd gotten lost," Royce Ann said a little uncomfortably.

"I ran into Rafael, and we took the long way back."

Royce Ann's eyes were faintly disapproving, not of Rafael but of Krista's failure to tell her about him. They were best friends; Krista had always confided in her, but she'd forgotten to tell her that she and the strange, silent Mexican were lovers. And their relationship *was* intimate; they had the special, tender look of lovers.

She managed to get Krista alone during the intermission in the fireworks display. On the way to the bathroom she asked, "How long has this been going on, Krista?"

"About a month." She smiled serenely. "I'm sorry you don't approve."

"It's not my place to approve or disapprove. Why didn't you tell me? We've always told each other everything."

"I know how you feel about him."

"Look, I don't think I like Rafael Contreras, but—" Royce Ann raised her hands to stop Krista's interruption "—but I don't know him. You could have told me, Krista. Why did you want to keep it a secret?"

After establishing that Royce Ann's need for the bathroom had been merely a ploy to get Krista alone to talk, they sat down on a bench. Krista turned her serious blue gaze on her friend. "Rafael's very different from most men we know, and there are a lot of people around here who don't like him because of those differences. I didn't want anyone telling me it's wrong, to stay away from him, that he's not good enough for me. He's a good man, Royce Ann."

She dropped her gaze to the ground for a moment, then looked at her friend. "You don't know what it cost him to come out tonight and sit with you and the others. He's a very private man, Royce Ann. He knows what people think of him; he hears the things they say. He knows showing up with me tonight will mean nothing but gossip, and none of it flattering to him. He asked me if I minded being seen with him, as if I might be ashamed.... He's kind and gentle and tender. He's a good, honest man, and I love him, Royce Ann."

Royce Ann impulsively hugged her. "You're special to him, too—you made him smile. I wish you all the happiness in the world, Krista."

Krista was laughing along with her friend, but she had to wipe a tear from her eye. "Thank you, Royce Ann. I know some people will disapprove, but I'd hate for you to be one of them."

"If he makes you happy, how could I disapprove? And I swear I'll never call him cold or inhuman again. I always assumed that he couldn't be hurt by insults. It was a stupid assumption. If he's kind and gentle and tender, he can't be cold and unfeeling, can he?"

"No, he can't."

As they started back to the quilt Royce Ann asked, like an excited teenager, "Has he said he loves you yet?"

"No." Krista smiled sweetly, a little shyly. "He said...he said he cherishes me." Then she pleaded, "Don't repeat that, okay? If it got out he might be hurt, or embarrassed, and he's been hurt enough."

Her friend was impressed. "Cherishes. That might even be better than saying he loves you. Of course I won't tell anyone, not even Jim."

When they reached the others Krista sat down in front of Rafael, then leaned back against his chest. He bent his head to whisper, "Did you reassure her that I'm not some monster?"

The floodlights that had been turned on for intermission went off. In the cover of darkness Krista turned her head. "That wasn't why—" Rafael cut off the flow of words with a kiss, and his hand came up to brush over her breast. The caress was brief, so no one could see, but it made her ache for more attention. "I'm running low on patience," she whispered.

"It'll be worth it."

"You're awfully sure of yourself, aren't you?"

"I'm sure of *us, cariña.*"

That was true. No matter what obstacles stood in their way, he was sure that he and Krista belonged together. Their love was too strong, too good, to be wrong. But a lot of good things went bad, and he'd have to be very careful that it didn't happen to them.

When the fireworks ended an hour later Krista refused Jim's offer of a ride home, and she and Rafael walked down the street to his Bronco. "Do you want to stop at your house and get some clothes?"

She nodded. "I need to tell Juana not to expect me until...when?"

"Sunday. Monday. Next week. Whenever you come back." Rafael concentrated on driving for a few minutes before asking, "What about your father? Are you going to tell him where you'll be?"

Krista laid her head back, letting her eyes close. She knew she should say yes, but she also knew what Art's response would be: an explosive outburst of temper. She was too happy tonight to let her father ruin it. "We'll see," she replied.

She was saved from being forced into a decision when they reached *la casa grande:* Art wasn't home. She packed a bag, told Juana where she would be and left again with Rafael.

Krista felt as if she were floating—no, sinking—through thick, soft, warm clouds that enveloped her like a cocoon. Her muscles had turned to jelly; her bones had dissolved into nothingness. The only things that kept her from disappearing completely were the strong arms wrapped around her, her lifeline to the world, to reality.

"Are you all right?"

The mustache tickled as Rafael bent his head to whisper the question in her ear, and Krista would have giggled if she'd had the strength. Instead she simply sighed. "Perfect."

"Was it worth the wait?"

"Oh, yes."

He stroked her hair between his fingers, then turned onto his side to face her. Black eyes held hers even in the darkness of the bedroom. "I missed you," he said intensely.

"Oh, Rafael, I missed you too." She wrapped her arms around his back and pulled him down for a kiss. "I missed you so much.... I love you so much...."

"Where are you going?"

Rafael had eased away from Krista and was standing up when she sleepily asked the question. He lay down again, on top of the sheet, and leaned over to kiss her forehead. "I would give almost anything to stay in bed with you, *cariña,* but I have to work today."

"Oh, Rafael..."

"I'll get off around three or three-thirty. I should have told you last night, but I had other things on my mind."

Krista opened her eyes then and smiled devilishly, her blue eyes gleaming. "Show me the other things that were on your mind."

"Tonight."

She knew that if she persisted she could convince him that being late for work had its rewards, but she didn't have the energy. "Could you drop me off at the house to get my car? If you're going to work I might as well do a little shopping."

Rafael left the bed and disappeared into the closet. "Sure, but if you want to use the truck instead it's all right."

"You'd really let me keep the Bronco today?"

She liked that idea. The truck would be fun to drive, and it would keep her away from the house, away from her father. "Thanks. I'd like that."

Rafael came out again wearing jeans and carrying running shoes. "You'll have to pick me up this afternoon, but the rest of the day is yours."

"I have a lot of experience at picking you up," she teased as she began dressing.

"You never were very subtle, were you?"

"Couldn't afford to be. You were so intent on ignoring me that I had to be aggressive."

"Maybe I was playing hard to get."

"The only problem was that *I* wasn't playing. I was dead serious."

A smile came to him slowly. "So was I, *querida.*"

When they were ready to leave she asked, "Aren't you going to shave?" His jaw was prickly with a day's growth of beard, giving him a slightly unsavory appearance.

"Not now." He locked the door behind him before handing the keys to her. "You can drive."

The Bronco *was* fun to drive, and its owner remained relaxed and unconcerned in the passenger seat, something Krista appreciated. She remembered when Art had tried to teach her to drive twelve years ago. After two lessons he'd turned her over to Ruben and declared *his* car off limits to her.

"Will you be home this afternoon? I'll call you when I get off."

Home. She liked the sound of that. "I don't know," she said as she stopped in front of the border-patrol station. "I'll just be here around three, all right? I don't mind waiting."

Rafael gave her a quick, hard kiss, his beard scratching her tender skin. "Be careful."

"You, too." Krista watched him get out of the truck. A few long strides took him inside the building and out of sight. She shifted into gear and drove away.

The day passed quickly, because she was happy and contented. She puttered around the house, making the bed, taking cuttings from the plants she'd given him, gathering the clothes they had hastily shed the night before. After lunch in town and a little shopping, she went to wait for Rafael at three o'clock.

Pulling into the parking lot behind her was Royce Ann. She parked next to the Bronco and went around to lean against the fender. Krista sat in the driver's seat of the truck, the door open and her feet dangling.

"I hate this heat," Royce Ann said without preamble.

Krista grinned. "And hello to you, too."

Royce Ann pushed a strand of black hair from her forehead, then sipped from the extra-large cup of iced Coke she held. "Hello, Krista. I see you're waiting for Rafael. I hate this heat." She spoke slowly, her Southern drawl even more pronounced.

"It isn't so bad."

A van pulled into the parking lot, followed by a Dodge Ram four-wheel drive. Royce Ann waved to her husband. "There they are."

Jim Stone looked hot and sweaty in his uniform. Rafael looked cold and dangerous in his street clothes.

"He looks like one of those border bandits that attack the illegals," Royce Ann whispered as Rafael's easy, unhurried stride carried him toward them.

Krista nodded in agreement as she slid to the ground. He was dressed in jeans and a denim vest left open to expose one very nice chest. Around his forehead he had tied a red bandanna, his usually neat hair tumbling over it. He was scowling and looked fierce. Savage.

"He may be kind and gentle," Royce Ann said in a hurried whisper, "but he scares the hell out of me." She moved away from the Bronco as Rafael reached them. "Hello, Rafael. Krista, I'm going to wait inside, where it's air-conditioned. I *do* hate this heat. See you later."

Rafael stopped less than a foot in front of Krista. Cold black eyes scrutinized her face; then slowly, beneath his mustache, one corner of his mouth rose slightly. "Your friend should have stayed around. I have a chilling effect on most people."

"Not me. Would you be embarrassed if I kissed you in front of those men?" She gestured to the three agents across the lot from them, but he didn't bother to look.

He placed his hands on her waist and pulled her snugly against him. "They probably wonder what you see in me. They think you must be too blind to see how unfeeling and inhuman I am."

She brushed a strand of his hair in place over the headband. Still smiling but more serious now, she softly said, "I love you, Rafael." His reaction—a slight tensing of his jaw, a narrowing of his eyes—prompted her to continue quickly. "I'm not asking anything of you. I'm not using you. I just want to be with you.... I just want to love you."

But I'm using you, his conscience cried. *God forgive me, I'm using you.*

"You're welcome to be with me as long as you want." His voice was a little huskier than usual, the only lingering sign of his guilt. "What about that kiss, *cariña?*"

She slid her arms around his neck and pressed herself against him. Instead of one kiss she gave him a series of them, nipping at his lips, nibbling his tongue, exploring his mouth in quick forays before withdrawing. Swallowing a groan, Rafael placed his hand on the back of her head, forcing her to hold still while he took control, thoroughly loving her mouth with his.

"Come with me, *cariña*," he murmured, his lips brushing her forehead. "Let me take you to the mountain and make love to you. I want to undress you and cover your body with kisses. I want to touch you, to know that you want me as much as I want you."

His erotic whispering sent a shiver chasing down Krista's spine and stirred a hunger deep inside her. "Yes. I do want you. Please take me away from here and make love with me. Let me have a part of you for the rest of my life."

"You are part of my life, part of my heart, part of my soul. For as long as I live you will be a part of me. Every sunrise, every moon, every wind, will bring memories of you."

Footsteps approached, and Rafael slowly raised his head. He didn't release Krista, though; he simply turned his head and asked, "What do you want, Martin?"

"Where are those papers I asked for?" Martin Thompson asked hostilely. He didn't like to see Rafael and Krista in an intimate embrace. It proved that he had been wrong about Rafael's attraction for Krista, and he didn't like being wrong.

"They're on your desk. The left side. I left them there this morning." To Krista he said softly, "Let's go."

She got into the Bronco and climbed across to her seat. "Why aren't you in uniform?" She buckled her seat belt, then turned slightly to see him better.

"I don't always wear one. Sometimes it's better if the people I'm talking to don't know who I work for." Like today, when he'd been questioning the illegals he met about smugglers in general and Art McLaren's people in particular.

She didn't question him further until they were on the highway. "You mean . . . sort of undercover."

He shrugged. "Sort of."

"Is it dangerous?"

"I suppose it could be. Does that worry you?"

"Yes."

"Don't let it. People are afraid of me. They don't bother me."

She gave his thigh a squeeze. "*I'm* not afraid of you."

"You barreled into my life without taking time to consider whether you *should* be afraid. That's the way you approach everything, Krista. To you the world is good and bright, and you see no reason to be afraid."

"Is that bad?"

Rafael raised her hand to his lips and tenderly kissed it. "Not always. Sometimes I envy you that. But sometimes it makes it easier for you to get hurt. Not everyone is as good and sweet and nice as you. Not everyone deserves your trust."

"You do."

She said it so simply that Rafael wanted to die. Her trust in him was implicit. What would his betrayal do to her?

"I would never do anything to hurt you if I could avoid it," he said very quietly. "Do you understand that, Krista?"

She gave a laugh. "Of course I understand. You're not that kind of person."

He silently prayed that she would still feel that way when she found out what he'd done. He prayed that she would be able to forgive him, and he hoped he would be able to forgive himself.

Once they left the highway the road was empty of other traffic. The truck climbed steadily on the narrow road, finally reaching the clearing where Rafael had parked the last time. Hand in hand they leisurely followed the steep path. When they reached the top Rafael spread out the blanket he carried and drew Krista down with him.

"I missed you," she said.

His eyes were serious. "I've missed you, too." He rolled onto his side, leaning his head in the palm of his left hand. "Talk to me, Krista. Tell me about yourself. What do you want? What makes you happy?"

"*You* make me happy. You're the best part of my life. And a family would make me happy." Her fingers moved up to glide through his hair, dislodging the headband and pulling it free. Her voice became soft and dreamy. "I want a husband and children. Oh, Rafael, I want a dozen children—beautiful little boys like their father, and little girls like—"

"Little girls like their beautiful mother," he finished for her. He often found himself dreaming about children, too, about daughters who were the mirror image of their blue-eyed mother. "What about your career? What if your dozen children interfere?"

"Who needs a career when you can have babies?"

"You don't support the women's movement with sentiments like that, do you?"

"Women's lib means the right to choose. If I choose a family over a career, that's my right. Besides, I *could* have both." Her hand dropped from his hair to his chest, where it rubbed sensuously over smooth skin. "What about your family, Rafael? Do you miss them?"

"Yes."

There was a tightness in his voice, warning her, but she continued without notice. "We were a horrible family. My mother couldn't even love me. I was one of the reasons she left Dad. She hated the house, the desert and 'that clinging brat.' That was me. She hated me, and I hated myself. It was years later, Rafael, that I finally realized I wasn't to blame for Selena's unhappiness. I couldn't accept responsibility for her. I couldn't control her anymore than you could control Rebecca and her father when they hurt you and Josefina and your family."

The lines of his body tensed, and his breathing was tightly controlled. He started to roll away from her, but something held him still, forced his eyes to hers. "Do you think that still bothers me?" he asked carefully.

"I think that even after twelve years you feel guilty as hell over that. You blame yourself, and you avoid your family. You hate yourself for letting those bad things happen."

"This is none of your business." His voice was harsh, his eyes turning to ice.

Krista nodded, gracefully accepting his rebuke and hiding her hurt with a smile.

"I'm not 'avoiding' my family."

"All right."

"It all happened a long time ago."

She nodded again. "A very long time."

"Halderman was a bastard."

Rafael couldn't stop the words. Honesty compelled him to admit that she was right, and each short, defensive sentence was born of the guilt he was denying. "It's better for them—not seeing me. I can only remind them of the sadness and pain."

"Rafael, you're their *son,* their *brother.* They love you, and seeing you would only remind them of how much they love you. They don't blame you for what happened. How could they?"

"I was responsible!" He rose to his feet and walked to the edge of the slope to stare out over the valley. He wanted to change the subject, to force the unpleasant memories back into a dark corner of his mind, and he wanted to regain the closeness he and Krista had shared only minutes ago. When he turned he gave a hesitant smile. "I'm sorry, Krista. You're right. I've avoided my family for seven years, and I rarely saw them for the five years before that, because I *do* feel guilty for the things that happened. I appreciate your concern, but I'm not ready to deal with that. I don't know if I ever will be. But I don't want to argue with you. The time we have together is too important to waste arguing. Please forgive me."

She welcomed him into her embrace, pressing her face against his chest. "I'm sorry, too, Rafael. I won't bring it up again." Her mood changed rapidly from regret to playful teasing. "You promised me something back there in town. Are you going to renege?"

"What?" he asked, pretending ignorance, though his eyes showed that he knew very well what she meant.

"You said you would undress me and kiss me and make love to me."

"*With* you. I always make love *with* you." He eased her onto her back and removed her shirt, then the rest of her clothes. While she lay there naked, trembling with anticipation, Rafael meticulously folded her clothes, straightened her socks, making a neat stack on the corner of the blanket. When he turned back to her, he merely looked at her, aware of her growing frustration but in no hurry to ease it.

"You are beautiful."

She reached out to him, but he shook his head and waved her hands away. "Be patient."

His hands moved over her, a mere fraction of an inch above her skin, and, without even touching, left a widening trail of goose bumps in its wake. The first place he made contact was with one coral nipple, and Krista whimpered. He drew his hand away and bent over her, and without touching any other part of his body to hers, he sucked the eager bud into his mouth for a gentle kiss.

As he had promised he covered her body with kisses until she pleaded mindlessly for him; then he shed his clothes and answered her pleas with his body, giving her all she could take. When she arched beneath him and gave a shattered cry, he joined her in sweet agony, emptying himself into the warmth of her.

"You are beautiful." Krista repeated his words to him as she drew her fingers across the stubble on Rafael's jaw and the softness of his lips to the silkiness of his mustache. "I love you, Rafael."

He lay on his back, his eyes closed, feeling warm and satisfied and lazy. "Why?" he asked softly. "Am I so different from the other men you know?"

She chose not to answer his second question. "I don't suppose any of us has a choice as to who we fall in love with. I think it just happens."

No, he certainly hadn't been given a choice. He hadn't even wanted to *like* Krista, but no matter how hard he'd fought, it had happened anyway; he'd fallen in love with her.

She would like to hear the words, he knew, but he wouldn't say them. When his part in her father's arrest came out she would be hurt and angry, and she would probably question everything he'd ever told her. When it was all over, when she could see that he had no reason for lying, then he would say it. Then he would tell her how much he loved her. But for now he could only show her and hope she understood.

"I want you again, *pequeña*. Making love with you is the nicest feeling...better than anything I've ever known. When I'm with you, I feel like that's where I belong. I've waited all my life to meet you." He pulled her gently to him and kissed her. His lips were soft, his teeth gentle, his tongue boldly stabbing into her mouth. His hands left off their caresses and tangled themselves in her hair, holding her head as his mouth became demanding, forcing a response from her.

Krista tried to move onto her back, impatient for him, but Rafael resisted. "I want to look at you," he muttered thickly, easily lifting her body onto his. "I want to watch you move. I want to see you take me inside you, and I want to see that it feels good for you. I want to see your face at that moment when everything explodes, *pequeña*, my little one, my love...."

Gentle fingers guided him inside her; then Krista sat still, her eyes moist with tears. He was a very special man, and she felt as if she might burst with love and happiness. She had never felt so rich, so blessed, as she did with Rafael. "My love," he'd said. Yes, he was definitely her love.

She moved slowly, rocking her hips, her small breasts swaying slightly. Rafael was content to lie still and give her total control, to let her do what she wanted with his body while he simply watched. His mouth formed a straight line, not smiling but not as harsh and stern as usual, because his eyes were soft and gentle. They were filled with the love that

he refused to put into words, though Krista saw and recognized it.

She felt that her release was near when Rafael reached his
own, and she forced herself to hold back, because his eyes
were closed. When he had relaxed and was looking at her
again she began moving against him. While somber, intense black eyes looked on, Krista, silhouetted against a
slowly setting sun, reached the moment "when everything
explodes" and sank slowly, tearfully, into Rafael's arms.

Chapter 10

"Nick and Carla Morris are having a party tonight. Everyone at work is invited."

Krista looked at Rafael, but he kept his eyes on the road. "Would you like to go?" she asked.

"Yes." He admitted it simply. Rafael, who chose to have little contact with anyone, wanted to go to a party. He wasn't sure why. Maybe he felt more sociable these days. Maybe twelve years of loneliness was catching up with him. And maybe he wanted to show Krista off, to let his coworkers who called him cold and unfeeling see the way she looked at him.

"All right."

"Krista..." He slowed to a stop at the junction of the dirt road and the highway. "Constancia Aranas will be there. She's dating Darren Carter."

A flare of jealousy coursed through her. A party sounded like fun; meeting Rafael's former lover didn't. When he saw them together—lovely, beautiful Constancia, and Krista—would he realize how wrong he'd been to choose her over the Mexican woman? Be gracious, she cautioned herself.

"That's okay," she said, feigning indifference. I have no intention of letting you get within ten feet of her anyway.

Sometimes, Rafael thought, it was as if he could see into her mind, see her thoughts and fears. He leaned toward her, and with one hand he traced the line of her jaw. "You're a very special lady, Krista."

She caught his hand and pressed a kiss to the palm. "No, Rafael," she disagreed. "You're the special one."

Almost everyone else had arrived at the Morris house by the time Rafael and Krista got there. She hesitantly got out of the Bronco, suffering yet another attack of nerves at meeting the beautiful Constancia. Maybe she should have worn a dress instead of jeans. Maybe, she worried, she should have taken the time to do something with her hair, instead of wearing it in her usual braid.

Rafael stopped her at the bottom of the porch steps. Gently his fingers moved across her cheek, down her throat, over her collarbone. "You are the loveliest woman I've ever seen."

"Thank you." She was grateful, not so much for the compliment but because he was sensitive enough to realize she needed to hear it.

He lifted her hand to his mouth for a kiss, then led her up the steps to the door. Nick Morris answered their knock, taking them through the house to the den.

"Drinks and food are in the kitchen," Carla Morris called. "Glad you finally made it, Rafe."

"Finally?" Krista asked him.

"They do this the first Saturday of every month. This is the first time I've come."

They were greeted by everyone in the room, and Krista was introduced to the few people she didn't know. There was no sign of Constancia, but Royce Ann wasted no time before explaining that she was in the kitchen.

When conversation among the men turned immediately to work, Krista withdrew. "Want a beer, Rafael?"

His eyes moved caressingly over her. "Please."

She was hesitant to enter the kitchen—down the hall and to the right, Nick had said. She could hear two women's voices, one of them Carla's, the other soft and melodic and accented. Taking a deep breath, she entered the room. Carla said something and left. Krista faced the slender, black-haired woman nervously and for a moment they simply stared at each other.

It was Constancia who spoke first. "I wonder if they'll be disappointed that they missed our first meeting," she said, a tentative smile on her lips.

"Probably. You're even prettier than the picture in the paper."

"Thank you."

From first grade Krista had been taught all the proper social graces, but she couldn't think of a thing to say to this woman who had been Rafael's lover.

Constancia understood her discomfort. "Rafael and I had a good relationship," she said softly. "It served its purpose, and when it was time, it ended. He wasn't hurt, and neither was I. It's time for better things for both of us. I've found mine, and I think Rafael has found his in you." After a brief silence she continued, "Shall we join the party before they come to see what we've done to each other?"

Krista agreed, first getting a bottle of beer and a can of Coke from the refrigerator. They walked down the hall together in silence. When they entered the den every eye was on them. They separated, Constancia going to Darren at one end of the room, Krista to Rafael at the other. He accepted the beer with murmured thanks. Black eyes searched her face; then he asked, *"¿Está bien?"*

She popped the top of her Coke. *"Está bien."* It was all right.

Richard Houseman joined them. He was tall, blond and handsome, but Krista's attention belonged to Rafael. "Rafe. Krista."

"Hello, Richard." She was surprised that she'd been able to remember his name. He was the man from New York who didn't like to be called Rick, Rich or, worse, Dick. "How do you like the desert after New York?"

"I don't care for it at all. I don't know how you people stand it. Of course, Contreras here is the only person I know who actually likes the desert. He must have ice water in his veins."

She lifted the can to her lips, slowly swallowing the cool liquid. When she lowered it again, she fixed a cool gaze on Houseman. "Not at all. Personally, I love the desert. I find it...sensuous. Strong." The look she gave Rafael left no doubt that her description extended to the man as well as the land.

Houseman seemed to have difficulty clearing his throat; he coughed several times, then muttered an excuse and left.

As soon as the man was gone Krista said flatly, "I don't think I like him."

"I got that impression."

"Hey, Rafe," Nick called. "How about a little poker?"

The term "poker face" could have been invented to describe Rafael. Not one flicker of emotion crossed his features while he played, whether he held nothing or a full house, whether he lost or won. The only time the blank mask ever shifted was when he looked at or spoke to Krista; there was always a tenderness there for her. It didn't go unnoticed by Houseman or by the others at the table.

Exactly two hours after they'd arrived Rafael pocketed his winnings, collected Krista from the sofa, where she was sitting with the other women, and said good-night. He wanted to go home, to get her away from all those people and alone at his house, where he could have her undivided attention. He had shared her long enough; selfishly, he wanted her to himself.

"Did I embarrass you, leaving so quickly?" he asked in the truck.

"Not at all. In fact, I was about to suggest it myself. Parties are all right, but I'd rather be alone with you."

Despite her answer, he still wondered. His behavior had bordered on rudeness. He hadn't even asked her if she wanted to go; he'd just ordered her to come along. Would her rich, sophisticated boyfriends ever have treated her that way? "I'm sorry," he said uncomfortably. "I don't go to parties often—but you could probably tell that by my behavior."

"There was nothing wrong with your behavior, Rafael."

It was another moonlight-and-shadows night. Occasionally she could see his face well; other times he was just a dark shadow in the darker night. When she could see his face, though, she saw that he was troubled. "If it would help to talk, I can listen," she offered.

How could he tell her that he was comparing himself to her other boyfriends, to the rich Europeans and famous Americans, and finding himself lacking? He wasn't even supposed to know about them.

When she saw that he wasn't going to accept her invitation to confide in her, she said, "Tell me about Constancia. About you and her."

They were in shadow again when Rafael began the story. When he'd been stationed in San Diego, he'd often patrolled the canyons adjacent to the border and east of San Ysidro. They were sometimes called *no man's-land* because of the bandits who hid there and attacked both illegals and border-patrol agents. Ramón Aranas was such a bandit. He was also *un pollero.*

Pollo, he exclaimed, was slang for the illegals; it meant "chicken." Their smugglers, or guides, were called *polleros,* "chicken handlers." Aranas was *un pollero* who often robbed and beat the people he was guiding across the border. One night he made the mistake of attacking Rafael and his partner, an officer with the Border Crimes Task Force, a unit of the San Diego Police Department that worked along the border. With one shot from the cop's gun Ramón Aranas was dead.

Later Rafael learned that Aranas had a wife, a pregnant twenty-two-year-old who was now a widow. He went to see her, to offer his apologies. A week later she lost the baby.

Over a month passed before he made the trip to Tijuana again to see Constancia. The visits continued, and when he transferred to Nueva Vida, Constancia, with no family of her own, followed, settling in San Ignacio.

By the time he finished the story they had reached the house, and Krista was curled up in his arms, wedged between his chest and the hard steering wheel. They sat silently for a long time, the sounds of their breathing mingling with the night noises.

"I always hated sharing a bed with someone," Rafael remarked while his hand found its way inside her shirt. "I felt trapped and crowded. The first night you stayed here, I was going to lie with you until you went to sleep, then go into the other bedroom."

He sighed softly, his warm breath stirring the hair at Krista's temple. "You fell asleep, and I thought I'd lie there just a minute longer, and the next thing I knew it was morning and you were in my arms, all soft and warm and golden. I never thought such a small bed could feel as empty as it does when you're not in it."

After another silence, during which he played lazily, almost absentmindedly, with her breast, Krista asked, "Would your parents like me?"

"They would adore you."

"And your brothers and sisters?"

"Them, too. Maybe someday . . ." That magical, mythical someday, when she was able to forgive him for his actions against her father, when he was able to forgive himself for Rebecca Halderman, when he could return to his family. Someday, when he could convince Krista to marry him, to be his wife, to have his children.

Krista fell asleep easily that night, secure in Rafael's embrace. She slept so soundly that he was able to leave the bed without disturbing her. He pulled on the jeans he'd discarded only an hour earlier and went into the living room, to his desk.

From the locked drawer he drew out the folder marked McLaren. He had consolidated the material on Art and

Krista into one neat, thick file. He spent the next hour and a half reading the pages that he knew by heart, studying the photographs that were etched in his memory.

It wasn't fair. This was an important case—busting Art McLaren was going to look damned impressive on Rafael's record. It wasn't fair that Krista had to be involved, that he had to fall in love with the suspect's daughter, that he had to investigate her along with her dirty father.

And it wasn't fair that he was at his desk, his mind on work, while the sweetest, loveliest woman in the world slept in his bed. Rafael returned the file to the drawer, locked it, turned out the light and returned to his bed. To Krista.

The next ten days were the best Krista had ever lived. She spent her days at Art's house, working in her second-floor room, and her nights with Rafael. Art knew she was seeing Rafael, but after his initial anger he said little about it. He was too preoccupied with his business to worry about his daughter. As for Krista, she was ridiculously happy.

Wednesday afternoon found her at work making a dress for Juana. The housekeeper's anniversary was coming up in a few weeks, and a McLaren original would be Krista's gift to her. It was a beautiful day, the dress was coming along well, and Krista didn't have a care in the world.

Then the air conditioner went on the blink shortly after lunch, and the heat began seeping through the thick walls and the doors and the windows.

Then came Royce Ann's phone call. "I have a message for you from Rafael."

Krista brushed her hair from her sticky forehead. "Okay, what is it? Is he working late?"

"No. He said for you to stay there. Don't go to his house until he calls you. Krista—" Royce Ann's voice was quavering, and she stopped until it was under control.

"Royce Ann, what is it? What's wrong?"

"He and Jim went out today, and Jim was attacked by this illegal, and Rafael saved his life, but…he killed the boy. Oh, Krista, he killed a sixteen-year-old boy!"

* * *

Krista turned out the lights, lit three small candles and opened the balcony doors. The air conditioner was still off, and the house was filled with stifling heat. Her light cotton skirt and tank top were damp, and her skin was slick with sweat.

She went out onto the balcony, but it wasn't much cooler there, and the night seemed so still and empty. She returned to her room, switching on the radio as she passed it. Music filled the air, moody, mysterious, and Krista threw herself across the bed to listen, willing her mind to stop working, to shut down completely.

Rafael stopped his truck about fifty yards from the big house. He cut the engine, switched off the lights and sat there. He knew which room was hers; he picked it out, dimly lit and still. He stared at the open French doors, wishing she would come out, needing to see her, but unable to go to her, to ask for company, for comfort, for her self.

Krista rose from the bed as the song ended and turned the knob to a country station. Rafael liked country music, so she was going to learn to like it. Tonight was a good time to start. It made her feel closer to him.

So many country songs were sad, and the mournful tunes deepened her own sorrow. Rafael was out there somewhere, hurting, and he hadn't turned to her, hadn't called to tell her what happened, or where he was, or if he was all right. At a time when he needed someone, he hadn't come to her.

She was amazed by her capacity for pain. Just when she thought she couldn't hurt anymore, the ache found deeper roots inside her and filled her again. Surely there was a limit to how much of this she could bear!

One sad love song followed another, and Krista knew she was going to burst into tears. She wandered out onto the balcony again, leaning against the wrought-iron railing that still held the heat of the sun.

Where was Rafael?

Slowly the dark outline of the Bronco took shape. Krista's fingers wrapped tightly around the railing as she leaned forward to look more closely. Her eyes squinted, then, becoming accustomed to the dark, relaxed again, and she saw the truck clearly—even the man inside.

Rafael had come.

She released her grip on the railing and went inside. Through her room, down the hall, down the stairs. She burst out onto the porch and hesitated there.

He was out of the truck now, standing in front of it. Slowly he started toward her, and she raced down the steps, heedless of her bare feet. She fairly flew out to meet him, throwing herself into his ready embrace near the fountain.

She was crying and trying to talk at the same time. She cupped Rafael's face in her hands and placed a half dozen kisses on his cheeks, his eyes, his mouth. "Are you all right?" she whispered.

"*Sí.*" He gathered her against his chest, hiding his face in the fragrant cover of her hair. He held her tightly, unaware that he was crushing her, but she didn't mind. She stroked his thick, springy hair with one hand, his back with the other, murmuring soft, meaningless words, sometimes only sounds.

"I was so worried," she said when he at last raised his head.

"I—I needed to be alone." He leaned his forehead against hers. "I'm sorry."

"No. Don't be." She rubbed her fingers along his unshaven jaw to his mouth, and he twisted his head slightly to bathe her thumb with a moist kiss.

"I tried to stay away," he admitted hoarsely, "I went out into the desert so I could stay away from you, but . . . I had to come."

She was hurt. "Why, Rafael? Why didn't you want to see me?"

"All I can do tonight is take. I can't give anything. There's nothing *to* give. I can only use you."

"That's all right. I can give tonight, Rafael. I have plenty to give."

He laid his hand against her cheek, his rough thumb wiping a tear from the corner of her eye. "You are so good, Krista, and I...I killed someone today. He was sixteen years old, and he'll never get any older, because I killed him."

"You didn't mean to."

"But the boy is *dead*."

"Rafael, listen to me. I know how much it hurt you to do that—I know how much you care—but it *wasn't* your fault. He was sixteen—that's not a child, not these days. If you hadn't stopped him, he would have killed Jim, and he would have attacked you. He *knew* what he was doing, Rafael. He *knew*."

Rafael tightened his embrace again. "Stay with me, Krista. Don't ever leave me."

"I'll always be here, darling, always." She cupped his face in her hands and kissed him hard. "My father's gone. Do you want to come in?"

He shook his head. "I want to go home, but I can't face the house without you. Come with me, Krista. Let's go home."

Rafael took her to bed as soon as they got to the house. He hadn't exaggerated earlier. He took her warmth and her love and her body and gave very little in return, but Krista didn't mind. She knew he needed her. She didn't mind giving, because when she needed him someday, he would give it all back.

She awoke alone Thursday morning, but she could smell Rafael's scent and feel the lingering warmth of his body on the sheets, so she knew he hadn't been gone long. She pulled on a robe from the closet and went in search of him.

He was at the corral with the horses, talking softly. He quieted when he became aware of Krista's approach, and the horses protested his sudden silence.

"Go ahead and talk to them," she invited. "They like the sound of your voice."

Rafael's eyes shifted first; then he turned his head so he could look at her. His face was expressionless, his eyes blank, giving no hint of his mood. She studied him, her own eyes clear and unwavering. He looked all right, she thought, though tired. She suspected that he hadn't gotten much sleep the night before. She had tried to stay awake with him, but the warmth of their bodies and her own weariness had drawn her into an easy sleep.

Rafael *hadn't* slept well. Long after Krista had drifted off he'd lain awake, remembering. When he did finally sleep he was tormented by dreams of a lifeless José Ruiz. He had awakened with a start, the softly glowing lights of the clock on the nightstand reading four-thirteen, and had decided that further sleep wasn't worth further dreams.

"How do you feel?" she asked softly.

He didn't know how he felt this morning. There was a sense of disbelief that he had actually killed someone, along with the sickening knowledge that it was true. He had been grateful to wake up next to Krista, but now he felt ashamed that she had seen him at his weakest, his most vulnerable. Once before he had claimed to be weak in his desire for her, but they had both known it wasn't true. He couldn't deny that last night he had needed her, needed her desperately, and he felt ashamed and bitter and defensive.

"I'm all right."

The three words weren't reassuring. Krista bit her lower lip, unsure what to say. She sensed his withdrawal, and she couldn't understand it. Last night he had wanted her, had needed her, but this morning he seemed to be erecting some kind of barrier between them, something she could feel as surely as if it were real.

"Would you like some breakfast?" she offered.

He would like her to go away and leave him alone, he decided, then immediately changed his mind. He didn't want to be alone this morning, not yet. It was too soon.

"Rafael?" She reached out her hand, but the instant it made contact with his arm he stepped back quickly, clumsily, as if burned by her touch. A dull flush appeared beneath his high cheekbones, but he offered no apology or explanation, and Krista knew better than to ask for one. "I'll start breakfast," she said. "Come in when you're ready."

She returned to the house, but he remained with the horses. From the window Krista watched him reach out to stroke each animal, his hands moving soothingly over their necks, and she wished he would touch her that way. Remembering how he had repulsed her own touch just minutes earlier, she shivered.

Obviously he was still troubled about the shooting. Well, that was normal, wasn't it? she asked herself. But she didn't know the answer; she didn't know anyone besides Rafael who had ever killed someone, so she didn't know what was normal and what wasn't. She didn't know how it was going to affect her, if Rafael was going to draw away from her and shut her out. She was very much afraid that he might.

The coffee was ready, the bacon was fried, and the eggs were almost done, but still he remained at the corral. Krista went to the front door, pushed it open and called his name. He gave no sign of hearing her, but after a moment he turned away from the corral and came into the house.

They sat at the table in silence. Krista managed to eat a slice of bacon, but Rafael didn't touch any food; he simply drank the coffee and stared out the window.

"Talk to me."

Rafael looked sharply at her. What did she want? Was she expecting him to behave as he had last night? Did she want him to show her again how weak he could be? There were no answers in her face; she was looking at the ivy she'd given him long ago, her index finger lifting a limp leaf.

"It needs water," she remarked, then turned her gaze to him.

Unaccountably angered, he reached across the table to the pot and jerked the plant from it, scattering clods of dry dirt over the table and their food. "I told you I didn't have time to take care of any damned plants," he almost snarled.

His uncharacteristic outburst both surprised and stung Krista, but she gave no sign of her feelings. She calmly rose from her chair and carried their dishes into the kitchen, returned for the plant and placed it in a glass of water, then returned again with a damp cloth to clean the dirt from the table. Rafael grabbed her wrist, determined to draw some sort of response from her.

"I can clean up my own messes."

"I don't mind." She transferred the cloth to her other hand and began wiping the tabletop.

He shoved his chair back, knocking it over when he stood up. "I don't need you cleaning up after me, or cooking for me, or feeling sorry for me. I don't need a damned thing from you, do you understand?"

He gave her a shake that finally made her look at him. "I understand perfectly," she said, her voice guarded. "But *I* need something from *you*. I know that you're upset, Rafael. I understand that. I know you need—"

"You don't know anything! You think you have the answers to all life's problems, but you don't! Tell me, Krista, how many people have you killed? How many times have you shot someone and seen them die right in front of you? You want to play the expert on what I need and how I feel, and you don't know what in hell you're talking about!"

Don't lose your temper, she counseled herself behind closed eyes. He's hurt, and he needs to be angry. Let him say what he wants.

"Since the day I met you, you've been pushing in where you don't belong, trying to run my life. Don't try to solve my problems, Krista. You can't even handle your own. You've got a mother who ran out on you, a father who can't stand you. Now you've pushed yourself on me. Don't interfere. Don't tell me how I feel or what I need."

He finally succeeded in getting the response he'd wanted. Blinded by tears, Krista freed herself from his grip without difficulty—he willingly let her go—and stumbled across the room and down the hall to the bedroom.

Rafael felt angry and frustrated and guilty. He hurt so badly inside, and now he'd passed on some of that pain to Krista, the one person in the world who didn't deserve his cruelty. He had selfishly used her last night, had taken everything she offered, and then had been unforgivably cruel this morning. He had no right to treat her that way, no matter how much he was suffering.

He went down the hall to the bedroom and slowly pushed the door open. Krista had gotten dressed and was sitting on the edge of the mattress, her hands folded in her lap. A small overnight bag sat on the floor next to the bed. She refused to look at him or give in to the tears that burned her eyes.

"Go home," Rafael said in his raspy, tired voice. If she went home he couldn't hurt her anymore, couldn't say anymore horrible things, and he wouldn't have to see that wounded look in her eyes. "Take my truck and go back to *lu casa grande*."

Krista had already made her decision. She couldn't bear the idea of going back to her father's house; she was sure Art would have quite a bit to say about the shooting, all of it vicious. So she had called Royce Ann and asked if she could stay at her house for a few days. "Royce Ann's coming over to get me," she said, her voice shaking slightly.

He squeezed his eyes shut, rubbing at them with the heels of his hands. He had put that quiver of hurt in her voice, and he despised himself for it. Now that he was calmer he couldn't believe that he had taunted her about her parents, that he had used things she'd told him in confidence to hurt her. If she asked him again how he felt, he would tell her. Miserable. Tortured. As if he'd been damned to hell.

"How is Jim?" he forced himself to ask.

"All right. You can go see him."

"I don't go to hospitals."

Krista rose from the bed and smoothed down her skirt. "I'll remember that if I ever come close to dying," she coolly responded. She walked past him and into the living room to watch for her friend from the window. Rafael entered the room a short time later, but she didn't acknowledge his presence until she saw the dust signaling an approaching car. She walked to the open door, then paused with her hand on the knob.

"Krista?"

She turned toward Rafael. He looked miserable, and she knew his behavior had hurt him as much as it had hurt her. She wanted to put the suitcase down and run back to him, but she wouldn't do it, not unless he asked her to stay.

He couldn't ask her. He couldn't. Until he'd worked through this anger and anguish that were eating at him, he couldn't be with her. "I'm sorry."

The words sounded inadequate to his own ears, but Krista appreciated them. She crossed the room to him, stopping only inches in front of him. "I'll be at Royce Ann's," she said softly.

He simply nodded.

"I love you, Rafael."

He pulled her into his arms for a fierce kiss that ended as quickly as it began. "Thank you," he whispered.

Royce Ann was waiting for her at the car. "Is Rafael awake? I wanted to thank him...." Her blue eyes had dark smudges underneath from a restless night.

"This isn't a good time, Royce Ann. Maybe in a couple of days."

"You want to talk about it?" Royce Ann cast a sideways glance at her friend, trying to read something, anything, in her face.

"No, not right now."

After the car drove away Rafael went out on the porch. The screen door banged a few times behind him before becoming still. For a minute he stood motionless, forcing taut muscles and nerves to relax. He closed his eyes and listened to the silence of the house, to the beat of his heart and the slow steadiness of his breath.

He was alone. He'd pushed Krista away at a time when she'd wanted only to be with him, to help him. He had hurt her, and she'd left him, but it was better this way. As long as she was gone he couldn't hurt her anymore. But he knew she would be back.

He was glad she had gone to Royce Ann's house instead of back to her father's. He wanted Krista away from her father, completely uninvolved. That way Houseman and Thompson couldn't order him to pump her for information on Art, and maybe the distance between her and her father would ease her pain when he was arrested. And when it was all over, when she found out about her father and Rafael, about the investigation and the drugs and the lies and the deceit, she would need a good friend like Royce Ann.

She'd been gone only minutes, and already Rafael missed her. When he'd dealt with his problems and she came back to him, he would do everything in his power to make sure she never left again. He would give her everything she needed to be happy.

Most of all, he would love her.

Chapter 11

Rafael looked at the face in the mirror before him and grimaced. He had slept poorly last night—and for five nights before that—and it showed in his face. His eyes looked sunken, with dark smudges beneath them, and his cheeks were hollow. The lower part of his face was prickly with a growth of beard, which he prepared to shave by lathering thick white shaving cream over his jaw.

As he shaved his thoughts wandered to Krista. With the passing of each day he thought less about Ruiz and more about her. It had been five days since he'd seen or talked to her, and he missed her more than he would have believed possible. He'd wanted to call her Thursday night, only hours after she'd left, but he had still been so angry that he'd decided to wait. As each day dragged out, his anger had faded and his pain had eased, and now he knew he could see her without lashing out at her. Today he would call her.

He rinsed off the shaving cream and dried his face on a fluffy red towel, then reached for his uniform shirt hanging on the doorknob. He was already wearing the dark green trousers. As soon as he put on the shirt he could leave for work, and the sooner he got through the day at work, the sooner he could see Krista.

A flash of memory stayed his hand as it touched the soft green fabric—that of Jim Stone being knocked to the ground, blood seeping from the bullet wound to soak the shoulder of his shirt. Though the wound hadn't been serious there had been so much blood…and it could have been prevented. Not the shooting, of course, but Jim could have come out of it with nothing more serious than a bruise.

Rafael went to his bedroom, where he found what he was looking for at the back of the closet. He hadn't worn it in a long time. Though it didn't weigh much, it could be almost unbearable on a hot day—and the desert was always hot. Still, the multiple layers of Kevlar fibers could stop just about any caliber bullet and some knives. It was a precaution that he would take from now on, for his own sake and for Krista's. He could stand the heat.

He put the vest on, adjusting it for maximum protection and comfort, then put on his uniform shirt. A glance in the mirror assured him that only someone very familiar with bullet-proof vests could tell he was wearing it. He turned away, gathered his revolver, keys and wallet and left the house.

Krista and Royce Ann finished a lunch of salad and fruit and carried their iced tea into the living room. Krista sat down in a white wicker chair that faced the picture window and looked out at the empty road. "It looks hot," she said.

"Haven't you noticed that the air-conditioning has hardly stopped running today?" Royce Ann asked, fanning herself languidly in spite of the coolness of the house. She pushed her black hair off her forehead with the back of her hand, then touched the cold glass to her skin. "That feels good."

Krista laughed, something she hadn't been able to do much of during the past few days. "You should be ashamed of yourself, Royce Ann, a Southern girl who can't stand the heat. What if you'd been born back in the days of the plantations, before air-conditioning?''

"I'd have moved up north," Royce Ann replied in her best drawl. "I also would have absolutely refused to wear all the clothes women had to wear back then. I would have shown them what a woman looked like without two dozen petticoats or crinolines or whatever they call them . . . What are you going to do?''

Krista's surprise showed in her eyes. "Do? About what?''

"Look, I love having you here, Krista, and you're welcome to stay as long as you want, but sooner or later you're going to have to *do* something. If Rafael doesn't come around, you're going to have to go to his house and make him see that he needs you. Especially since you can't go to your house anymore.''

Within an hour of her arrival at the Stone house Thursday, Art had shown up, demanding that she go home with him immediately. Her refusal had led to a shouting match, ended by Art's threat that if she didn't obey, she was never welcome there again. She had coolly replied that she would be by to pick up her clothes sometime in the next week.

"He wants to be alone, Royce Ann. He made that abundantly clear. When he wants to see me, he'll let me know.'' Though her voice sounded light, she was troubled by his failure to contact her. She had spent the last five and a half days at Royce Ann's house, afraid to leave for even short periods of time, afraid that he would call and she'd miss him. Now she knew she would, as her friend put it, have to *do* something. Jim was home from the hospital and back at work, so she was going to have to patch things up with Rafael or find a new place to live. She had imposed on her friends long enough.

She had refused to tell Royce Ann what Rafael had said to her to make her leave. Not even her best friend knew the things about her parents that she'd told her lover. Repeating his insults to her would require confessions about herself and her relationship with her parents that she didn't want to make to anyone else. Royce Ann had tried to reassure her, telling her that whatever he'd said meant nothing, because he'd been angry, he'd been through a traumatic experience. When Jim came home from the hospital and found Krista in temporary residence, he had shared Royce Ann's certainty. Rafael had to deal with his problem in his own way, he'd told her, but it certainly didn't mean that he didn't want Krista anymore. Give him time.

Time. The small, four-letter word brought a sigh from Krista. She had all the time in the world, but it didn't make waiting any easier.

The sound of a truck's engine caught her attention, and she looked out the large window in time to see a border-patrol truck turn into the drive. "Is Jim supposed to come home for lunch?" she asked, slowly straightening in her chair.

Royce Ann leaped to her feet and whirled around. "No, he isn't. What if something's happened? Oh, Krista, what if they had to take him back to the hospital for something?" Then her fear dissolved into a smile of triumph when the driver got out of the truck. It was Rafael. "I believe you have a guest, Miss McLaren," she teased. "I'll be in the kitchen."

Krista crossed to the door and stepped out onto the porch just as Rafael reached the top of the steps. They simply looked at each other for a long, long time; then she smiled coolly and said, "Hello, Rafael."

Behind the mirrored sunglasses his eyes narrowed. For a woman who claimed to love him, she certainly didn't look too happy to see him. Was she still angry about the things he'd said to her last week? Did she want to make him suffer a little now in return?

Krista was quaking inside. It seemed like forever since she had seen him, and he looked so good, so strong and handsome. She longed to feel his arms around her, to hear him call her *"cariña"* or *"querida."* "You look good."

"Do I? I feel rotten." He took a step closer to her. "I owe you an apology."

Her heart sank all the way to her toes. An apology? Was that why he'd come? Not to see her but to apologize? "No, you don't, Rafael," she said a little sharply. "I understand."

Her disappointment was so obvious that his fears eased a little. "I'm sure you do. You're a very understanding woman. But I want to give you the apology anyway." He went to her, pulling her against him so quickly and so unexpectedly that it took her breath away, leaving her so weak she couldn't have struggled if she'd wanted to. He lowered his head to hers, brushing his mustache across her ear, whispering, "I'm sorry, *cariña,* so sorry I hurt you. When you left I wanted to die, but I had to let you go."

"I wanted to stay," she breathed.

"I would have hurt you more. I'm sorry *cariña,* but the way I felt last week, I was no good for you." His mouth moved to hers, tenderly taking possession of it. His tongue moved to part her teeth, but she was ready for him, leading him hungrily into the warm, moist darkness of her mouth. He took only a taste of her, then put her away from him. She made a sound of protest, but he refused to budge. "If I keep kissing you I'll never be able to leave you, and I'm supposed to be working now," he explained with a rueful smile.

He reached down to smooth his hand over her hair, while his eyes drank her in. She was so damnably, achingly beautiful, and she was his. She loved him. He wanted to kiss her and never let her go, but instead he took a step back and looked at her again. This time his gaze took note of the faint circles under her eyes and the weariness in her face, and he knew that the last week had been difficult for her, too. His heart ached because she'd suffered such distress, yet he rejoiced that she cared so much about him.

"You look lovely," he murmured.

"You look tired. Have you been sleeping all right?"

"Without you? I told you, my bed is empty without you."

"I'll be there whenever you want me."

"I want you tonight." Then he almost grinned, following as her eyes dropped lower and lower, finding the proof that his words were lies. "I want you now, too, but I don't have the time, and you're worth far more than the few minutes I could offer."

Krista smiled then, that dazzling smile that affected his body, his entire sense of being, and for a moment he considered forgetting his job for the afternoon. But his sense of responsibility was too great, and there was always tonight.

She laid her hands on his shoulders and stood on her toes to press a kiss to his lips. "I love—" The words forgotten, her hands moved quickly over his back, then his chest, and her eyes were questioning. She pulled away and walked to the end of the porch. When she turned Rafael was watching her somberly. "You're wearing a bullet-proof vest."

He nodded.

"I'd forgotten about the danger...."

"The danger is always there, Krista. This just evens the odds a bit."

This time she nodded. "Be careful, Rafael." She returned, throwing herself into his arms and hugging him tight, vest and all. "Please be very careful. I love you."

"The only happiness in my life is with you, Krista. With you I have hope. No matter what I do—" he had a brief mental image of José Ruiz, lying dead on the ground "—I know I'll find peace with you." He kissed her quickly, then walked to the steps. "I'll be home between four and four-thirty. Do you still have the key?"

She nodded. He'd given her a house key the day he'd let her use his truck; it was still on her key ring.

"Be there for me," he said hoarsely.

"I will. I love you, Rafael."

They were the last words he heard from her as he walked away.

"Well?" Royce Ann asked excitedly when Krista reentered the house. "I didn't hear much talking, so I assume you were making up instead."

"I thought you were going to be in the kitchen," Krista scolded with a mock frown.

"I was, but since you didn't bring him in, I figured it was safe to come out. Besides, it's hard to eavesdrop from the kitchen." Royce Ann dropped her playful teasing. "Did you get things settled?"

Krista nodded. "I'm going home this afternoon."

"Home meaning with him?"

She nodded again.

Royce Ann gave a whoop of excitement. "That's great! Now I won't have to watch you mope sixteen hours a day and listen to you pace the other eight. I'm happy for you, Krista!"

They spent the next hour talking; Krista was finally able to really enjoy Royce Ann's company. The afternoon quiet was frequently broken by their laughter, until Krista was forced to say goodbye. "I'm going to go to Dad's house and get some of my clothes," she said as they walked out to the Mustang.

"It's been nice having you," the black-haired woman said, giving her a hug. "I hope nothing like this happens again, but if it does, remember you're always welcome here."

Krista's response was halted by the passing of a border-patrol truck. Inside were Darren Carter and Martin Thompson. She and Royce Ann watched them until they were out of sight. "They must be so shorthanded while Jim's at a desk that Martin has to go out. He really hates that," Royce Ann said. "Let me know how it goes."

"I will." Krista turned to get into her car but was distracted again, this time by a helicopter flying overhead. When the noise was gone she said goodbye and drove away.

At the McLaren house Juana went upstairs with Krista to help her pack. Krista had decided to take just enough clothes for a week or two, and Juana would pack the rest and store them for her until she knew where she would be living. She and Rafael hadn't made plans; she didn't know if he wanted her to live with him or if he would prefer that she find a place of her own. Though he didn't seem to mind sharing his home with her, he was still a very private man. Oh, well, apartments were plentiful in Nueva Vida. If Rafael didn't want them to live together, she could easily find a place in town.

"You're happy, aren't you?" Juana asked, carefully folding clothes into the suitcases on the bed.

"Very." Krista's smile said it all. "He's a very special man, Juana."

"What about your father?"

Krista shrugged. "You've been here since I was born, Juana. You know what it's like for Dad and me. He never really cared much what I did. He only dislikes Rafael because he's..."

"Because he's Mexican. I tried to warn you, Krista. Your father has no objections to hiring us. But that's the extent of his involvement with us. He'll never approve of a son-in-law who's Mexican." She closed one suitcase and reached for another. "Are you sure you want to make this choice?"

"Rafael cares about me, Juana. He really does. How could I turn that down in favor of a father who...who can't stand me? Rafael's never said he loves me, but he does care. I know it."

"Love is a word that doesn't come easy to your Rafael. You can see it in his eyes, in the way he treats you, but it may be a long time before he says it." Juana paused in her packing to draw Krista into a motherly embrace. "Señor Contreras is a good man, Krista. Always trust him, and be happy with him."

"Oh, I will, Juana. I promise that.... You've been the closest I ever had to a mother, and though I've never said it, it meant a lot, knowing that you were here. Thank you."

The ringing of the telephone interrupted the emotional exchange, and Juana moved to the nightstand to answer it. She spoke briefly, her eyes remaining on Krista as the younger woman brought an armload of dresses from the closet to sort through. When Juana hung up she uttered a silent prayer and crossed herself.

It had been Royce Ann Stone. She'd said very little; she'd just asked Juana to keep Krista there until she and her husband could arrive. She had sounded so somber that the housekeeper knew something had happened to Rafael, and the news wasn't going to be good.

Krista didn't notice Juana's preoccupation. They finished packing and were carrying her four suitcases downstairs when the doorbell rang. Art came out of the office, Juana hurried to the door, and Krista waited at the stairs.

Like any woman who loves a law-enforcement officer, Krista dreaded seeing a uniform and an official car in the middle of the day when Rafael was working. The fact that Jim had brought his wife, who looked as pale and frightened as the day after he'd been shot, increased Krista's fear. Her throat was too dry to swallow, and her hands were trembling so badly that she had to push them into the pockets of her skirt.

"Is he all right?"

Her voice sounded remarkably calm. She couldn't believe she could sound so normal when she thought she was going to collapse.

"I don't know." It was Jim who answered. "He was shot three times. His vest stopped two, the third one went into his abdomen."

Royce Ann slipped her arm around Krista's shoulders. "They've flown him to a hospital in El Paso. We'll drive you there, okay? Juana, are these her bags?"

"Take these two." The housekeeper indicated a large suitcase and a smaller overnight bag.

"I forbid you to go."

Everyone turned to stare down the hall at Art McLaren, varying degrees of surprise on their faces. Except Krista. She had expected no less from her father. "Let me carry the big one, Jim; your shoulder's not healed yet," she said, still sounding incredibly calm. "What happened?"

"He was ambushed by Gregorio Ruiz."

Ruiz. That name was beginning to arouse a surge of hatred in her when she heard it. "Gregorio?"

"José's brother."

"Damn it, Krista, did you hear me? You will not go to the hospital to be with that bastard!" Art was livid.

Krista ignored him. "Thank you for helping me pack, Juana," she said, and the housekeeper hugged her.

"He'll be all right, Krista. I'll pray for him."

Krista switched her purse to her left shoulder and picked up the bigger suitcase, then left the house, followed by Jim and Royce Ann. Art was left staring in outrage.

It was fifty miles to El Paso, and they traveled the entire way in silence. Krista stared out the window, alternating between silent prayers and attempts to determine if this was real. It was all a terrible mistake, she told herself more than once. She'd seen him no more than two hours ago. How could he be in a hospital now, hurt, or possibly dying?

They were met at the hospital by an El Paso-based border-patrol agent who introduced himself as Dave Brown. He was a tall man who matched his name—brown skin, brown hair, brown eyes. He informed them that Rafael was in surgery, his condition critical. Gregorio Ruiz, shot once by Rafael, was in good condition and in protective custody.

Krista was grateful in some small corner of her mind that the boy hadn't died. He was seventeen, a year older than José, Brown told them. If Rafael had killed him, even in self-defense, his guilt would probably have destroyed him.

She had taken up a position at the window of the waiting room when they arrived and hadn't moved since. After an hour or so Brown brought her a cup of coffee. He was interested in her. He'd heard a few rumors from other agents about Contreras—that he was ruthless and hard, more machine than man, someone to be feared. He must have something going for him, he thought, to have a woman like this. He hoped the news that eventually came for her would be good.

It was five-twenty when the doctor in stained scrub clothes came into the room. He wore a white lab coat with an embroidered patch that identified him as T. R. Sawyer. "Mrs. Contreras?"

He looked expectantly from Royce Ann to Krista, then at the two men. "Is there no Mrs. Contreras?"

Krista had frozen in place for a moment, but now, eager to hear news of Rafael, she moved toward the doctor with an easy grace, despite her fear. "Not yet. How is Rafael?"

Dr. Sawyer wasted no time on platitudes. He could see from her eyes that she was tired and sick with fear. "Mr. Contreras is doing fine, considering what he's been through. He'll be spending some time in ICU, but we don't expect any problems."

Krista's knees turned rubbery as a wave of relief rushed over her. "He's really all right?" she asked, clasping the doctor's hand in hers.

"Really. He's a very lucky man. If he hadn't been wearing the bullet-proof vest he would have died. One of those shots hit right above his heart." He shook his head in wonder, then went on to what he knew would be her next question. "You can see him in about an hour, but just for a few minutes."

A few minutes wasn't enough, would never be enough. She wanted to spend every hour of the rest of her life with him, to make sure she never again came so close to losing him. "Can I stay with him?" She could see him preparing to say no, and she begged, "Please. This past week has been so hard for him, and he doesn't like hospitals at all. He hates them, and he never goes near them." She followed the words with the smile of an angel. "It'll make us both feel a lot better."

"I'll make you a deal, Miss—"

"Krista McLaren."

"Krista. You go with your friends and eat some dinner, and when you come back I'll let you stay with him until he wakes up. After that we'll see, all right?"

She nodded eagerly. "Thank you, Dr. Sawyer."

Dave Brown left them then, and they went to the hospital cafeteria. Though Krista made a selection from the menu, she was too nervous to eat much. "What about his family, Jim? Will they be notified?"

"As far as I know he doesn't have any."

She shook her head. "He's got parents and grandparents, and twelve brothers and sisters, and nieces and nephews and everything."

Royce Ann and Jim stared at her. "You're kidding. Where do they live?"

"In Mexico. He never said the name of the town, though. Wouldn't it be in his file at work? Don't you have to give a number for an emergency?"

"Yes, but…well, I looked at his file once, and there was nothing there. I just assumed he didn't have anyone."

"I bet he's got their addresses at home, probably in the desk," she said softly to herself. "But I don't know if he'd want to call them. He hasn't seen them in years…." She would ask him when he woke up, she decided. As long as he wasn't dying, she didn't have the right to call them without his permission.

The Stones finished eating; then Jim convinced Krista to leave the hospital long enough to get a rental car. He had to return to Nueva Vida that night, and it would save her the trouble of getting one later. Royce Ann offered to stay with her, but Krista refused. Jim needed his wife, too, and Rafael was going to be all right. She wanted to be alone with him.

When she returned to the hospital a nurse showed her into a small, dimly lit room. The back of the bed was pushed up against one wall, and Rafael lay there, still and pale and to Krista's untrained eye, hardly breathing. The nurse started to leave, but Krista stopped her. "Are you sure he's all right?" she asked in a shaky whisper.

The woman smiled. "He's doing fine. And he's on a monitor, so if anything goes wrong we'll know it right away. We're just down the hall if you need anything, okay?"

"Okay." Krista remained where she was until the door had swung shut behind the nurse. Slowly, her fingers clutching her purse tightly, she moved to the bed and reached out to touch Rafael's hand. His skin seemed so cold, and he made no response to her touch. "Oh, Rafael," she whispered. "What did they do to you?"

The bed was surrounded by equipment that she'd seen only on television shows, machines she couldn't identify, and there were IV needles stuck into his arms. On his chest were two horribly ugly bruises, each about the size of a fist, from the first two bullets. They looked awful, but she could imagine how much worse the wound from the third bullet looked where it had entered unprotected flesh.

He looked weak and vulnerable, not at all like the strong man she knew. What had it taken to make him like that? His health and strength had drained away in the six hours since she'd last seen him at Royce Ann's house.

The night dragged out, each minute seeming like an hour. Krista's relief turned again to worry as he continued to sleep, breathing shallowly, hour after hour. She knew it was good that he was having no problems, but shouldn't he be waking up soon? What if he wasn't sleeping but was in a coma? He must have lost so much blood; what if the trauma was more than his body could bear?

"You look awful. You're going to scare him when he wakes up."

Krista turned from the still figure in the bed who'd hold her attention for hours to see Dr. Sawyer in the doorway. "When will that be?"

"I really can't say. Don't worry, Krista. He's resting, and that's the best thing for him now. His vital signs are good, and they brought him in by chopper, so there wasn't much of a delay in getting him into surgery. He's fine—but what about you?"

She looked surprised. "I'm all right."

"You need some sleep."

"Later. I want to stay here." She turned to look at Rafael again, and the doctor moved to the other side of the bed. "I saw the helicopter," she said softly. "I was at Royce Ann's house, and Rafael came by on his way out. When I left we saw his boss heading in the same direction, but we thought he was just out in the field because Jim got shot last week, and they're shorthanded. Then the helicopter flew over. I didn't even think . . . Today's the first day since I've known him that he's worn that vest.''

"You make sure that he always wears one from now on.''

"Oh, I will, I promise.''

"I've got to get going. If you insist on staying awake, the least you can do is sit down for a while. You've been on your feet for hours.'' Dr. Sawyer pulled a chair from the corner of the room to her side of the bed, and she gratefully sank down into it. "I'll see you tomorrow.''

"Thanks, Doctor.''

There was so much noise, so much confusion. He knew the smells. He remembered them from before, the last time, the only other time he'd been in a hospital.

He knew the sounds, too: the squeaking of the nurses' rubber-soled shoes; the beeping of the monitors; the soft whooshing of some machine. He knew the smells and the sounds, but none of that mattered. He was in the hospital, he'd had surgery, and he was hurting. And he didn't know why. He couldn't remember that. Why was he there?

It was his dream—that nightmare that had plagued him for so long—only this time it was more real, more vivid. He felt the pain, the fear. And this time there were new faces, new names mixed with the old.

Like Gregorio. The name matched a face, a boy's face. He couldn't have been more than seventeen, a year older than his brother José. But José was dead, because Rafael had killed him. Was Gregorio dead, too? Had he also killed Gregorio? He tried to ask, but he couldn't force his mouth to work, couldn't make the words come out.

His head ached, and he felt as if his brain had stopped functioning. There was awareness but no memory, questions but no answers. Why would he kill a boy? Why would Gregorio want to kill him? Did he work for Rebecca's father? Was it all Rebecca's fault? Damn it, why couldn't he remember?

He struggled to open his eyes. His vision was blurred; then it cleared, and he saw multiple images of everything, including the woman. The blond-haired woman who must somehow have been responsible for what had happened to him.

"Rebecca?"

Krista had leaned forward in the chair to rest her arms on the bed, her head down. She straightened as that single, hoarse word whispered through the air. For a moment she couldn't draw any breath into her lungs, and when she finally succeeded, it stung. Her eyes stung, too, with the sudden appearance of hot tears.

Rebecca. He'd said he no longer loved Rebecca. He'd said he cherished her, Krista, that he would be hers for as long as she wanted him, and now he was calling Rebecca. Had he lied? Did he still love the other woman? Was that why he was attracted to Krista, because she reminded him so much of Rebecca?

Rafael wouldn't lie, she insisted. He wouldn't use me to replace her.

Unless he did it subconsciously. She'd known his love would be strong and deep and intense. Too strong to die, too intense to be forgotten. So he'd satisfied it with another woman who looked like Rebecca, who had the same background. One he could pretend, subconsciously, was Rebecca.

He moved restlessly and despite her tears Krista reached out to lay her hand over his. "It's all right, Rafael," she whispered, her voice quavering. "You're all right."

His fingers clenched hers, then relaxed and he slept again. Krista laid her head on the bed and softly cried.

She stayed by his side for the rest of the night and through the next day, holding his hand, murmuring soft, comforting words to soothe him when he became agitated by his dreams. He spoke often, but only in Spanish. A nurse who spoke the language listened once, then merely shrugged. He was rambling, she said. Just disjointed sentences that meant nothing. He never spoke Krista's name, but she comforted herself with the fact that he didn't speak Rebecca's name again, either.

At last he became lucid. His eyes were open and finally focusing, but he couldn't see Krista, who had moved to the window for a few minutes. "Krista," he murmured, slowly rising onto one elbow. "Want to see Krista."

She hurried to him, sitting on the edge of the bed. Her touch was very gentle as she eased him down again. "Don't try to move, Rafael."

He gripped her hand weakly. "Oh, God, Krista, it hurts," he moaned.

"I know it does, darling, but you're all right." She stroked her fingers through his hair, dislodging bits of sand and dirt that had accumulated when he'd fallen. "Don't try to talk, all right?"

He ignored her advice. "What happened?"

"You were shot."

He nodded slowly. His voice got stronger, his eyes more alert. "Gregorio. I couldn't remember. I thought...the nightmare..."

"What nightmare, Rafael?"

"The hospital...Rebecca. I thought it was the nightmare again."

Krista looked down, her gaze settling around his mouth. She couldn't meet his eyes. "Would—would you like to see her? I can find her. It might take a few days, but I know I could find her, and she would come...."

His fingers tightened around her hand slowly. He saw the signs of last night's tears, and he asked quietly, "Why would I want to see Rebecca?"

She couldn't answer without crying again, so she remained silent.

"What did I say last night, Krista?" He was puzzled, but he kept his voice calm and even. He knew he couldn't have said anything to make her believe he still cared for Rebecca Halderman, because those feelings were dead. He wondered briefly if he had talked about the investigation, but that wouldn't explain her offer to find Rebecca. "Krista?"

"You wanted her," she whispered.

"Did I say that?"

"You said her name." Through her wet lashes she saw his mouth curve up slightly, and she raised her head to look at him.

"I've been in the hospital twice, Krista. The other time was because of Rebecca. I was dreaming, Krista.... I couldn't remember what had happened, why I was here. All I could remember was what she'd done to me. I don't care about her, *querida*. How could I, when I have you?"

She was dismayed to feel the tears on her cheeks again, to hear them in her voice. "It's all right if you want her."

"I don't. Rebecca Halderman means nothing to me. God, Krista, don't you believe me?" He cautiously pulled her down to him, cradling her with one arm against his chest. "Quiet, *querida*," he soothed, stroking her hair. "*Está bien.* It's all right, my love."

"My love," she repeated, her tears drying. She moved off his badly bruised chest and wiped her cheeks. "You are my love," she said, her voice vibrating with intensity. "I love you, Rafael."

"Then come back down here where you belong," he growled, pulling on her hand.

"And where is that?"

"In my bed, my arms, my life." He was very serious, his face set in familiar hard lines, but his eyes were gentle. "You've taken my heart and my soul, Krista. You filled all the empty places in them. There's no room for anyone else in my life but you. I'll never let you go."

"I'll never try to go," came her promise. Rafael wondered what she would think if she knew that she would soon break that vow when she found out about him and her father. But he meant what he'd just said: he would never let her leave him. As long as she loved him, he would never let her go.

He held her for a while before gently pushing her away. "You need to rest, *cariña*."

She tried to argue, but she was too tired. She kissed him goodbye, then asked at the nurses' desk about nearby motels. As soon as she checked in at one just down the street she called the hospital and left the number, so they could contact her if anything happened; then she undressed and collapsed into bed.

The next morning, after a hearty breakfast, she returned to the hospital. Rafael looked and felt much better, which was evidenced by the kiss he gave her.

A nurse's aide came in, carrying a tray, which she set on the bedside table. In the middle of the tray stood a glass of juice.

"What's that?" Krista asked curiously.

"Breakfast."

"Interesting. I'm glad I ate my pancakes and eggs and bacon before I came."

"Please don't talk about it," the aide teasingly pleaded. "He's on a clear-liquid diet—nothing but water and Jell-O and juices for the next few days. Don't tempt him with tales of food."

Rafael liked being tempted, but it wasn't the food; it was the mere sight of Krista, wearing a lavender dress and looking lovelier than ever. As soon as the nurse left them alone he reminded her that they were supposed to have been together two nights before.

"But we *were* together. You were in that bed, and I was sitting in this chair."

"That isn't quite the way I planned it," he growled.

"Well, sweetheart, I'm not the one who went out and got myself shot, so don't blame me. How do you feel?"

"I'm okay."

"Will there be some kind of investigation into the shooting?"

"They came by early this morning." Rafael pushed the table away and motioned for her to sit beside him. She did, but pulled the tray back and picked up the glass. "Drink this."

"No."

"Come on. You have to."

"I'm not thirsty. I'm hungry."

"Rafael, you heard what she said—clear liquids for the next few days. Then you can have food."

"No, then I get full liquids. Milk, cream soup, pudding and ice cream. *Then* I get real food. I'm hungry now," he grumbled. He pushed the glass away, but Krista was persistent.

"Listen, you've got to do everything they say before they'll even consider letting you out of here, and the things we can do with our time together are going to be strictly limited as long as you're here. Drink your breakfast so we can go home sooner."

He grudgingly allowed her to hold the glass while he sipped the juice through a straw. "It tastes awful," he said when he finished.

"You'll get used to it." Krista put the glass on the tray and moved the table back. When she spoke again, her voice was serious. "Rafael?"

"Yes?"

"I love you very, very much. I don't ever want to be away from you like last week again."

He gathered her into his arms, wincing when she bumped the bruises on his chest. "You're never going to lose me, Krista," he reassured her in a whisper. "I can promise you that. We're going to spend the rest of our lives together and raise beautiful children. We'll be together always, my love."

Chapter 12

It was a typically hot desert day, the air so dry that breathing was difficult, but to Krista the day seemed so gorgeous. She was taking Rafael home from the hospital. Royce Ann and Jim had brought the Mustang to El Paso the previous weekend, along with some clothes for Rafael, and now Krista watched as the nurse helped him into the small car. She stowed the suitcase in the trunk, then slid behind the wheel.

After a long silence Rafael quietly, unemotionally, told her about the shooting. "I was afraid out there, Krista," he finished. Afraid that he might die and never again get to hold her or kiss her, never get to tell her how much he loved her. Yet he still hadn't told her. Not really.

"It's natural to be afraid," she said with a gentle smile. "Just proves you're human."

He laughed, then stopped with a grimace and pressed his hand to his abdomen, lightly touching the healing wound. "There are a lot of people around who would be surprised to hear that."

He was tired again by the time they reached his house.

"Come inside and lie down."

"Only if you lie down with me."

"I've been waiting for the chance." She slipped her arm around his waist, and they went inside the house together. "Welcome home, darling," she whispered, kissing him.

She helped him undress, and he eased himself into the bed. "Take your clothes off and lie with me," he demanded. "I want to look at you."

Blushing, she obeyed him. He reached across, his hand shaking slightly, and brushed his fingertips across her breast, gently squeezing her nipple into hardness. "I thought I might never see you again," he hoarsely whispered. "Never get to tell you how important you are to me . . . how much I need you. You are my life, Krista. Without you, I would have died out there, because you give my life reason . . ." His hand fell back to the bed, and his eyes slowly, unwillingly closed. "Don't leave me, Krista," he pleaded in an almost silent voice. "Please don't leave me."

She blinked the tears from her eyes. "I love you, Rafael," she told the sleeping man. "Oh, God, I love you." She drew the covers up over them, tucking the sheet around his shoulders; then she lay down again, snuggling close to his warmth for the first time in two weeks.

Finding Rafael still sleeping soundly when she awoke, she slipped from the bed, pulled on one of his shirts and left the room.

She had planned to be back in New York before the end of May, and here it was the beginning of August, and she didn't want to go. She wanted to spend the rest of her life in this small house in Nueva Vida—or at least as long as Rafael remained there. She would be like Constancia if he didn't marry her—she would follow him from town to town. But she wouldn't go back to New York, not without him.

She went to the desk to write to her landlord and to Tracy. Tracy Lord would tell the various people involved with her work who would need to know. She didn't even consider whether the move might affect her career. If she couldn't continue with her line of clothes from Nueva Vida, she would find a new job, she decided—like mother and wife. That sounded like more fun anyway.

The letters were brief. She told her landlord that she would be in the city before the end of the month to gather up her things. That would leave plenty of time for Rafael to be completely healed, she thought. She began looking for envelopes—he must have some somewhere. The first two drawers in the desk turned up nothing, so she closed them and pulled open the third one.

The third drawer was usually locked, though she didn't know that; she reached down to pick up a thick file, to see if there might be any envelopes underneath it. There weren't. The file was heavy, and filled with papers and clippings. She wondered what it was, then decided it must have something to do with his job. She could feel a label on the underside, and she started to turn it over to see what it said.

Rafael rose slowly from the bed. Ignoring his clothes, he walked down the hall, his right hand lightly covering his wound, his left rubbing his eyes. He moved silently, giving Krista no warning of his approach. When he saw her sitting at his desk with the file that was unmistakably hers, he uttered a sharp curse. "Krista!"

She turned, the file still upside down in her hand, and gave him a smile. He felt relief wash over him. If she could still smile like that, then she didn't know what she was holding. She hadn't read any of it.

"I didn't know you were awake."

"Of course I'm awake," he said petulantly. "You said you'd stay with me, but when I woke up you were gone."

She placed the file back in the drawer and shut it. "I'll come back if you want. I was just looking for some envelopes. I wrote a couple of letters while you were asleep, and I thought I'd get them ready to mail."

"I don't have any envelopes. I don't write to many people," he said, a sardonic tone in his voice. Then he sounded just tired again. "Please come back in the bedroom."

When they were comfortably settled in the bed again, he moved Krista into the circle of his arms. "You didn't know what you were getting into when you offered to stay here with me, did you?"

"Oh, yes, I did. I've been watching you snap at the nurses and doctors for the last week."

"I'm sorry I'm in a rotten mood. If I could make love to you, I wouldn't mind staying in bed all the time, but since I can't..."

"It won't be long till you get all the loving you can stand, I promise," she assured him. And the sly way she smiled at him left no doubt that she fully intended to keep that promise.

Krista was a patient, charming and cheerful nurse, and Rafael grew stronger each day. It wasn't long before he was well enough for Krista to keep part of her promise. By the time he had been okayed to return to work she had done a most thorough job of easing his frustration and satisfying her own hunger, too.

She'd told him about the fight with her father, and he'd immediately suggested that she live with him. He wanted to keep her close; he wanted her in his bed every night and every morning.

Her living there didn't sit well with Thompson and Houseman. On Rafael's first day back at work they raged at him for the problems he'd created.

"You did it on purpose, didn't you? You removed her from McLaren's house so we couldn't get any information from her, didn't you?" Houseman accused.

"Yes."

Rafael's straightforwardness threw Houseman off a bit. He had expected evasion, not a terse admission. "Why?"

Rafael refused to answer that question in front of Thompson, but once he was alone with Houseman, he said darkly, "I'm already going to be in enough trouble with Krista over this. I won't use her. I won't let you involve her in this mess."

"She might already be involved!"

But Rafael couldn't be swayed. "She isn't. She knows nothing about it."

Richard Houseman rubbed his neck wearily. He seemed to remember having this conversation before. He hadn't been able to change Rafael's mind then, and he wasn't going to change it now. He wasn't even so sure any longer that he should try. Nothing they'd found pointed to her involvement. "Did you know she gave notice on her apartment? She isn't planning to return to New York."

Rafael didn't know, but it was just as well, since he had no intention of letting her return. According to Houseman's information McLaren's business should be shut down by the beginning of September. As soon as Rafael could convince Krista that she had to forgive him because of their love, he was going to marry her. He didn't even let himself think of the possibility that she might not forgive him, might not marry him. It *had* to happen. If there was a God in heaven, it had to happen.

"The shipment's due tomorrow. He's going to be making two more; then he's retiring. There will be one last shipment around the end of the month—supposedly over five hundred kilos of high-quality cocaine—and that's when we'll get him. That's over a thousand pounds. Not a bad haul."

No, not bad at all. That would bring Art enough money to live comfortably for the rest of his life, even with his expensive tastes. Unfortunately, there wasn't much use for that kind of money in prison.

Rafael wondered where Houseman got his information. He must have one of McLaren's employees on his own payroll to keep him informed. Just like Ruben Gonzales kept Rafael informed.

The shipment didn't arrive.

For the first time in months there was no shipment, and this close to the end of the case, it made Houseman nervous. "Let's go to New York," he suggested the next Monday. "See what's going on."

Rafael looked wary. "When?"

"Tomorrow. Don't worry, Thompson will approve your travel."

Who cared about approval? "Krista's going to New York tomorrow."

The blond man was silent for a moment; then he said, "Get her flight numbers. We'll make sure we get there either earlier or later. Tell her you're going to El Paso—something to do with the kid who shot you—and you have to stay a few days. We should be back by Wednesday or Thursday. Is she going on business?"

"Yes." That had been all—no explanation. Just "business."

Rafael was troubled. He didn't like lying to Krista. If he lied to her now, how was he going to convince her that he wasn't lying when he told her that he loved her?

"Look, if it bothers you that much, tell her the truth. Tell her her dad's a big drug dealer, that you've been using her to find out information about him," Houseman said sarcastically. The look Rafael gave him was one of pure hatred. He rose from the chair and left the small office.

Thompson entered the office minutes later. "Is Contreras giving you trouble?"

"Not really." Houseman was beginning to wonder if Rafael should be dropped from the case, but he said nothing to Martin Thompson. He was starting to understand Rafael's dislike of the man.

A half hour later Rafael returned to work. He dropped a piece of paper on Houseman's desk and walked out without a word. Richard picked it up, smiling slowly. It was Krista's flight schedule—airlines, flight numbers and departure and arrival times. No, Contreras wasn't giving him trouble. He would keep him on.

It was a bad dream—just a nightmare. Like the day she'd been told that Rafael had been shot. A nightmare too awful to be true. But it was true. It had been true with Rafael, and now it was true with her.

"Decided yet who to call?"

Krista lifted her gaze to the man seated across from her at the desk. Tyler McKenzie. Detective Tyler McKenzie. "I—I don't know. If Rafael were home I could call him, but he had to go out of town on business. I don't know...."

She felt numb—and had for the past hour. The trip had gone smoothly until she had gone to retrieve her suitcases from the luggage carousel. There had been no sign of her second bag, so she prepared to wait, but suddenly two men in suits had flanked her. One took her suitcase from her, while the other flashed an ID and a badge. Tyler McKenzie, NYPD. Amid stares and curious whispers they had hustled her through the crowd to a waiting car.

They had arrested her, Krista McLaren, who had never taken any drug stronger than aspirin, for possession of cocaine with intent to distribute.

"I know some attorneys here," she continued in that breathy, not-quite-sure-this-is-real voice. "I guess I could call one of them.... Wait! I know that man."

McKenzie glanced over his shoulder at the tall blond man across the room. "Houseman?"

"Yes. He's with the border patrol." What was he doing here? He was supposed to be with Rafael; they were going out of town, the two of them, to check out a lead on one of their cases.

"Nah. DEA."

She looked back at McKenzie. "What?"

He realized he shouldn't have told her, but the mistake had been made, so he continued. "Richard Houseman is with the DEA. He's in and out of here all the time." He watched Krista and saw her stiffen. The response interested him. "You know, drug enforcement. Now the smaller guy with him—he's border patrol. Out of New Mexico."

Krista found "the smaller guy," half-hidden behind Houseman and a cop the size of a linebacker. He wore a well-tailored, plain black suit. The stark black of the suit and the soft white of the shirt emphasized his dark skin, his black hair.

Ten minutes ago Tyler McKenzie hadn't believed his prisoner was guilty of the charges, but her response to seeing a drug-enforcement agent made him rethink her innocence. She certainly was shaken up by the man.

She sank back in her chair. "I don't understand," she murmured. "Why didn't he tell me he was coming to New York?"

"Houseman, could you come here a minute?" McKenzie called.

Houseman left the others at the desk and sauntered toward Detective McKenzie. When he saw Krista the color drained from his face. Any appearance of relaxation disappeared, and he became as tense as she was. "What are you doing here?" he demanded harshly.

McKenzie filled him in on her arrest. Houseman ran his hand through his hair. "Oh, my God," was all he said.

Krista stared at Rafael, willing him to notice her, and he did. With that uncanny sense that told him when she was near, he turned, his eyes going directly to her. He walked away from the giant of a cop in midsentence, went straight to her and knelt in front of her.

"Krista." He reached for her hands and found them cold and trembling. His eyes searched her quickly, thoroughly, for any sign of injury. "Are you all right, *querida?*" He could think of no reason for her to be there unless she had been the victim of some crime—a robbery, or perhaps an assault. Again his eyes sought confirmation that she was unhurt, and she supported it verbally.

"I'm okay. Why are you here, Rafael? You told me—"

He laid his fingers over her lips. "Later. Why are *you* here?"

"I've been arrested."

He almost smiled. Good, upright Krista, who had never broken any laws in her life other than the speed limit, arrested? The idea was laughable. But no one was laughing. They didn't even smile. Rafael rose to his feet, keeping one of her hands in his. "For what?"

McKenzie told him, and Rafael's fingers tightened around hers. *That bastard!* he cursed silently. *Damn Art McLaren to hell!* No wonder Houseman had missed the last shipment. McLaren had used his own daughter as the courier.

Krista stood up, too. "Rafael, I didn't know it was in my suitcase," she said tensely. "I swear to you, I don't know where it came from."

He raised one hand to her hair and smiled. "I know, *pequeña.*" He knew her—he loved her. He knew Krista would never get involved in her father's schemes. He slid his arm around her waist and pulled her to him, encouraging her to lean on him, both physically and emotionally.

Krista remembered that she should be angry with him for being in New York and not telling her, but she was too frightened and too grateful for his support. Whatever the problem, she was sure that he would handle it for her; he would take care of it. His lie would wait until later.

"Can we talk to you, Tyler?" Houseman asked. "In private?"

The man agreed and led the way to an interrogation room. Krista was left alone at the desk. The conversation took only a few minutes; then the three men returned. "All right, Miss McLaren, you can go," McKenzie said, ripping up the report he'd been working on.

She rose to her feet. "That's it?" she asked weakly. He smiled. "Be thankful that you have such good friends. And the next time you visit the city, be careful what you carry in your bags."

Rafael took her arm and led her from the building. Richard Houseman accompanied them to the car, asked for the address of her apartment and drove them there. He wanted to question her a little more about the drugs. Tyler McKenzie was a good cop, and he felt Krista was innocent. Contreras was convinced of her innocence, and Richard was leaning more in that direction himself, but he needed more information.

"Who knew you were coming to New York, Krista?" Richard asked as soon as they were seated in the living room.

She lifted her shoulders in a weary shrug. "Rafael, Royce, Ann, Juana."

"Who is she?"

"My father's housekeeper." She went on with her list. "My father, Tracy Lord, Jack Marshall."

There was no need to ask who the last two were; Houseman was very familiar with the names. "Was anyone supposed to meet you at the airport?"

"Tracy." Krista's forehead wrinkled into a frown. "I wonder why she didn't show up. I just assumed she was late; then McKenzie and his partner came and said I had to go with them. I'd better call Tracy and tell her I'm home."

"Later," Rafael said. He tugged at his tie, loosening it. "How did everyone at *la casa grande* find out about your trip?"

"Tracy called this morning after you left and asked me to bring some stuff from Dad's house, so I called to ask Juana to pack it in a small bag for me."

"What did she say?" Richard asked.

"Oh, I didn't talk to her, not then. Dad answered. He said he'd have her do it. When I stopped by I just took the suitcase. I didn't look in it. I talked to Juana for a minute, but I didn't stay very long, because Jack Marshall was there with my father, and I don't like him. Besides, Dad and I aren't on the best of terms these days. Where do you think it came from—the cocaine, I mean?"

"South America," Richard said with a wry grin. "Maybe Colombia."

"That's not what I meant. How did it get in my suitcase?"

Houseman shrugged her question off. "Look, I know you've been out of town for a long time, but do you by any chance have some coffee? I sure could use a cup."

"I think there's some in the freezer. I'll see."

As soon as she left the room Houseman said in a low oice, "You think McLaren and Marshall put the cocaine n her bag?"

Rafael nodded. His eyes, focused on the hallway, were old and angry, watching for Krista to reappear.

Houseman was grim. "I don't think the thought's occurred to her yet. McKenzie said that a couple of seams in he suitcase had been intentionally cut. They wanted her to et caught."

Rafael had already reached that conclusion. "They're uspicious."

"Why? Why would McLaren set his own daughter up?"

"Because he knows he's being investigated. He may not now by whom or how close we are to getting him, but he nows something's going on."

It fit; it was the only explanation. The bag had been ocked when it was checked onto the plane, and it had still een locked when it was unloaded in New York. Thanks to he baggage handlers' roughness and the weak seams, hough, the suitcase had broken open when they were unoading it, and a few packets of white, powdery substance ad fallen out. They had called airport security, who in turn alled the police, and they found three kilos of quality cocaine in the suitcase.

"If she didn't get caught, then Lord was supposed to remove the cocaine before Krista saw it. So Art's sending a varning: back off, or Krista will get hurt. To you?"

Rafael agreed with his guess. "Lord must have stayed out of sight to see what happened. When she saw McKenzie, she eft."

"McLaren's a real bastard. It's going to be a pleasure to get rid of him."

A slow smile crossed Rafael's lips, and the other man ook it as a sign that Krista was coming down the hall behind him. "We're going to have to tell her something soon," Rafael said quickly, quietly.

Krista set a tray on the coffee table, then handed a cup of strong, black coffee to Houseman. "Once you taste this you'll probably regret asking. Rafael makes much better coffee than I do," she said apologetically. "So... what are you guys doing in New York? Why did you tell me that you worked for the border patrol? And why did you let me believe him, Rafael?"

Rafael was staring into the coffee she'd given him, pretending not to notice her questions, so Houseman answered. "I believe I told you I was temporarily with them, which I sort of am. As for being in New York—I'm just following up on something, and I needed some help. Since Rafe is still on desk duty, Thompson decided it would be best to let him come instead of one of the other guys. He's already shorthanded, with Rafe still under the doctor's care."

The explanation made so much sense that Krista didn't even consider that it could be a lie. And it was true that he had said the job with the border patrol was temporary. She directed the next question to Rafael, who was sitting silently beside her. "Why didn't you tell me you were coming here?"

"I told you I had to go out of town on business. I don't know much about what Richard's doing, and I didn't know if it was all right to tell anyone about it, even you."

She tilted her head to one side to look at him, and he met her eyes, though with some difficulty. Then she grinned impishly. "All right, I'll accept that. Whatever the reason, I'm very grateful that you two are here. I didn't know who to call or what to do."

"Glad to have been of some help," Houseman responded. "Rafe, I'm going home. Why don't I pick you up in the morning at nine?"

Rafael nodded once. Houseman swallowed the rest of his coffee, said good-night and left. Rafael turned to see Krista. "Is it okay if I stay here?"

"Do you really think I'd let you stay anywhere else? There are too many beautiful women in New York for me to turn you loose without protection."

"I've got the only woman I want right here." He leaned
ver to kiss her, then pulled her to her feet. "Show me your
edroom, Krista," he challenged, "and we'll see who needs
rotection."

She was more than happy to comply.

"Rafael?"

He grunted in response, too tired to speak.

"If Richard works for the DEA, then he's investigating
omeone in Nueva Vida, isn't he?"

"Probably."

"I wonder who it is."

He pretended not to hear her.

"Rafael?"

"What?"

"Do you think Jack Marshall's involved? I never have
ked him—he gives me the creeps."

"I don't know, Krista. Go to sleep. It's been a long day."

Another few minutes passed; then she asked, "If it is
Marshall, do you think he's going to get my dad in trou-
le?"

Frustrated with the topic of conversation, Rafael reached
or her and yanked her across the bed and beneath his body.
'Your bed is too damned big," he growled before his mouth
overed hers.

Krista gave up her questions and turned her mind to the
nan who was filling her with his need, taking from her and
iving in return. By the time their sudden, fierce lovemak-
ng ended she had completely forgotten what she had been
alking about.

"Rafael?"

He grimaced in the darkness, pressing his face against her
air. "What?"

"I'm very glad you're here. Good night."

"Good night, *cariña.*"

The care that Houseman had taken in booking their
lights so that his and Rafael's didn't overlap Krista's was

wasted; the three shared a row of seats on the flight home from New York to Atlanta, then on to Dallas and El Paso before finally taking a short commuter hop to Nueva Vida

It was Houseman's first chance to really watch Krista an Rafael together, and it was the first time he truly began t regret getting Rafael involved with the case. It was plain t see that the two were in love, and it was also plain to see that Rafael was worried about the effect of his part in the investigation would have on Krista. Personally, Houseman couldn't see that there would be much of a problem; she loved the man so much she could probably forgive him anything. They would soon find out what her reaction would be, though. She'd gone on asking questions about Marshall and the cocaine, and Rafael and Houseman had agreed, however reluctantly on Rafael's part, that she was going to have to be told something. Otherwise they feared she might go to Art, and tell him her suspicions about his employee and reveal Houseman's true job to him. They couldn't afford to have him tipped off this close to the end

"Have her come in to the office tomorrow," Houseman told Rafael outside his small apartment. "We'll talk to her then. And for God's sake, keep her away from the old man and a telephone. Don't let her blow this for us."

Rafael somberly agreed. He knew how to keep her busy. He was going to make love to her all night, make her think of no one but him. It might be the last chance he had.

Rafael was nowhere to be seen when Krista arrived at the office the next day for lunch, but Darren Carter, seated at his desk, told her to go into the small conference room at the end of the hall. It was a dreary room, barely large enough for the scarred wooden table and the chairs that circled it. Three of those chairs were occupied by Rafael, Houseman and Thompson. A fourth chair, on the opposite side of the table from the men, was pulled out for Krista.

She looked puzzled. "Am I interrupting something?" she asked.

"No. Please sit down." Houseman gestured to the empty chair, and she slowly circled the table to take it. Her eye moved quickly to Rafael, but he was staring at the table-top, and he refused to meet her gaze. He looked colder and harder than she'd ever seen him, and she knew something was wrong. She was about to hear something that she didn't want to hear, but her legs were too weak to follow her brain's command to take her out of the room.

Houseman glanced at Rafael. He had offered him the opportunity to talk to her first, to explain everything, but the man had refused. That left Richard stuck for a way to tell her. He decided to be blunt.

"Krista, we know who put the cocaine in your suitcase. The DEA's been after him for about eighteen months now. We brought the border patrol in about five months ago, because in addition to smuggling cocaine and various other drugs, the man also smuggles illegals. Rafe and Thompson and I have been working this end, and we've got people in New York and Miami, too. It's a pretty big operation, and we're about ready to shut it down."

He paused to see if she had any questions, but she remained silent. She wasn't sure her voice would work; she wasn't even sure if she understood what he was saying.

"After what happened to you in New York, we decided it would be best to bring you in—to tell you everything we know. You got too curious about what was going on, and we can't risk letting these people know that we're about ready to move on them. We're trusting that you won't warn them."

"It's Jack Marshall, isn't it?"

"He's involved, but he's not the boss."

The boss. She knew with a sinking heart what he was going to say, and she didn't want to hear it. It couldn't be true. It didn't make sense. "He doesn't need the money from something like that," she whispered. "And why else would he do it, if not for money?"

"Who, Krista?"

"My father. That's who you're talking about, isn't it?"

Hearing the anguish in her voice, Rafael tensed, a muscle in his jaw jerking. She hadn't realized the worst of it yet, and she already sounded heartbroken.

"Your father doesn't have nearly as much money as you think. Those oil wells in Texas were sold years ago, and it takes huge sums of money to work the desert. And Art McLaren likes to live well. He's used to the luxuries of life, and when he found out he couldn't afford them anymore, he found a new source of revenue. He started smuggling illegal aliens. It was a short step from there to drugs. There's no mistake, Krista. I promise you that."

She looked at Thompson, who was fiddling with an unlit cigarette, then to Houseman, who was openly sympathetic, and finally to Rafael. He was still staring downward, the lines of his face hard and unyielding. There was no emotion there, nothing. And then she realized what Houseman had said. The border patrol had been involved in the investigation for the last five months. Rafael had been working on it for the last five months. It had been four months ago that she had come to Nueva Vida. Four months since she had gotten involved with him.

She looked so shocked that Houseman knew immediately she had made the connection. He wanted to kick Rafael, to jerk him out of the chair and make him face her, convince her that she was wrong, but instead Contreras just sat there, avoiding her eyes and looking guilty as hell.

She thought she was going to be ill. She was going to break into tears and fall apart in front of the three men. What a wonderful day—to find out that her father was a drug dealer and a smuggler and that her lover was a dedicated federal agent, willing to make any sacrifices for the sake of his job. Willing to make love to her, to pretend to love her, to tell her all those lovely lies—just so he and his partners could send her father to prison!

The silence in the room was deafening. Finally, when Krista thought she could stand it no longer, Rafael spoke. "Leave us."

Houseman and Thompson exchanged glances at Rafael's sharp command, then left the room. The door closed with a click.

"I always knew you were dedicated to your job," she said in a pain-filled voice so low that Rafael had to strain to hear.

'But sleeping with the person you're investigating—that's utting it close. Don't you have a code of ethics? Or don't thics matter when you're trying to arrest a criminal?''

Rafael moved his chair around the table next to hers. 'Look at me, Krista.''

Slowly she pulled her gaze from the table to his face. The old blank mask had disappeared, and his eyes were alive vith emotion: anger, sorrow, heartache—and love. "You veren't part of the investigation to me, Krista. You know hat.''

Did she? All she knew was that he had never wanted an ffair with her, had never come right out and said he loved ter. Her lower lip trembled, and she made an effort to hold tack her tears. "I thought I knew you, but I was wrong. I hought you were good, and honest. I thought I could trust ou. Oh, God, I was so wrong. You used me. You made ove—had sex—with me to find out what you could about ny father.'' The tears were coming, and there was no way he could stop them. "What have you done to me, Ra- ael?'' she whispered sadly.

"I *made love* with you, cariña. It wasn't sex, not ever,'' te insisted, his voice raspy, vibrating with intensity. "I never vanted to hurt you, Krista, but I needed you so much. I teeded you so I could live.''

Krista closed her eyes and gave a nearly hysterical laugh. 'Stop it,'' she sobbed. "No more lies. I can't bear any- nore lies.''

She was hurting badly, Rafael realized, and right now he couldn't help her. He moved away from her sadly. "Go thead and hate me, Krista,'' he said, hating himself far nore than she ever could. "When the hate's gone, you'll still ove me, and I'll be waiting.''

She didn't reply until she reached the door on the other ide of the room. Then she turned to look at him through ter tears. "I wish I did hate you,'' she whispered. "Then it vouldn't hurt so much.''

Chapter 13

There was no pleasure in being right when it threatened to destroy you, and Rafael definitely felt shattered. He'd known all along that it wouldn't be easy for Krista to find out what he'd done, but he had expected anger, not that heart-wrenching pain he'd seen in her face. She doubted the truth of everything he'd ever said and done; she doubted that he'd ever cared at all for her. The irony of the whole thing was that he'd never gotten one bit of information from her that could be used against Art. The only thing he'd ever found out was that she was innocent, ignorant of Art's business.

Krista packed her clothes and drove back into Nueva Vida. Though she knew she would be welcome at Royce Ann's house, she checked into one of Nueva Vida's few motels. She'd been there for several hours, stretched out on the bed and staring dry-eyed at the ceiling, when the phone calls started.

She didn't want to talk to anyone, so she ignored the ringing. The caller was persistent, though, calling every fifteen minutes like clockwork.

Half an hour after the last call someone knocked at the door. The knocking turned to pounding, and she pulled the pillow over her head. She stayed like that until she heard her name bellowed in a furious voice. With a sigh she got to her feet and went to open the door for Richard Houseman.

"Why the hell didn't you answer the phone?" he demanded, running his fingers through his blond hair.

"I think I made it rather obvious that I didn't want to talk to anyone. What do you want?"

"Can I come in?"

"Might as well, unless you want an audience." She gestured, and he looked around to see curious guests at the nearby pool staring at them. She walked to the bed and sat down, drawing her knees to her chest. Houseman closed the door and paced the length of the room.

Krista was determined not to make it easy for him. She watched him, her eyes wide and clear and empty, offering no easy way for him to start. As he'd done earlier that afternoon, he decided to be blunt.

"Contreras is miserable as hell," he blurted out.

Krista had expected something about her father, not Rafael. For an instant she looked surprised; then her expression closed, becoming cold and hard. As he watched the transformation Houseman wondered briefly if she'd learned that from Rafe. It was so much like his response to things that it was uncanny.

"Krista, he didn't do this to hurt you. Can't you see that?"

"You surprise me, Richard. I never figured you and Rafael for friends."

"Funny, I never figured you for stupid. The man doesn't need friends. He needs you."

Krista's temper flared, and she started to rise from the bed. She stopped herself in time, though, and sank down again. "*I* never thought I was stupid, either. Now I know just how stupid I can be. I know men like you and Rafael can't be trusted . . . ever."

"He's in love with you," he insisted.

"Oh, please, Richard. He never told *me* that, and I fin
it difficult to believe he told you." She managed to soun
incredibly bored, without even a hint of the tears that wer
building inside her.

"He didn't. He didn't have to. Any more than you had t
tell me that you love him."

"I made a mistake, and it's costing more than it wa
worth," she replied. "Don't make it worse, Richard." Sh
changed the subject, asking in a pleasantly pitched voice
"When are you going to arrest my father?"

Houseman was immediately on guard. "I don't know."

Krista could see that he was trying to decide if she coul
be trusted with any more information about the case, an
she smiled sardonically. "Don't worry, Richard. I owe m
father less than I owe Rafael. I don't plan to tell him any
thing. Let him pay for what he's done."

"You're not that cold." Whether or not she approved o
what Art had done, family loyalty would demand that sh
help him.

"I've been in Nueva Vida four months. You know wha
I had to do to make him notice I was here? I had to go to bec
with a Mexican—a Mexican who was getting a lot of attention for killing a sixteen-year-old boy. He didn't care where
I was all those nights before, who I saw, what I did. But he
cared about the Mexican."

She shrugged. "We're not a normal family, Richard. I
hardly know Art. To you he's my father. To me he's someone who never wanted anything to do with me. I have no
father, not in the real meaning of the word. My family consisted of other kids whose parents didn't want them, kids
who were dumped in boarding schools, like me. It's funny—
he was afraid the great McLaren name would be shamed by
my affair with Rafael, and the whole time he was smuggling drugs into the country, getting rich off other people's
weaknesses. What the hell did he think *that* would do to the
family honor?"

"I'm sorry, Krista."

She smiled faintly. "Four months ago the biggest problem in my life was boredom. I was tired of New York. Now... I've been arrested. I've spent hours at the hospital worrying over a man who betrayed me from the very beginning. I've been kicked out of my home. I've found out that my father's a drug dealer and that the man I thought I loved is every bit as dishonest and unethical as my father.... I'd take boredom any day."

Houseman sat down on the edge of the built-in dresser. "What are you going to do?"

"I don't know. Right now I'm going to feel sorry for myself a little longer. Then... I don't know." She looked up, her eyes narrowing suspiciously. "Why are you here?"

"Because I don't like the way things turned out today. I'll be honest, Krista. I'm still not sure I trust you. I'm not sure you're as innocent as you appear to be. In my business, though, you learn not to trust people, and fortunately for you, no one else shares my suspicions. Especially Rafe. I gave him a chance today to tell you about your father himself, alone, but he wouldn't. I think he was afraid to."

"He had good reason to be afraid. If we'd been alone he probably wouldn't have walked out of that room alive. Do you want something else from me?"

"Maybe a chance to let him explain what he did, how he feels."

"Why should you care? You just admitted that you two aren't friends. What difference does it make to you?"

"We're not friends," he agreed. "Except for you, I don't think he's ever let anyone get close enough for that, has he? But I respect the man, and I don't think you're being fair to him."

The laugh that came from her sounded wild. *"Fair?"* she echoed. *"I'm* not being fair? You don't know what you're talking about, and you don't have any right to be here at all, so go away and leave me alone! Just leave me alone!"

Houseman got to his feet. Before he left, though, he laid a card on the dresser where he'd been sitting. "My local number is on this card," he said quietly. "Let me know when you've made your decision. Goodbye, Krista."

Rafael went for a long drive into Mexico when he got of work that afternoon. On his way back he stopped at th Blue Parrot for dinner, sitting in the back booth, looking s fierce and formidable that even the waitress was hesitant t approach him. After he finished eating he thought abou going to the office—anything to avoid going home to ; house that he knew was going to be empty. But, callin; himself a coward, when he left the bar he headed for home

He didn't need to check the closet or the dresser drawer to know that Krista's things were gone. He felt it in the si lence. The house had lost its warmth, its friendliness. H undressed, took a shower, then lay down in the bed they hac shared.

It was a long, lonely night.

Krista saw Rafael the next day. Having eaten nothin; since breakfast Friday, she was forced by her rumblin; stomach to go out for lunch on Saturday. She had the bac luck to choose the restaurant where Rafael and Richard Houseman were finishing their lunch. She stood in the doorway near the sign that read Please Wait to be Seated her expression frozen, and swore to herself that she would not speak, would not react in any way. Not even when Rafael approached her after paying for his meal and stopped right beside her, speaking her name in that raspy voice that she loved so much.

She might have been carved from stone for all the response she gave. Marble, Rafael thought. Beautiful, cold marble. She stared straight ahead, completely motionless, hardly even breathing. He thought that if he touched her the marble might crack and fall away, but he didn't want to see what was underneath. He'd had nightmares about the pain he'd caused her, and he couldn't bear to see it again. Wounded by the lack of love in her beautiful blue eyes—by

he lack of any feeling at all—he silently walked out the door
and left her standing there.

Houseman stopped in front of her. "Are you enjoying
this, Krista?" he asked sarcastically before following the
other man out.

She stood there for a moment, her eyes squeezed shut,
until the waitress asked, "You want smoking or non-
smoking?"

Krista looked at her as if she didn't understand the words.
"Smoking...?" she repeated in a daze. "No. I—I don't..."
Her hunger forgotten, she turned and left the restaurant.

"The shipment is due tomorrow." Houseman waited for
Rafael's response, but none came. "Did you hear me?"

The other man nodded once. "The shipment is due tomorrow. Over five hundred kilos. Where?"

"Here. He's bringing it right through the border checkpoint. Can you believe the nerve of that bastard?"

Rafael rubbed his eyes. It had been a hell of a week; he
really didn't know how he'd gotten through it. He was
learning to sleep a little, though he still reached for Krista a
half dozen times each night, still wondered for a brief minute each morning where she was before the truth struck him
with fresh pain: she was gone. He'd lost her, and he didn't
know if he could ever get her back.

"Do you want to be there tomorrow when we get Mc-
Laren?"

Rafael shrugged. "Yes." Not that it mattered much to
him one way or another, but he had nothing else to do.

"Eight o'clock, my apartment."

Rafael left the conference room that Houseman was using as an office and returned to his desk. A message was
propped up on his phone, and he reached for it. The name
McLaren leaped out at him, and his heart skipped a few
beats. Krista had called him! he thought excitedly; then his
happiness faded with the realization that the first name
wasn't Krista. It was Art. Art McLaren wanted to see him
at *la casa grande* as soon as he could come.

He stared at the piece of paper as if it could give him the answers to the questions whirling in his mind. What did Art want with him? Had he heard that Krista was no longer living with him? Or had he somehow heard about the investigation? But there were no answers on the paper. Only Art McLaren held the answers.

Art was waiting for him. He ordered Rafael to follow him, then climbed into a pickup and drove off. They were several miles from the house when Art stopped. They had crested a hill that gave them a broad view of McLaren land.

Rafael walked over to Art, who held out a pair of binoculars. "Look out there. Krista's dependable—came out to exercise her horse just like always. No one else can ride him, you know."

Hesitantly he took the glasses and turned them in the direction Art had indicated. First he saw no sign of life; then he turned slightly, and a big black stallion and its rider appeared. He swallowed hard. It was Krista and Diablo. He started to lower the binoculars, but Art said, "Keep watching."

As he did, four more riders approached. Leading them was Jack Marshall.

"I know you're onto my little...sideline," Art said, smiling smugly. "I'm retiring tomorrow. My final order is due then. If you arrest me, if you interfere in any way, she won't come back from this ride alive. You know how easy it is for someone to die out there—especially someone who comes from the city, who knows nothing about survival in the desert. She could get thrown from her horse, wander off, not hear the men calling.... She'd die slowly. You know that, don't you? Painfully." He shook his head with regret. "Hell of a way for a girl to die."

Rafael took one more look. Krista was frightened, and Diablo, protective of his mistress, was wild-eyed, ears flattened back. Rafael lowered the binoculars and turned icecold eyes on her father. His face, as usual, was emotionless, but his eyes were full of fury and anger and something else, something that brought a smile of triumph to Art's face: anguish.

"What do you want me to do?" he asked, his voice low and cold and empty.

"Call off whatever you've got planned for tomorrow. I want my shipment, without any trouble from you. And forget about the investigation. I won't be bringing in any more people or drugs after tomorrow, and I want to be left alone for the rest of my life."

Rafael nodded once. "Tell them to bring her back."

"Not yet. They'll bring her back tomorrow night. It isn't that I don't trust you, Contreras, but... I like to play it safe." Art smiled, accepting the binoculars that Rafael held in limp hands. "Then we have a deal?"

The word came out unwillingly. "Yes." A deal that Rafael couldn't make; he didn't have the authority. Houseman would never go along, not even to save Krista's life, but Rafael needed time, time to plan.

"I'm pleased that you're so reasonable, Contreras," Art said, unable to resist the urge to rub it in. "I half expected you to refuse. I would kill her, have no doubt about that, but it does seem such a waste, doesn't it? It's a little disappointing, though. I didn't think you would ever allow any one to interfere with your work, especially a woman. You've become too human, Contreras. Now you have a weakness."

In silence Rafael walked to his truck, got in and drove away across the parched grass. Now he had a weakness, he thought cynically. Krista was one hell of a weakness.

He felt frozen as he drove back to town, refusing to let himself think or feel too much. He had to stay calm. He needed a plan, and he needed help.

Houseman was still in the office, several strangers with him. He didn't bother to introduce them, but Rafael knew they were fellow DEA agents, there to take part in the arrest. Rafael stood silently, and after a moment Houseman asked the three men to leave them alone for a minute.

"They have Krista."

Houseman looked puzzled. "Who has her?"

"McLaren's people."

"You mean she went to her father's house?"

"I mean," Rafael said sharply, "that McLaren sent her out with Jack Marshall and three others. They're going to kill her if we arrest him tomorrow."

"Damn! How did he find out that we're going to bust him tomorrow?"

Rafael shrugged. "He said to call off what I've got planned, that he doesn't want any trouble from me. He didn't mention anyone else. I don't think he knows about you."

Houseman was relieved. "He probably thinks you found out about the illegals, then stumbled onto the drugs. If he doesn't know about us, then we're all right. Where'd they take her?"

"I don't know. There are dozens of places out there to hide."

Richard Houseman walked to the door and stared out, his hands thrust deep in the pockets of his slacks. He tilted his head back, closed his eyes and considered their options. When he turned back to Rafael the answer was written on his face. "We can't call it off."

"You want to let them kill her."

"Of course I don't, damn it!" Richard studied him for a long moment, then asked the question that he knew would anger the other man, but he had to know. "Are you sure they kidnapped her? Are you sure she didn't go along willingly? She has to know that you'd do whatever you could to help her. You *would* call the whole thing off if it were up to you."

Rafael's entire body tensed. He radiated outrage, but when he spoke his voice was low and quiet and tightly controlled. "I saw her face. She was terrified. She's afraid of Jack Marshall, and she knows what's going on. She knows they're going to kill her."

"I can't help you, Rafe. The DEA has spent a lot of time and a lot of money on this case. I can't go in and tell my bosses that we had to call it off because we thought one possibly innocent woman might get killed. I can't do it." He dragged his hands through his hair in frustration, spitting out a low curse. "Can you track?"

Rafael nodded.

"Are you good?"

"The best here." But was that good enough? he agonized. Was he good enough to save Krista?

"I can't help you, but if you wanted to go tonight to see what you could do, I couldn't stop you, either. How many men are with her?"

"Four when I saw her."

"Can you find her and take care of them?"

Rafael closed his eyes briefly and saw again the fear on Krista's face when the four men had intercepted her. He would find her and free her, he vowed, or die trying.

Tracking was a combination of skill and luck. Luck was with Rafael in that he knew what direction they had been heading and precisely where to go on McLaren's property to pick up their trail. Skill was going to be necessary because he had to wait until the sun had set, giving them at least a four-hour head start. He couldn't risk being seen on McLaren's land, and he was going to have to track by flashlight.

He took only the most basic equipment: a strong flashlight with extra batteries; a notepad; a pencil; a measuring tape; and a tracking stick. The last was a sturdy walking stick with rubber-band markers. Once she was on foot, two successive prints would give measurements, marked on the stick with the rubber bands, that would be invaluable in following her trail: the length of her foot; the length of her stride; and the step interval—the distance between the end of one step and the beginning of the next. His job would be made easier by the fact that Krista was the only woman in the group, and also by the fact that she was wearing sneakers—some part of his mind had noticed that through the binoculars—while the men were most likely wearing boots. When they dismounted from the horses the size and shape of her prints would make telling her tracks from those of the men simple, and the tracking stick would make following them much easier.

As the sun set lower in the western sky he changed to a dark shirt, jacket and jeans. He threaded his holster through his belt and added a .357 Magnum. On the table next to a rifle lay extra ammunition for the two guns, a razor-sharp hunting knife, a canteen of water and some granola bars.

He chose the better of his two horses and set out for the place where he had last seen Krista. He found the five sets of tracks right where he expected them. Though only a few hours old, they were already starting to disappear; the ground was soft and sandy and couldn't hold a print long. Swinging to the ground, he held the flashlight far out to one side so that its beam was cast directly across the tracks, creating shadows and making the prints more visible. Since he knew that Krista had ridden out alone, then been joined by the other four, he was able to separate Diablo's tracks from those of the other horses. If the horses separated, at least he would know which direction the big stallion had gone.

An hour's ride led to harder ground, and signs became harder to find. He relied on flat spots, small areas where the dirt had been leveled by the weight of the horses, and areas where the small rocks and pebbles had been pushed into the dirt or uprooted from their beds and scuffed forward.

Three hours into the search Rafael was kneeling beside some of the few clear prints. Two of the horses—neither one Diablo—had broken off and headed south. A third one had joined the others from the south, and those four had continued northward. Rafael was unsure which group to follow. If they suspected he might follow them, they would split up to confuse him, but which group had Krista?

He decided to continue tracking Diablo. The stallion's tracks showed that he was still being ridden and was under control, and he knew that the horse was skittish around anyone but Krista. He was betting that she wouldn't be separated from her horse, and he'd better be right, he thought grimly, because Krista's life depended on it.

He was rewarded some three hundred yards later. The party ahead of him had stopped to rest, and among the prints he found were flats—tracks with no separate, elevated heel, consistent with the sneakers Krista had been wearing—whose size indicated that they belonged to a woman. There were also three distinct sets of heels—tracks with a separate, elevated heel—all belonging to men.

Rafael drew out the notepad, pencil and measuring tape, then made quick sketches of each of the four tracks, drawing them exactly to size and adding all markings—patterns on the shoe soles, cuts, irregularities. Next he used the tracking stick to follow Krista's tracks. They led away from the men and the horses, and her stride became greatly extended: she had started running. One of the men had followed, and Rafael found evidence of a scuffle twenty yards away.

He stared at the tracks leading back to the horses. Again Krista's stride had altered; this time the left side was consistently shorter than the right. She was limping; she had suffered some sort of injury in her attempt to escape. She knew she was in danger, and she was scared. That thought tore at Rafael's gut. He could imagine her terror, and he swore he would make them all pay for it when he reached them. No one would ever be allowed to make her suffer such fear again.

It was almost dawn when he noticed the smell. Smoke. They had built a fire somewhere up ahead of him—not far, judging by the smell. He was almost there; he had almost found her. The tracks led him to the mouth of a small canyon. Close inspection of the bushes that grew there showed several leaves turned at odd angles, the undersides showing. They had almost returned to their natural positions, meaning that it had been some time since they were disturbed. Several more leaves near the ground had been stepped on by the horses. Rafael turned them over to examine the bruising on the bottom sides. Fresh wounds were usually dark green; then they gradually turned black, then

either gray or light brown. These leaves were practically
black.

Rafael left his horse and disappeared into the canyon. H
hoped to spot Krista and her guards. If he could catch them
while they were still sleeping he would have a better chanc
of getting her out safely, without putting her in any mor
danger than she was already in.

The ground was hard, the sleeping bag inadequate pro
tection against the chill air and the millions of little rocks
but Krista was so tired that her body ignored the discom
fort and slept. Her sleeping bag was in front of a large rock
facing the three men and the dying fire some twenty fee
away.

They were careless, letting her sleep so far away, Rafae
thought. They probably thought she was helpless, though
no one would come after her. They were wrong. He move
in silence through the early-morning light, then knelt be
side her. Very carefully, very slowly, he pulled the zipper o
the sleeping bag down. Knife in hand, he reached inside t
find her ankles. They were tied loosely together, and h
sliced easily through the rope without disturbing her. Re
membering the fall she'd taken in her escape attempt, h
checked her left ankle and found it swollen. He cursed si
lently. She would have trouble walking, and running woul
probably be impossible. But that was all right. He coul
carry her.

When Krista felt a pair of strong, warm hands move up
her body she stiffened. Just before they reached her own
hands, she raised hers, which were tied together with a
length of rope, and hit her attacker under the chin, forcing
his head back. She felt something cold and heavy fall onto
her stomach, and she opened her mouth to scream, but the
sound was cut off by a hand over her mouth and a frantic
whisper, "It's me, Krista! *Querida,* it's me!"

Her eyes flew open, and she stared up at Rafael. When he
saw that she recognized him, he uncovered her mouth and
picked up the knife that he had dropped, then freed her

wrists. "Can you walk?" he asked, pushing the sleeping bag out of the way.

She had no idea whether her ankle could support her weight or not, but she nodded anyway. Rafael sheathed the knife and moved back to stand up. He froze when he felt cold, hard metal against the back of his head. He became completely motionless; his breathing stopped. He was astounded when Krista smiled faintly at the man behind him and reached out her hand to him. Didn't she realize the guy was holding a gun to Rafael's head?

She did, but she didn't stop. "It's all right," she whispered. "It's Rafael."

The gun was removed; then a familiar young voice said mockingly, "It's not smart to get so involved looking at pretty ladies that you don't hear someone come up behind you, Contreras." Eduardo put away the gun and came around to help Krista up. "I'm going with you."

Rafael stared up at him. There were a million questions running through his mind, but now wasn't the time to ask them. He rose fluidly to his feet. "Let's get out of the canyon," he ordered. "Then I'll come back and get the horses."

They took Krista between them, Rafael's arm around her waist, Eduardo's around her shoulders. Between the two of them they were able to support most of her weight, but there were still painful twinges in her ankle, and she had to keep her jaw clenched to stop herself from crying out. They had gone only ten or fifteen yards when her right foot landed in a hole and she was forced to step down hard on the injured ankle. Rafael felt her grab at his jacket, and he lifted her, but it was too late to stop her groan.

Diablo recognized his mistress's distressed voice. Untethered, he started toward her, drawing curious whickers from the other horses and waking the men.

They heard shouts and curses, and Rafael looked around for a place to hide. The only cover was a boulder barely large enough to shelter one person. Another quick survey showed that they weren't far from the canyon mouth. He released Krista, shoving her into Eduardo's arms. "Get her out of here! My horse is right outside. Take her and head south."

"I'm not going!" Krista argued, but Rafael didn't even look at her.

"If anything happens to her, Eduardo, I'll kill you," he promised in a deadly calm voice. "Go."

"No!" she cried, but Eduardo unceremoniously flung her over his shoulders and started off at a slow jog. She was heavy for the boy to carry, but he had decided at the beginning that he wouldn't let them kill her. Contreras's threat was just a little added incentive.

Marshall and the other man were closing in, and Rafael dived behind the boulder as the first shots were fired. He pulled the Magnum from its holster, took careful aim and squeezed the trigger.

Hitting a moving target in the dawn light wasn't easy, and his first two shots missed. They had the effect, however, of forcing the two men to seek cover, giving Eduardo precious extra time to get away with Krista.

Krista was furious. "Put me down!" she shrieked. "I'm going back!"

Eduardo obeyed her only when he reached the horse, but he didn't put her on the ground, he settled her into the saddle. "Get out of here!" he ordered.

"What are you going to do?"

"I'm going back in there to even the odds."

She had been disappointed when he joined them last night. Though she had met the boy only once, she had liked him. But only a few hours after his arrival he'd told her that he would try to help her get away. Now he was going back, endangering his own life to help Rafael. Her eyes stung with tears. "I want to go with you," she begged. "Please, Eduardo, let me go."

He shook his head. "You can't help. He could die, lady, and then they'd kill you. He would have died for nothing."

He jerked his head in the direction behind her. "That's south. Go on. We'll catch up."

There was more gunfire, and Krista flinched. Tears rolling down her cheeks, she reached for the reins and urged the horse in the direction Eduardo had indicated. It took all her strength and willpower to stop herself from turning back into the canyon, but Eduardo had been right. She couldn't help Rafael now.

She didn't ride far before turning the horse around to face the canyon. She sat frozen in the saddle, listening to the gunshots, imagining the worst and praying for the best.

Rafael was reloading his revolver when Eduardo dashed toward him, falling and rolling the last few feet. He flashed a white grin at the older man. "It's good that I'm quick on my feet, huh?"

"Why didn't you stay with Krista?"

"She's all right. She's probably waiting at a safe distance."

A bullet hit the rock directly above their heads, and the soft stone splintered, raining down on them. Rafael rolled onto his stomach and peered through the low bushes in the direction the shot had come from. He took aim at a patch of faint blue and pulled the trigger with a slow, deliberate squeeze. Next he heard a cry, and the blue patch didn't move again.

"That leaves Marshall," Eduardo called.

Even as he spoke, so did Marshall. "I'm coming out, Contreras! Don't shoot!"

Eduardo made a gesture of disgust. "He's a coward except when he's threatening helpless women."

They watched the man appear from behind the clump of sage, his hands above his head. "Did he hurt her?" Rafael asked, never taking his eyes off the man.

The boy knew that if the answer was yes, Rafael would kill Jack Marshall right there; he could see it in his face. He was grateful he didn't have to lie. "No."

Slowly Rafael rose to his feet. Holding the gun loosely in his right hand, he moved from the protection of the boulder and started toward Marshall. When he was about ten

feet away Marshall's right hand dropped behind him. H
was smiling coldly when he pulled out a small pistol that ha
been stuck in the back of his belt and pointed it at Rafael.

"You can kill me," Marshall said, "but you're going t
die, too."

The shot surprised Rafael. It didn't come from his gun
and he knew Marshall hadn't fired, because he was the tar
get. A red stain was spreading to cover the front of the othe
man's shirt, and he fell to the ground. Then Rafael remem
bered the gun Eduardo had pulled on him earlier, and h
turned to see the boy standing behind him.

"Is he dead?" Eduardo asked shakily.

Rafael nodded.

Eduardo paled, and the gun slipped from his fingers
Rafael went to him, laying his hand on his shoulder
"*Gracias,* my friend."

He went to gather the horses, silently urging Eduard
onto one. He swung onto Diablo's back, grateful that th
stallion remembered him from the times Krista had ridde
the animal to his house. Slowly, side by side, they rode ou
of the canyon.

Krista gave a cry of thanks when she saw them and race
the horse across dangerously uneven ground, reining in nex
to Diablo. For a moment she and Rafael just looked at eac
other; then she leaned across, reaching for him. He wrappe
his arms around her, lifting her onto Diablo's back, cra
dling her against the solid strength of his body.

Tears burned her eyes, and she hid her face against his
chest so he wouldn't see them, but he felt them, wet on his
shirt. "Did they hurt you?" he demanded coldly.

She sensed that his anger was directed at the men and no
her, and she shook her head. "No, they didn't hurt me."

"They scared you."

"I'm all right. Thank you, Rafael—and you, Eduardo.
Thank you so much."

Rafael stared straight ahead. *Thank you?* He had just
risked his life for her, and that was all he got? *Thank you?*
"Look at me, Krista."

She kept her head down, her eyes locked on his shirt.

"Damn you, look at me!" he shouted.

People and horses alike were startled by his shout. Diablo sidestepped nervously, and Eduardo wisely guided his horse some distance away.

Rafael grabbed her chin in one hand and forced her head up. "Damn it, Krista, I love you!" he growled in a low, raspy voice. "You've spent enough time condemning me for what I've done. Now you're going to start forgiving me."

"Forgive you?" she asked in disbelief. "You used me! You betrayed me! You took my love, knowing that it was all just part of your job!"

"*You* weren't my job. Your damned father was! Krista—" He stopped himself. Anger would get him nowhere, and after the ordeal she'd been through, she didn't need his anger. So he took a few deep breaths to calm himself, then said softly, "Forgive me, Krista. Please, *querida.*"

"I want to," she said sadly, "but I don't know if I can trust you again, Rafael." But even as she said the words, she knew that she had no choice. Rafael was her love and her life, and she needed him. Without trust, how long could their love survive? And without love, how long would she survive? The thought brought her to tears again, and he let her cry, murmuring soft Spanish words of comfort in her ear.

When her sobs quieted he lifted her face. "I can't change anything I've done, Krista. I can't magically erase all the hurt, or my betrayal. But I love you, and I can make you happy. You're never going to be happy without me, Krista. You love me, and you need me, and I need you. Give us a chance, *cariña.*"

"I don't know if I can," she whispered sadly.

Grimly he accepted that—for the time being. "Do you want to ride Diablo or my horse?"

"Can I stay here? Diablo doesn't mind."

He agreed solemnly, but one corner of his mouth lifted in a half smile. She might think she couldn't forgive him, that she couldn't trust him, but she was wrong. She still loved him. She knew he loved her, and she trusted him. She just didn't know it yet.

Rafael glanced at his watch. If they headed west to cross the highway, then turned south, they could make it to Jim Stone's house in a couple of hours. Krista would be safe there. He called to Eduardo to rejoin them.

"How did McLaren find out about my investigation?"

"How did you find out what was happening at his house?" Eduardo replied.

Rafael cursed softly. "Ruben."

"If you caught McLaren, he wanted you to be grateful for his help. If McLaren got away with it, he wanted *him* to be grateful, too."

When they reached the Stone house Jim was already in uniform, preparing to leave. With a curious glance at Krista and Eduardo, he motioned Rafael to the side. "I don't know what you and your buddies from New York have been up to, but all hell broke loose at the McLaren place this morning. Thompson just called. They're busting just about everyone over there, a couple of people have been shot, and he's calling us in to assist. Do you know what it's about?"

"Smuggling."

"Illegals?"

"Cocaine." Rafael saw Krista watching them, saw the question in her eyes. He asked it for her. "What about Art McLaren? Did they get him?"

Jim raised one eyebrow. "That's one way of putting it," he said cynically. "He's dead."

Epilogue

Rafael stood on the porch, leaning one shoulder against the post. He wore only a pair of low slung jeans, and he had a red bandanna tied around his forehead. A sheen of perspiration covered his chest and arms, but he didn't really notice the heat. August in the desert was always hot.

It was quiet around the house as he pulled open the top of an ice-cold can of Coke. He'd given up alcohol a long time ago. He had taken advantage of the quiet to get some work done around the house, but that was finished now, and he had nothing to do but wait and think.

Five years had passed since Art McLaren's death. It didn't seem that long, and yet it seemed like forever. His death had been an unexpected end to the smuggling case. Sad. No one really missed the man; no one had really mourned him. Krista had probably been the only person in the entire world who cared about him, and he had destroyed the last of her love by giving the order for her death.

Rafael's gaze turned to the desert again, in the direction that Krista had gone. Usually he accompanied her on her

daily walks, but today he'd remained behind to get the la:
minor repairs done around the house so they could enjoy th
rest of his vacation. Running the Nueva Vida station was
job he enjoyed, but it had a tendency to encroach on h
personal time. He needed this vacation.

A flash of bright turquoise caught his eye. Krista cam
into sight first, moving slowly in the late-afternoon hea
Her long blond hair was pulled into a ponytail, then braide
to keep it off her neck. She wore a sundress, part of her la
est collection, made of lightweight cotton in a shade of tu
quoise that flattered her deep golden skin and blue eyes. Th
dress was loose fitting, hiding the slight roundness of he
stomach and leaving plenty of room for further growth.

Impatient to be with his family again, Rafael left th
porch and went to embrace them. He swung sixteen-month
old Julia into his embrace as Miguel raised his arms. "Me
también, Papa," he said in his childish voice, and Rafae
lifted him, too.

Alejandro looked disdainful. "I can walk," he saic
making a face at his brother and sister.

Krista laughed. "It's a good thing you can, Alex, 'caus
I don't think your dad can handle all three of you."

"I know, and you can't because of the baby," he sai
importantly. "That's why it's good that I'm a big boy. I ca
help."

As soon as they got close to the house the two younges
wriggled down, and all three children ran into the yarc
Krista and Rafael stopped near the corral, where Diabl
came over to nuzzle his mistress. Krista pushed her hand
into the pockets of her dress and leaned against the fence.

Rafael walked a few feet away, then turned back to loo
at her. His black eyes moved slowly, like a caress, over he
body, over the slight swell of her stomach. The evidence c
the child growing inside her was becoming more noticeabl
every day. He reached out to trail his fingers over her bell
before letting his hand drop to his side again. "You'r
greedy," he remarked. "Four children in five years."

"I want a big family—like yours. We have a lot of love to give."

Again his eyes moved over her, and this time he felt his body respond. In the almost five years they'd been married—and the six months before that—one thing had never changed: the intense desire he always felt just looking at her. He'd never wanted a woman the way he'd always wanted Krista, and his desire for her hadn't diminished one bit. Even now he wanted her. He wanted to find the peace he'd always found in her body, in her love.

Krista was looking at her husband with a measuring gaze that was filled with love. He was so quiet, keeping everyone at a distance except her and their children. He needed solitude and quiet, the way she needed him. They were so different, and yet so alike. They had something that few people ever found—love and contentment and respect. Rafael was her best friend, and she was his. She couldn't believe that she had ever considered giving up everything they had together simply because of his role in the investigation into her father—but maybe she never really had. Even when she was telling him that she didn't know if she could ever trust in him or his love, she had known that there was no future for her without Rafael.

"The kids need their dinner; then it's bedtime."

The faintest hint of a smile touched her lips. "I think so. Then maybe you and I..." Her voice trailed off, and she moved closer to him.

Rafael reached out to slide his hand inside the rounded neckline of her dress. His callused fingers rubbed across her breast before they found the flat little nub that responded instantly to his touch. "Do you know what you do to me, señora?"

Smiling smugly, she reached down to undo the button of his jeans. "I think I do," she said softly, teasingly, as her fingernail moved up and down his zipper. "If you'll help me with the kids, we'll see if I'm right."

Hand in hand they crossed the barren ground to the lush yard. As soon as she'd learned she was pregnant with Alejandro, Krista had insisted that they haul in dirt and plant some grass, which required an incredible amount of water. Children needed grass to play on, she insisted, and Rafael was more than willing to go along with her desire.

"Vengan, mis hijos." Rafael picked up Alejandro, and Krista herded the smaller two into the house. She fixed dinner, while Rafael washed three little faces and three pairs of hands. After they ate she bathed Julia in the bathroom they'd added on to their bedroom, while Rafael bathed the two boys in the other bathroom. The children were read bedtime stories, then tucked into their beds.

Alejandro was last. After kissing him, Krista left Rafael to settle him into his bed and went to their bedroom at the end of the hall.

"Pero no quiero to go to bed," Alejandro said determinedly, and Rafael hid a smile. One of these days they were going to have to put a stop to the kids' style of speech. As Rafael taught Krista Spanish, Alex picked it up and incorporated it into his own speech. Miguel, and even Julia learned it from him.

"You have to, *hijo mio,"* Rafael said patiently. His patience with the children was infinite, even when he was aching to be alone with their mother. "Your mom and I are going to bed, too."

"But you and Mom don't have to go right to sleep when you go to bed," the small boy pouted. *"Está bien. Ahora* will go to sleep, *pero mañana,* no way."

Rafael bent to kiss his cheek; then he left the room. He found Krista standing in front of the grouping of photographs on the wall. He put his arms around her from behind and rested his chin on the top of her head.

"I like this picture," she said, pointing to the one in the center.

It was Rafael's favorite, too. It had been taken almost two ars ago at the annual Contreras family reunion. In the nter stood Krista, pregnant with Julia, and Rafael. They re surrounded by his brothers and sisters, nieces and phews, aunts and uncles and cousins. Next to Rafael was mother, holding Michael. His father, with Alejandro on s shoulders, was beside Krista.

"I love your family." She turned her head to smile at him. love you."

He pulled her over to the bed with him, holding her so se that her hair stirred with his breath. "You told me once at none of us has a choice who we fall in love with, that it's mething that just happens."

"It's meant to be," she said with a smile.

"Yes...meant to be... Even if I could have chosen, queña, I would have chosen you. The first time I met you, the Blue Parrot, I knew I could love you."

"But you still kept me at a distance."

"You scared me, señora. I didn't know you. If I let you t close to me, I thought I'd fall in love with you and you'd e me.. like Rebecca."

Slowly he began easing her dress off. When all their othes were out of the way he made love to her tenderly, ressing and stroking her, kissing her, whispering softly to in Spanish. This time, though, she knew what he was ying. She could translate the words of love, and she fer-ntly, joyfully repeated them to him.

It was dark. Beside her Rafael lay quietly, silent but vake. His arm curved out to hold her close to him, against m. Through the window she could see the twinkling stars, e brilliant moon. The light reached inside the room, athing their bodies in its soft golden glow. It was a beau-ful night, all moonlight and shadows, like that first ght....

Krista sighed happily and turned her head to press a kiss to Rafael's chest. "I love you, *querido*," she whispered.

The words pleased him and made him smile. "I know *pequeña*, my little one. And I love you."

He turned to her again, and she smiled dreamily. Yes, was a beautiful night. A beautiful night for lovers.

*   *   *   *   *